Death Benefits

Death Benefits

A **Ruby Lake** COZY MYSTERY

KIRSTIN DIANNE

DEATH BENEFITS

Published by Painted Skies Publishing

Leander, Texas

paintedskiespublishing.com

First Edition

Library of Congress Control Number: 2025908752

ISBN 979-8-9988143-2-7 (hc)

ISBN 979-8-9988143-1-0 (pb)

ISBN 979-8-9988143-0-3 (ebook)

ISBN 979-8-9988143-3-4 (kdp)

To John, for a million beautiful memories

Chapter One

Ava Andrews thought she had heard it all. After several years of investigating employment complaints, she had come across a number of excuses and crazy stories. Now this was preposterous.

"Tell me the rest of the story, Des. What was Pete's explanation for kissing his female employees this morning?"

Ava recently joined Ruby Park Senior Living as the new Director of Human Resources. Desiree Sparks, Des to her friends, worked on Ava's team. Ava had received an employee complaint via email earlier that morning. Since she was tied up giving a presentation, she had asked Des to speak with the employees involved right away.

"Join me, and I'll fill you in." Des raised her coffee cup and motioned for Ava to enter her cozy office. The rich aroma of hazelnut filled the air.

"Great." Ava walked in and stood by the wooden desk. Dressed in a chiffon blouse and pencil skirt, she looked polished.

"Pete said, you know this is Employee Appreciation Week, and nothing shows I care more than an innocent peck on the cheek."

Ava raised her eyebrows. "You're kidding."

"No, I'm not." Des shook her head. Her pixie hairstyle and wide eyes accentuated her curious nature.

"Did he show any sign of remorse?"

"On the contrary, he acted like I was infringing on his territory," said Des. "When I reminded him of the harassment policy, he appeared to be anxious."

"Mind if I take a look at your investigation notes?"

Des handed Ava a manila folder that contained her hand-written notes along with a neatly typed summary. Ava took a seat facing her. She crossed her long legs, tucked a lock of her hair behind her ear, and scanned the report.

"I see one of Pete's employees reported his actions as creepy and surprising," said Ava.

Des nodded. "That was Kim."

Ava read further. Kim claimed that her manager, Pete Reinholtz, came up behind her, swooped down to drop an envelope on her desk, and then gave her a quick kiss on her left cheek. The two other women in the Facilities Department shared a similar account. Inside each of their envelopes was a gift card from Pete to a local restaurant. Lady Luck was popular for its happy hours, greasy burgers, and pull tabs. Interestingly, the department's only remaining male employee, Todd, received a gift card to a bait and tackle shop and not even so much as a hand shake.

Kim stated she'd been reluctant to report this to Human Resources at all, but she knew he was out-of-line and violated the center's policy. She had asked Des to keep her name confidential because she didn't want to make waves with Pete. Renee said she didn't understand why this was being made into a big deal.

Ava read a direct quote aloud from the third employee,

Candace. "I'm comfortable working for him, but I don't want him to kiss me again because it gave me the heebie-jeebies." Glancing at the rest of the draft report, she saw that the disciplinary action section remained blank.

Ava retuned her attention to her competent HR generalist and asked, "Has Pete received any prior corrective action or complaints of sexual harassment?"

"Not that I'm aware of. There's nothing like that in his personnel file. But honestly, that surprises me. I've known Pete for years, and he can be very difficult, if not downright rude. His director, Cheryl, documented one conversation she had with him after he yelled at an accounting clerk during a staff meeting. He manages the accounting support team as well as facilities. That was over a year ago."

"Okay, thanks. What a way to kick off Appreciation Week. But it should be smooth sailing from here. Right?"

"Knock on wood." Des smiled. "I know you've be planning this celebration since you joined us. It's going to be great!"

The first week of June was the unofficial start of summer in Minnesota, and Ruby Park kicked it off with their annual Employee Appreciation Week. Ava had been looking forward to leading the festivities.

"Thanks for dropping everything this morning to meet with his team. We both know how important it is to enforce our Code of Conduct," Ava said.

Des nodded and asked, "How was your presentation this morning?"

"Judging by the feedback, I think it when really well. The department heads were particularly interested in our retention rates and turnover data. Plus, they hadn't seen our employee demographics in that level of detail before."

"Our growth has been amazing," Des said. Ruby Park had become the largest senior care residence in Garrett County.

Ava smiled as she stood. She waved the folder in her hand and said, "I'll visit Pete before the end of the day. I'm curious to see if he understands how serious this is."

"If you want my opinion, he probably doesn't, but I doubt it was sexually motivated. At least the employees didn't take it that way. He's self-absorbed and likely thinks they'd appreciate this kind of attention from him."

"We need to change that way of thinking. I'll talk to Cheryl first. Thanks again. I really value your opinion." Ava stepped out and headed back into her office.

Following a budget meeting with the leadership team, Ava took the opportunity to speak with Cheryl, Ruby Park's Chief Financial Officer. Cheryl was shocked to learn about Pete's behavior, and she supported issuing a formal warning.

"Kissing employees is a serious accusation. Even if it was meant to be innocent," Cheryl said.

"I've seen employees terminated for less than this. Pete is a manager and should know better." Ava pointed out. "However, a key point in this case is that the staff didn't feel harassed or harmed."

Cheryl responded, "Pete can be thoughtless. If his team is comfortable working with him, I'd like to give him another chance, as long he understands nothing like this can happen again."

"All right, I agree. I'll remind him that any kind of retaliation is unacceptable. Would you like to sit in on my conversation with him this afternoon?"

"Please go ahead without me. I have to meet with the auditors." Cheryl glanced at her watch and added, "I might be in the conference room for the rest of the day. Thanks for handling this, and keep me posted."

"Will do."

Ava returned to her office in the Administration wing where all her teammates were working at their desks. Ava enjoyed the hum of keyboards clicking, printers printing, and phones ringing. She quickly lost track of time screening resumes for a nurse manager opening while fielding frequent questions.

During a quiet moment, Ava took her almost forgotten lunch out of her mini refrigerator. Because it was mid-afternoon, she wouldn't have to make dinner before her workout that night. She quickly ate the turkey and spinach wrap at her desk, which allowed her plenty of time for one of her favorite daily routines: walking through the senior living facilities and its gardens. Her college mentor once told her it was important to stay connected with the organization's mission and the people they served. She kept that value close to her heart.

Ava made her way down the wide corridor that led to the modern assisted living facility. It had been renovated the year prior following the addition of a new independent living building on the grounds. She entered a large community room used for events and popular activities. It was happy hour for the residents, so she knew exactly where she'd find him. Her favorite person in the world over the age of eighty was sitting in his wheelchair at a table with a few of his buddies. The activities manager and her assistant were busy distributing bingo cards.

"Hi Grandpa!" Ava called out.

Her mother's dad, Charles Johanssen, had moved into his assisted living apartment last winter after a stroke left him wheelchair bound. Getting to see her grandpa almost daily was the greatest benefit of working at Ruby Park. It gave her mother, Grace, peace of mind as well.

"Well, isn't this a pleasant surprise?" Charles Johanssen grinned from ear to ear. "You just missed your mother, honey. She stopped by for a visit before taking her car to the shop. We took a nice walk through the garden."

"Good for you. I was going to offer to take you outdoors, but it looks like you're all set to play bingo. How about I stop by tomorrow?"

"You know you're welcome anytime, day or night."

"Can I get you anything before I go?"

"Another beer wouldn't hurt, would it?" Charles asked with a sly grin.

"Of course not. Coming right up," Ava gave him a warm hug. She returned with a tray and served small glasses of Pilsner to her grandpa and his tablemates. "I hope you win a few rounds and share your earnings with these guys." Ava smiled brightly at Charles. She knew their prizes consisted of a choice of cookies or chips.

She waved goodbye to her grandpa and his friends. As she headed toward Pete's small office at the very end of the hallway, she willed her renewed happy mood to carry her through the rest of her work day. She spotted Pete at his desk.

Pete was an average-looking man in his early forties. He wasn't someone who would stand out in a crowd. His hair was thinning, and he wore black slacks and a plain collared shirt. He rose from his desk chair when she reached his doorway.

"I've been expecting you. Come in," he said in his gravelly voice.

"Good afternoon," Ava said as she closed the door and took a seat in his office. "As I mentioned on the phone, I wanted to follow up after the incident this morning."

"About that, I'm embarrassed, and I apologized to my team earlier," Pete said.

"Why did you feel that kissing them was appropriate in the first place?"

He directed his small, brown eyes away from Ava. "I guess I feel like my team is my second family. It was a friendly greeting."

Ava reviewed the Center's policy with Pete and advised him to never touch anyone without requesting their permission. He then responded that nothing like this would ever happen again. After she issued a written warning to Pete, she made herself a mental note to schedule the center-wide employee sexual harassment training.

As she walked back to Human Resources, she thought the conversation went about as well as could be expected. Pete's voice was flat, and she couldn't judge his sincerity.

The institutional clock in the main hallway warned Ava that she had worked later than she'd planned. She was looking forward to her much-needed yoga class tonight and had to rush home to change clothes in record time. As she packed up her carryall bag, she realized she'd left her Stanley water bottle in Pete's office. She threw her bag over her shoulder and headed back down to retrieve it.

The Administration wing was quiet now as most of her colleagues had left for the day. Approaching Pete's office, Ava could hear his voice. She peeked in. His back was to her, and he was talking into his cell phone. She saw her water mug on the edge of his desk. She intended to step in quickly, wave to him, and grab it.

Pete gave a swift kick to his waste basket, and it clanged against the wall. "I don't know how long I'll be stuck in this hell hole," he growled. "My plan is to set up a new CPA practice once that's all in order."

Ava stepped back to avoid being seen.

"Can you believe that blonde witch gave me a warning? Who the hell does she think she is? She's almost as bad as Cheryl. These chicks think they run this place. I'll show them a thing or two."

He's talking about me. Ava whirled around deciding to exit discretely through the side doors. She stepped outside to the now half-empty employee lot where her Ford Bronco Sport awaited. Before climbing into the driver's seat, she caught a glimpse of Pete through his office window. He stopped pacing, looked out at her, and closed his window blinds.

Chapter Two

AVA RUSHED THROUGH the garage door and into her home where she was greeted by her biggest fan. Reliable as always, Sophie sat inside the doorway with an out-stretched paw which Ava took in her hand.

"Hello baby, I'm here to feed you dinner. How was your day?" Her golden retriever responded with a loud thump of her tail. Her enthusiasm was barely containable, and Ava laughed. Sophie wriggled her entire body as she padded into the mud room. Located between her garage and kitchen, this space doubled as her laundry and Sophie's dining room. Her pup's message was clear—dinner first, then a trip outside. Ava set her large tote bag down on the bench, measured a cup of canine crunchies, and poured them into a white ceramic dish. A refill of fresh, cool water completed this dinner routine.

Ava loved her new life in Ruby Lake, Minnesota. She had settled comfortably back in her picturesque hometown during the early weeks of spring. She still couldn't believe she was here. Ava recalled that she couldn't race out of her small community fast enough when she moved to Minneapolis to attend the University of Minnesota. A degree in psychology and a student position as a recruiter at the University's Human Resources Department sparked her interest to this field. This passion inspired her to complete an MBA program while working full-time to build her career.

She had led human resources teams at the University followed by a large medical center in Minneapolis. At the age of thirty, her ambition, hard work, and resilience were rewarded, and she took her place as the youngest member of the executive team at Ruby Park.

Of course, a referral from her friend and neurologist, Dr. Suni Patel, didn't hurt either. Suni had seen first-hand how the daily demands of shouldering other people's stress had contributed to Ava's chronic migraines. Ava had agreed to Suni's offer to contact a colleague about a newly created position at her home town's growing senior living community. She was finally listening to her advice on making some lifestyle changes and slowing down a bit.

Jeff Wheeler, who served as Chief Executive Officer at the Ruby Park facility, was happy to hear about Ava's credentials. Before long, Ava was saying her goodbyes to her work team, her apartment in Bloomington, and to a four-year relationship with her ex-boyfriend.

Ava's new position as a department head afforded her the ability to finally purchase her first home which was something she and Grant, her ex-boyfriend, used to dream about. That is, until he surprised her by purchasing a townhome on his own. Over the past couple of years, Grant had been so busy growing his law practice at his father's firm that he had barely had time to see Ava, let alone settle down.

No one had been happier to learn of Ava's return to Ruby Lake than her mom. A successful real estate broker, Grace didn't lose any time offering a list of charming homes in the area to view with Ava. After all, she knew purchasing property ensured a long-term commitment. During a long weekend visit, Ava and Grace swapped opinions and decorating ideas while viewing over a dozen houses. Her mom subtly attempted to persuade Ava to select a property in her parents' neighborhood, but Ava instantly felt at peace when she walked into a cozy rambler with a million-dollar view of Ruby Lake.

Located in the newer Park Hills neighborhood, the home was nestled in the rolling landscape. The cluster of houses was adjacent to the golf course community and was connected to trails along the lake. Her neighborhood association included lawn maintenance and snow plowing, a major convenience for a single woman living in Minnesota.

Even better for Ava, she'd finally been able to adopt a dog from a rescue shelter. She let Sophie outside and stood still for a long moment, allowing the wonderful pine and flowery scents of her backyard soothe her soul. She recalled the day she met Sophie. It had been love at first sight that Saturday afternoon. Ava took the overgrown puppy for a short walk around the shelter's grounds and then sat in the lawn to inspect her skin and fur. The lanky dog climbed into Ava's lap and licked her face.

Ava was glad she came prepared with a leash and collar because she realized right then she was taking the fur baby home with her. The shelter staff explained she was a stray, wearing a collar with no identifying tags when picked up by animal control. All Ava needed to do was complete an application, promise to have Sophie spayed at the local veterinary clinic, and pay a $50 processing fee.

A cold nose touched Ava's palm as Sophie licked her fingers. "Let's go in, Sophie. We'll have time to relax on the patio when I return from class."

The second-best thing about owning her own home was her newfound closet space. She regarded her bedroom's walk-in closet as her private boutique. It wasn't decked out with custom cabinetry, but a girl could dream. Ava had asked her dad to install a small crystal chandelier after she'd moved in, and she now enjoyed the light-flickering effect it cast on the walls. Her wardrobe was meticulously organized by season, activity, color, and length. Ava quickly selected yoga attire from her athleticwear, pulled her caramel blonde hair into a ponytail, and headed out the door.

With a few minutes to spare, Ava stopped in the ladies' room at the Ruby Lake Community Center. She walked past the main office where she was surprised to see her yoga instructor, Brooke, standing across from Pete Reinholtz.

The two appeared to be arguing. Pete's beady eyes were trained on Brooke. He held her by the wrist, and she yanked it away from his grip. While Ava couldn't make out their words, she heard Brooke's raised tone of voice and noticed her face was beet red. Pete caught Ava's concerned gaze through the office window and grimaced.

Ava immediately dropped her glance and proceeded toward the gym. "Wow, this is a big turnout tonight," Ava said through the buzz of the members gathering in the community center gymnasium. She quickly rolled out her yoga mat next to Jenny, her human resources assistant.

Jenny nodded. "Once school lets out, participation will drop to half. All the moms in class will be busy picking up kids from day camp or running them to softball practice and soccer games."

Ava had been attending yoga class two to three days per week for the past few months and had never known Brooke to be late. In fact, Brooke made a point of being on the stage in front of the gym with soothing music playing well in advance. She discouraged tardiness because she said it upset the participants' chakra.

A few minutes later, Brooke bounded up the few stairs to the gym's stage. She stepped on her mat and surveyed the group. Wide-eyed and frazzled, she said, "I apologize for being late. Let's start by taking a few deep breaths. Slowly inhale, feel your breath expand in your stomach, now make an audible exhale." Ava heard the collective "woosh" made by her classmates. Brooke led this exercise a few more times before guiding the class into their yoga poses.

An hour later, Ava walked out of the center with Jenny by her side. Ava received a text from her mom asking to pick her up at Woodcrest Coffee House and Brewery.

"Hey, I'm headed over to Woodcrest to grab a bite to eat. Would you like to join me?" Ava aked.

"Thanks for the invite, but I promised my dad I'd stop by." Jenny shrugged her shoulders. "I'll take a rain check."

"Absolutely, see you in the morning."

Within a couple of minutes, Ava parked at the curb in front of her town's most popular watering hole which was owned and operated by Lauren and Matt Nicholson, her sister and brother-in-law. They served food along with fresh brewed coffee and craft beer until closing time.

Ava found her mom and sister sitting in green velvet armchairs in front of a coffee table. Ava took a seat on the aged leather sofa directly across from them. A gorgeous Turkish rug lay on the polished cement floor. Ava surmised her mom and sister had just completed a round of Connect Four—wooden circles from an oversized version of this childhood favorite were spread out on their low table. Woodcrest held Game Night every Monday evening, and enthusiastic groups of families and friends surrounded tables adorned with puzzles and board games.

Anyone who saw the Andrews women together could easily tell they were related. Their fair Norwegian skin tone and blonde hair came from Grace's side of the family. However, Ava's mane was a shade darker, and instead of her mom's and sister's blue eyes, hers were a deep brown so intense they almost appeared black. She shared that trait, as well as her height, with both her older brother and her dad.

Grace smiled warmly. "Thanks for meeting me here, honey. You were already in town, so I didn't think you'd mind. This will save your dad a trip."

"Anytime, mom. When will your car be ready?"

"Randy said the day after tomorrow. By the way, I met a really nice man when I dropped my car off. He's restoring his father's classic Ford Mustang. I believe his name is Jack. I haven't seen him in town before."

"That's Jack Lindstrom," responded Lauren. "Matt knew him in college. They played baseball together for a year, or maybe it was two. He's a couple years younger than Matt. He's single, Ava," Lauren added in her sing song voice that meant she was up to something.

Ava rolled her eyes and changed the conversation by focusing on their mother. "How are the plans coming for the Fourth of July Jubilee?"

"We finalized the agenda, but we could always use more volunteers. It's going to be so much fun. You two are coming, aren't you?"

"Of course we'll come, Mom," Lauren said. "Matt and I will be serving barbeque and grilled chicken sandwiches from our food truck at Lakeside Park during the softball tournament."

"That's wonderful! Ava, I hope you're reconnecting with your old friends. How is Shannon?"

"She's doing great. You have to see what she's done with Rosie's flower shop. She's expanded their gift selections with home décor and jewelry. Most of it is made by local artisans like herself. She's planning to market a line of her own jewelry. I'm really proud of her."

"I'll stop to check it out. Her new inventory should draw more customers to the square," Lauren said.

"Shannon is selling me flowers at wholesale for a fundraising event this week. I think I told you I suggested we have a dessert auction to raise funds for the Ruby Park Food Pantry. My boss, Jeff, thought it was a great idea."

"You girls are so creative," replied Grace. Remember when you and Shannon sold bracelets and key chains at the end of our driveway? Most kids held lemonade stands, but you always enjoyed making things."

"That's right. I feel bad for your mail carrier." Ava laughed. "She had no choice but to pass by our stand, and she was so sweet. I'm sure she had more painted rocks and beaded jewelry than she knew what to do with."

Grace patted her eldest daughter's arm and asked, "Do you still see Suni regularly?"

"Not nearly as often as I'd like now that I've moved. You know we were only college roommates in Dinkytown for two years, but we reconnected when she started her fellowship at the Minneapolis Medical Center. Hey, did I tell you she and Raj are getting married early next year?"

Lauren accepted a carry-out bag from her husband and said, "I'd be happy to set you up with one of Matt's friends. Just say the word."

Matt had a charming, wholesome face. He gave Ava a sympathetic grin and put his hand on her shoulder in a gesture of support before he walked back to the kitchen. He knew his wife liked playing matchmaker.

Grace continued her train of thought. "It's so important to keep up these connections, girls. There's something very special about having old friends who knew you when you were young."

"It's good be home," Ava said.

"I'm so glad my daughters live in the same community again. Now we just need to convince your brother to stay put after this new business venture wraps up. Otherwise, I'm worried he'll want to live in Texas permanently. Maybe he'll return for good after he completes this secret project he's been working on with your father."

Lauren stood and handed the takeout bag to Grace. "It's good for Reid to be out on his own, but I miss him too. I'd better check on the staff and let you two drive home to Dad. He's probably waiting for his dinner."

Chapter Three

AVA WOKE UP to the sound of rumbling thunder. She picked herself up from her sofa and clicked off her television set. She stepped up to the large patio doors, searching for signs of rain.

"Don't worry, Sophie. It's just a passing storm."

CRACK—BOOM! Lightening split the brooding sky. A man stared back at her from the trees behind her property.

"Aah!" Ava jumped back. Sophie uttered a loud bark, pressed her nose against the glass, and let out a slow growl that sounded like a lion purring. The hair on Ava's arms stood on end.

In an instant, the sky turned jet black. Ava gathered her composure and looked out again. Smaller flashes of light danced across the darknesses, but she couldn't see anyone—just the brief outlines of grand oak and maple trees bending in the whipping wind.

"Come on, Soph." Ava flipped on all the light switches to illuminate her living room and kitchen. Then she retreated to her bedroom suite.

"Should I call the police?" Ava asked her pup. "And say

what? That a man is on the nature trail after hours? I'm sure they'd get a laugh out of that."

Her bedside clock read 12:34 a.m. *Why would anyone be out in this weather?* Ava pushed a heavy arm chair from its spot near the window across her room until it pressed up against the door. Then, she withdrew her baseball bat from underneath her bed.

The rain began slapping against the glass. *Whoever that was, he's going to get soaked—serves him right!* Guarded by her dog, Ava sat upright leaning against her headboard, gripping her wooden bat. She had every intention of staying awake all night.

Ava yawned. *It's 6:30 already?* She rubbed the back of her stiff neck.

Sophie thumped her tail and whined. Ava understood this as a not-so-subtle demand for breakfast. After pulling her chair away from the door, she served breakfast to her faithful companion.

A number of thoughts passed through her mind about the night before. She rubbed her temples. *That was so scary.* Had the man intended to break in? At that frightening consideration, Ava dashed through the rooms to make sure she was alone.

Ava showered and dressed in less than thirty minutes. She grabbed the potato, ham, and spinach quiche she had baked for her team the day before, pleased with how well it turned out. She planned to reheat it in Lauren's commercial oven when she stopped by her sister's coffee shop on her way to work.

The Woodcrest Coffee Shop and Brewery occupied the

prominent corner of Lake Boulevard and Oak Streets in Ruby Lake's historic town center. The square was actually a "U" shape formed by three streets that surrounded the original town hall. This provided the foundation for shops and restaurants to view the lake that shared the town's name. Lake Boulevard served as the fourth road bordering the square, but it also wove around the entire eleven miles of the lake's circumference providing access into the historic downtown as well as to neighborhoods, parks, and recreational facilities.

Once Ava arrived, Lauren took the quiche from her hands and immediately placed it in the oven. While filling a carafe of coffee and bagging fresh muffins for her employees, Ava told her sister about spotting the man during the storm overnight.

"Who was it?" Lauren asked with alarm.

"I don't know—it happened so fast. Geez, I was terrified."

"Of course you were. You have to have someone install a security system right away. You never know what kind of weirdo is lurking around, trying to get in. You're a single woman, Ava. You need to be careful."

"I don't need to be reminded of my relationship status. I've never felt unsafe in Ruby Lake before. Now that I'm wide awake, I realize I let my imagination run wild. I like the idea of having a door camera, though. Do you know anybody who can install one?"

"I'll have Matt take care of it today. Give me your house key, and I'll have him find someone. Or maybe he and Randy can do it themselves if the hardware store has a system in stock."

"You're the best."

"Stop by after work tonight for dinner. Then you can pick up your key."

"I'll never pass up an invitation. See you after work." Ava

was pleased. Cooking for one was too much effort, and she'd had her fill of salads and soups, her go-to convenience foods.

Several minutes later, Ava found herself at Ruby Park. The senior living community included two buildings facing Ruby Lake with outdoor patio area and gardens woven throughout its grounds. The first residential building was comprised of independent living apartments for adults over the age of fifty-five. The second, larger facility contained assisted living apartments, memory care studios, a nursing home, and a rehabilitation unit.

Des greeted Ava with a cheerful smile. "Let me help you with that coffee carafe. What's all this?"

"I made a quiche to share for breakfast. A little something to show my appreciation."

"Wow, this is awesome. Thanks."

"Sure, let's set in on the conference table. I'll set out plates and forks."

"How was yoga last night? I heard Jenny caused a scene."

"Yes," laughed Ava, "Her Apple watch started ringing during the middle of our Warrior III pose."

"I bet Brooke didn't like that."

"You know it. When it rang a second time, Jenny got so embarrassed. She ran out into the hall to reset her watch but forgot she left her phone in her purse. She didn't realize pausing her watch wouldn't make her phone stop."

"Did her face get all red?"

"Yes, poor thing. But Brooke was truly the only one who got riled up by the distraction."

"She takes teaching very seriously. Expects everyone to be ready well before class starts—no excuses," Des said.

"Which reminds me, Brooke was late for class for the first

time. I saw her talking with Pete Reinholtz right before class was supposed to begin. Actually, they appeared to be arguing. That may be why she was so flustered."

"Really? Brooke and Pete are both around my age. We all knew each other in high school, but I'm not aware of any connection these days. I wonder what sparked that."

"Who knows. Anyway, thanks again for recommending yoga," said Ava. "It's just the right amount of exercise that I need to wind down after work."

"I wish I had more time these days. Between attending my boys' baseball games and preparing for Harper's graduation, I don't have an evening to spare. I'm thrilled their summer break starts soon."

"Please don't rush our short summer along. You know fall will be just around the corner!" Ava was teasing, but it was true. Minnesota's temperate summer weather only lasted about twelve weeks, and kids returned to school the day after Labor Day. The leaves would then change to their spectacular gold, amber, and ruby shades by late September. As a child, Ava had thought Ruby Lake must have been named after the lovely deep shade of red that the oak, maple, and aspen trees boasted as they flickered on autumn breezes.

In grade school, Ava learned her town was actually named after its first Mayor, an Irishman named Patrick Ruby. By the twentieth century, the small community's largest ethnic groups were of Norwegian, German, and Irish decent. Her second-grade class took a short walk to the town's center to visit the old town hall and the statue of Patrick and his wife, Bridget.

Ava secretly wished she hadn't learned that part of her town's history, preferring to imagine her lake reflecting its rich color during her favorite season of the year. But she held another special connection to its name, as the ruby gem was her birthstone. Ava often wore a gold and ruby ring, a birthday gift from her parents. Glancing at the deep red stone on her right hand gave her an instant reminder of home and family, which had been especially comforting after she moved to Minneapolis for college.

Ava looked forward to catching up with Des each morning. Although Des was ten years Ava's senior, they had many common interests and had become fast friends. Des had started working in the human resources office right after she'd graduated from high school. She had a natural way with people and was the perfect fit for the generalist role.

Ruby Park Senior Living had doubled in size during the past decade to meet the needs of Garrett County's aging population. Jeff Wheeler had known he needed to add an executive to his team which created the opportunity now filled by Ava.

"What's on your schedule today?" Ava asked her colleague. "I know we have the employee recognition prize drawings again at noon."

"Yes, five prizes each day. Jenny and May are free to help you in the cafeteria," Des replied. "I've got that grievance meeting with the service union before lunch. Talk about bad timing. Appreciation Week is supposed to be fun."

"Just treat today's meeting as an opportunity to listen and collect information. There's no requirement to reach a solution today," Ava said. "We'll make a decision once we've reviewed their case and all of the relevant information."

"When you put it that way, it really relieves the pressure." Des breathed a sigh of relief.

"You'll be great. Stacey, our director of nursing, asked me

to stop by this morning. She said it's urgent. Remember, we still have the resident's reception tomorrow, the fund-raiser, and the picnic to look forward to."

"I do love the annual picnic. I can't wait for you to participate this year. The leadership team serves the staff, and it is always a big celebration."

"I'm also looking forward to the dessert auction. I'm willing to spend a fortune on anything rich with chocolate."

Jenny popped her head into Ava's office. "Yvonne is here. She asked for a minute of your time."

"Des and I were just finishing up." Ava stood and greeted Yvonne as Des exited. "Hi, come on in."

Yvonne, the Center's rehabilitation manager, marched in with her arms crossed over her chest. "Sorry to interrupt. One of our physical therapists called in sick again today. She has a history of calling in to extend her weekends. I don't know what I'm going to do with her. The other therapists are upset that she's off frequently on Mondays, and they have to pick up the slack. It's not fair."

"Has she given you any reason for needing these days off, like a new medical condition?"

"Not that I know of. It seems like she's just not taking enough responsibility."

"Have you issued any corrective action for absenteeism?" Ava asked.

"No, but I've told her a couple times that I need her to be more reliable. I entered notes in the timekeeping system."

"Terrific, that will help us track a pattern. Can you get me a list of the days that she called in for the past six months? If it's excessive, we can speak with her together to see what's going on."

"I'll look back at the time records and will get back to you." Yvonne turned and trooped out of Ava's office.

"Thanks Yvonne. I hope your day gets better," Ava called out.

Ava looked up as Jenny stepped into her doorway. "What's this?" She eyed the beautiful gift basket wrapped in gold cellophane that Jenny was carrying.

"It's addressed to Human Resources. I went to pick up our mail, and it was in on the counter."

"Who's it from?"

"I don't know. There was a sticky note attached to the wrap with HR written on it, but nothing else."

"Maybe the card is inside. Let's take a look." Ava carefully untied the sparkling bow, and Jenny pulled back the sheer gold wrap.

"It's a chocolate tower from See's Candies, my favorite!" gushed Jenny. "But I don't see a gift card."

"This is my lucky day. I was just telling Des that I've been craving chocolate. Let's all take a break. I hope the donor comes forward so I can send a thank you note." Ava moved the basket from her office to the adjacent conference room, setting it down next to their breakfast. Her team: Des, May, Jenny, and Noelle joined her at the conference table and enjoyed quiche and chocolate while Ava began summarizing the week's remaining activities.

Dean from Accounting stepped in. "I'm sorry for interrupting. Can I leave these reports for you, May?"

"Of course. Help yourself to some candy," May pointed to the gold basket.

"Don't mind of I do." Dean glanced through the chocolates and chose one. "See you guys later." Dean smiled holding a delectable candy bar in one hand while balancing an armful of envelopes in the other.

"As I was saying," Ava said, "morale was very positive in the employee cafeteria yesterday. Everyone was excited about the prizes you purchased for the drawing. Since there was a huge buzz about it, we'll likely draw a bigger crowd today. Also, thanks for handing out all the Appreciation Week T-shirts yesterday afternoon. I already saw a bunch of people wearing them this morning."

Jenny held up her hands. "Everybody will wear their T-shirts on Friday. The picnic-goers will be a sea of matching blue T-shirts."

Des turned to May. "I think this year's design is the best yet. Great job!"

The group agreed and gave May their praise. Ava was enjoying the camaraderie of her team. She looked at each of them warmly and felt grateful she was now one of the family.

Ava said, "Remember, we'll need all-hands-on-deck tomorrow morning to set up for the dessert auction. Okay, let's get back to work. I promised Stacey that I'd meet her in the Nursing Home."

After Ava crossed the lobby that linked the administration offices to the residences, her first stop was the Assisted Living Center. As she drew nearer to the game room, Ava could see Charles pulled up to a table playing checkers.

"Hi Grandpa," she said, giving him a big hug. You're looking incredibly handsome today."

"Here's my Ava. What do you mean today, young lady? How do I look every other day?" Her grandfather grinned from ear to ear, "You better watch out Norm, now that my good luck charm is here." Charles beamed with pride whenever Ava came to visit.

"That's not fair. We're all tied up, two all. This here's the tie breaker," Norman teased.

"Have you seen Grant lately?" asked Grandpa. "Ole told me during breakfast this morning that Grant's talking about running for mayor in the fall."

"Oh really? I hadn't heard that. I haven't seen Grant since he helped me pack up my apartment in Bloomington."

"I sure wish you two would resolve whatever your disagreement is about. You know your grandmother and I were together for sixty years before she passed."

"And you two were perfect for each other. As for me and Grant… it's complicated Grandpa. We weren't meant to be."

"You kids always say 'it's complicated' when what you really mean is that you are too stubborn for your own good. I like Grant. He's family as far as I'm concerned."

"Would you like me to stay a while and give you a ride over to the Minnesota Room?"

"No, let us men battle this out to the finish. I appreciate the offer though, but I can use the exercise. I'll get myself over there in plenty of time."

Ava planted a kiss on Charles' cheek. "I love you, Grandpa."

"I love you more, Ava. See you soon."

Ava continued to stroll leisurely through the Assisted Living Center because she was a few minutes early for her meeting with Stacey. While the nutrition team was cleaning up after breakfast service in the Rose Dining room, residents were maneuvering their wheelchairs and walkers to win the best view of today's entertainer in the adjacent Minnesota Room.

She recognized Thomas who'd been their featured attraction about six weeks prior. Ava waved hello, and he responded with a bow. Thomas was a one-man band complete with an accordion, trumpet, bongos, and a harmonica.

"Would you like some help?" Ava asked.

"I've got it all under control. Been doing this for many years," Thomas said.

Ava wondered how he was able to manage moving all that equipment himself using only one trolley, but there he was, carefully unpacking his portable speakers and karaoke machine as if he were reversing a Tetris puzzle. At nearly seventy years old, he was the youngest person in the large activity space—or had been, before she stepped in.

"Break a leg," Ava said to Thomas as she continued down the corridor. "I'll try to catch the end of your show when I return from the nursing station."

Thomas gave her a wink. Ava considered the contrast between acceptable corporate behavior and the everyday residential life of these senior citizens. A wink or simple kiss on the cheek seemed to be second nature among men of her grandfather's generation, and their wives probably wouldn't want it any other way.

Ava approached the locked entrance to the skilled nursing unit and swiftly entered the security code. Moving toward Stacey's office on the left, she overheard her talking with a nurse at the nursing station. Ava waited in the hallway, allowing them to finish their conversation. Moments later, the nurse stomped past her.

"Come join me," Stacey said to Ava.

"Is she alright?" Ava asked, referring to the disgruntled nurse.

"Yes, just a little misunderstanding about the schedule."

"What can I do for you?" asked Ava.

"You know, we're holding our June reception for all of the residents tomorrow. This year's dessert was supposed to be strawberry shortcake. But we have a problem... the strawberries are missing!"

"Excuse me, we lost the strawberries? How many are we talking about?"

"We received a huge delivery yesterday morning from Sweetwater Farms, who graciously donated the fruit for this event. I went into the kitchen for a brief inspection while the team was out serving residents, and there were no strawberries to be seen. I have no idea why someone would steal that many strawberries."

"Why would you think the strawberries were stolen?"

"I don't trust our new nutrition manager, Cody. There's something fishy about him. He's always goofing off with the employees, and I don't think he holds them accountable. I'm sure you've seen all those tattoos, and what's with the nose piercing? It's not a professional image. I think he's better suited to be a line cook at Lady Luck."

"Have you asked him about the missing strawberries?"

"Not yet. I was hoping you would help me. I'd like to have you as a witness."

"Okay, since we have the time now, let's call Cody and invite him to speak with us."

Stacey snatched up her desk phone and quickly typed in a four-digit internal extension. "Cody, meet me in Human Resources in five minutes. Yes, Ava's office."

Ava didn't appreciate Stacey's rudeness toward Cody. Treating others with respect was at the heart of her leadership style. "We could have spoken with him right here, but my office it is. Let's head up there."

Ava knew from experience that an unexpected meeting request with human resources caused folks to feel as if they were being summoned to the principal's office. It was her goal to change that perception here at Ruby Park. Jeff had asked for her direction in changing the work culture, and she was committed to creating an open-door atmosphere.

Walking back out to the main corridor, Ava smiled as she heard a group of residents singing "Roll Out the Barrel" along with Thomas.

The two women sat down in Ava's office. A few minutes later, Cody knocked on the door frame before he entered. Seeing both Ava and Stacey sitting at the small round table in the corner, Cody's face flushed.

"Please join us," said Ava in her friendly tone. "We have a few questions. I understand we recently had a large delivery of strawberries. Is that correct?"

"We received several bushels of strawberries yesterday," said Cody. "We began rinsing them and—"

"They are missing!" exclaimed Stacey. "Exactly when were you rinsing them?"

"Yesterday afternoon after the lunch rush. I asked a couple of the assistants to help me with prep."

Stacey continued her tirade. "Did you know my nephew, Dave Sweetwater, donated these strawberries specifically for our resident appreciation reception tomorrow? Exactly where are they? What did you do with them?"

"Stacey," Ava inserted, "let's allow Cody to continue his story."

Cody took a deep breath. "As I was saying, we began rinsing the strawberries and noticed many of them had white mold."

"Mold? I don't believe that!"

"It's true. We can't serve any strawberries that had mold on them or were in the same container as berries that had mold. Nearly three-fourths of the delivery was visibly spoiled. Since it was a donation, I didn't call Sweetwater Farms for a replacement. I appreciate Dave's generosity, but I prepared a new plan for tomorrow. We have enough canned pineapple to make pineapple upside-down cake for the reception instead."

"Well, that's not what we had in mind at all," Stacey gave a dismissive wave of her hand.

"That's the best my team can do with the available food supply on hand. Besides, the residents love upside-down cake."

"You better hope our employees do too!"

"Cody, you said three-fourths were ruined. What about the remaining berries?" Ava inquired.

"As I said, we can't serve them here, but I let the kitchen staff take home small packages of the berries that didn't appear to have mold with instructions on how to clean them. The rest were thrown away."

Stacey and Ava spoke at once. Stacey demanded, "So you think you can just—" while Ava was asking a question.

Ava held up her index finger, and implored Stacey, "Please let me finish."

Stacey let out a huff.

"Cody, is it standard practice to give food away to staff?" Ava continued.

"It happens on occasion, but not often. Never with fresh food ready to serve. Just when there's something unusual like this. Like a couple months ago, we allowed staff to take stale baked goods home. When I called the bakery to report the problem, they agreed to deliver fresh rolls, but they didn't want a return of the stale items." Cody looked Ava in the eye with a panicked expression. "I'm sorry. Is there anything else you need from me?"

"No, thank you. I appreciate your time, Cody. You are free to go back to what you were doing."

Ava closed the door after Cody exited. "This didn't need to be an inquisition, Stacey. Why are you so worked up about this?"

"You heard him—he admitted he let the staff take berries home. I don't think the nursing staff get free food. Why should his? How do we know the strawberries were spoiled anyway? I know my nephew would have only donated the freshest fruit."

Ava sensed Stacey's family pride was wounded. "I'm certain Dave intended to donate fresh berries. It's really unfortunate this happened. But given the short time frame, I think it was gracious of Cody to find an alternative, don't you?"

"Maybe, but I am telling Jeff about this. I don't think it's right that Cody can just give away food whenever he wants."

"I'll also mention it to Jeff when I update him on tomorrow's events. I know all of Senior Living is setting up for the reception tomorrow. I'm sure you have plenty to do this afternoon."

Stacey took that as her cue to move on. "You're right, I'll see you tomorrow morning."

Ava studied her *To Do* list. She realized she only completed two of the dozen or so tasks she had listed for today. Just then her phone rang. The extension listed was from a nursing station.

She picked up the receiver. "Hello, this is Ava. How can I help you?"

"Hi, can employees get married?" asked the feminine voice on the other end.

"Yes, anyone over the age of eighteen can get married in Minnesota without parental consent."

"I mean, can employees marry other employees?"

"They sure can. Congratulations!"

"Thanks, bye," said the voice on the other end as the line disconnected.

Ava smiled broadly. *My faith in humanity is restored.*

Chapter Four

"I THOUGHT THAT WENT well," Ava said to May Tran, her payroll and benefits coordinator. They had completed the day's prize drawing in the cafeteria and were returning to their department on the second floor. "The Fitbit seemed to get the biggest reaction. That's a good sign for our wellness program, don't you think?"

May replied cheerfully, "I was thinking the same thing. We could look at getting fitness bands, yoga mats, and kettlebells for future give-a-ways."

Jenny was sitting at her desk near the entrance to the Human Resources suite with a long look on her face.

"What's up Jenny?" Ava asked. "Is something wrong?"

"I was waiting for you to come back. Please don't fire me." Jenny's face and neck turned red with white spots.

"It can't be that bad. What happened?"

"Ginny from Administration came in and asked if we received a chocolate basket. I said we did, and I thanked her for it. Oh my gosh, Ava, she said that it wasn't from her. Actually, she said the gals from the Hospice Unit sent it. It was their contribution for the dessert auction tomorrow."

Ava burst into laughter. "Oh no. That's hilarious! I thought you were going to share bad news."

"You're not mad?"

"Of course not. How could I be? It was a simple misunderstanding. There were no instructions with the basket. It is Appreciation Week, and we do receive food gifts from time to time, right?"

"Yeah."

"You poor thing—you should see the look on your face. It really is okay."

"What are we going to do? Ginny was really mad when I told her we ate it all this morning."

"I bet she was," Ava laughed even harder imaging the scene. May was laughing so much that her eyes welled up.

Jenny raised her eyebrows. "Ginny glared at me and she asked, 'You're kidding right?' and I said no, we really ate it!"

"When I stop laughing, I'll give Ginny a call to let her know that I'll replace it. No harm done. I'll run to the Wooddale Mall after work to pick up more candy and gift wrap. We'll fix it in the morning. The Hospice Team will never notice."

"What are we missing?" Des asked. She and Noelle were carrying lunch trays from the cafeteria. "We could hear you laughing from down the hall."

May regaled the group with a colorful description of Jenny's story. "Poor Jenny was white as a ghost. That is until she broke out in hives. I thought she was going to pass out."

Now everyone was laughing, including Jenny. "I thought I was in big trouble. You know how uptight Ginny is, and she'll probably tell Jeff. I'll pay you back, Ava."

"No, thank you. I've got this. Let me go give Ginny a call."

Ava headed to her desk. She pressed one hand to her side which hurt from laughing so hard.

After Ava spoke with Ginny and set the receiver down, her phone rang again. She didn't recognize the incoming number which included a Minneapolis area code.

"Human Resources, Ava speaking. May I help you?"

"Hello Ava, my name is John Carlson. I'm the Human Resources Director at A to Z Medical Supplies in Bloomington. Um, I am calling to share a complaint that I received from a member of our sales team who works closely with an employee at Ruby Park Senior Living Center. Is this a good time to talk?"

"Sure. Go ahead, John."

"This is a little awkward, but I need to bring this to your attention. Lindsey Green is one of our product account representatives who serves your center. During her recent visit, she met with your buyer, Pete Reinholtz. Lindsey informed me this morning that Pete asked her to demonstrate the fit of a new line of adult diapers."

"Oh, my goodness," responded Ava while grabbing a notebook and pen to take notes. "Did she tell you exactly what he asked her to do?"

"Yes, um he asked her to put the diaper on and demonstrate how the leg openings would remain snug to her body."

"Did she do what he requested?"

"Yes, she put one on over her pants."

Ava asked, "Did Lindsey say why she agreed to this instead of saying no?"

"Lindsey told me she felt extremely uncomfortable, but as a newer sales rep, she wanted to complete the sale and didn't want to risk losing your facility as a client. She said she felt intimidated by Pete and that during her drive back, she was angry and humiliated. She was crying when we spoke. As she's our employee, I'll offer her any support she needs form our end, but I felt you would want to be aware of Pete's actions. Lindsey will no longer be your account rep moving forward. Our sales manager will be in touch with your Chief Financial Officer in the near future."

"I completely understand. It's a very serious complaint, and I realize the gravity of this matter. I assure you that I'll look into this immediately and will bring our CFO, Cheryl, up to speed. Can you provide me further details on the date and time this occurred? Were there any witnesses?" Ava asked.

"No, they were in Pete's office with the door shut. Let me doublecheck on the time… Here it is. I see she was there last Friday from approximately two to three p.m."

"Thank you for your discretion and for bringing this to my attention. I'll get back to you, John. Can I use the number that you called me from, or do you have a direct line?"

"Yes, you can reach me at this number," said John. "Thank you, and have a good afternoon."

Ava glanced at her calendar. She and Des had a standing joke that complaints of bad behavior piled in during the full moon. Sure enough, it would occur that week. But this was no laughing matter. She sent a meeting invite to Cheryl to speak first thing the following morning and began preparing her investigation questions.

⋞

At the end of her workday, Ava stopped at the Coffee House and Brewery to pick up her house key.

"Hey, Ava," Lauren said. "Would you like a burger or a salad?"

"I'm sorry, but I can't stay for dinner. I just came by to pick up my key. I have to run over to Wooddale Mall to replace a gift basket." She quickly updated her sister regarding the chocolate mishap earlier.

"Here you go." Lauren laughed as she handed over the house key. "Matt and his friend from the hardware store installed your system this afternoon. He said to tell you that he took Sophie out about an hour ago."

"You guys are amazing."

"Anytime. Here's the manual and the instruction card with the code. It's just like mine… Pretty straight forward."

"How much do I owe you?"

"You can work that out with Matt. Come by for dinner tomorrow night—promise?"

"I promise. Thanks!" Ava left the restaurant and climbed into her vehicle. Since Sophie had been taken care of, she could spend more time at the mall.

During her drive to Wooddale, Ava's mind drifted. She was so grateful she'd traded rush hour gridlock traffic for small-town living. She didn't know anyone in the city who would drop what they were doing to help her out at home. Ruby Lake might be a 'blink and you miss it town' to those driving past on the interstate, but it was her home now, and she wanted to protect it just as it was. If the secret got out about how great their community was, mobs of city dwellers would move here and change it. She'd certainly witnessed suburban sprawl over the past decade.

Ha, get serious. Ruby Lake would never become a suburb. Not unless Clearwater or Kimball transformed into a booming metropolis… and that wasn't going to happen any time soon.

Once she arrived at the shopping center, Ava went directly

to Sees and quickly filled a shopping basket with treats. She replaced all the items her team had eaten that morning and grabbed several extra for good measure. Glancing at her watch, she decided she had plenty of time to browse the shops and indulge in some much-needed retail therapy.

As it turned out, browsing store displays and picking up a new pair of sandals brightened her day. She had barely thought about work at all, aside for the dessert auction… and the matter of meeting with Cheryl and Pete the following morning.

Ava imagined his small, piercing eyes. Was that a physical trait, or was he distrusting? While Pete acted apologetic when she talked with him on Monday afternoon, he was clearly angry on his phone a few minutes later. She realized she didn't know him at all. They'd never spoken one-on-one before that conversation. No doubt he was avoiding make waves while receiving a warning. She decided to put her work thoughts on hold again until tomorrow.

At the food court, Ava purchased teriyaki chicken to go. Then she carried her dinner, the chocolate goodies, and her new espadrilles back to the parking lot. It was time to go home.

❧

Following the evening news, Ava picked up her nearly empty popcorn bowl and water glass. Dumping the old maids into the garbage, she remembered she'd forgotten to take her waste bins to the curb for trash collection early the next morning.

She opened her double garage door and wheeled the large blue container to the end of her driveway. Meanwhile, Sophie ran in circles around the front yard. Fog was building, and the moon and stars were covered by a heavy layer of clouds. Except for the porch lights on the neighboring homes, it was relatively dark outside.

Ava saw a black Toyota Prius parked on the opposite side of the street where it came to a the dead-end. The hatchback appeared out of place sitting near the trail head. Its lights were off, and she couldn't see anyone inside. Perhaps the owners had lost track of time and were making their way back from an evening hike.

She returned to her garage to collect the recycling bin. As she planted it down on the curb, she gazed across the street again and thought the car had moved forward since she first saw it.

"Hey Ava," called a friendly voice.

Ava turned her head the opposite direction and saw her neighbor who lived two-doors down. He was wheeling his waste bin.

"Good evening, Bill," she said.

"Looks like we might be in for some rain again overnight. That was some storm we had last night."

"It sure was. Everything is really greening up."

"Say, I noticed you had security cameras installed today. Have you had any trouble?" Bill asked.

"No, but I figure, you can't be too careful," Ava replied.

"That's right. Let us know if you ever need anything," Bill said.

"Thanks, have a great evening!"

Ava patted her right hand against her thigh and issued a command to her dog. "Sophie, come." The lanky pup trotted along as they returned to the garage. Ava pressed the button to engage the electric garage door and watched it begin to close. As she stepped back inside her home, she heard the screech of a car peeling out as it sped down the street. She quickly moved to her front window, and saw the black car was gone.

After double checking that her exterior doors were locked, Ava switched on her alarm per the instruction card. Feeling a bit unnerved, she decided it was time to turn in. She padded into her bedroom, secured her door, and glanced under her bed to make sure her baseball bat was within reach.

Chapter Five

"WANT TO TAKE a walk?" Ava called. At the word 'walk,' Sophie scrambled to the foyer, nearly crashing into the front door.

"Isn't this a beautiful morning?" Ava asked shortly after they stepped onto the nature trail at the end of her street. She loved catching the sunrise and particularly relished Minnesota's long summer days. In June, the sun rose around five-thirty in the morning and didn't set until about nine at night.

After hiking nearly three miles round trip, Ava coaxed her panting dog back to the trailhead in Park Hills.

The shrill sound of emergency vehicles pierced the peace of the morning. A rescue vehicle and an ambulance sped down the highway, their sirens growing loader. Even after her years of working at a hospital, this urgency still affected Ava. She felt goose bumps form on her arms. Help was on its way which gave her hope that the injured or sick person would soon receive the assistance he or she desperately needed.

A few minutes passed, and a police vehicle whizzed by at top speed. She assumed there must have been an accident on the highway. Ruby Lake had one lone traffic light which regulated traffic coming off the highway onto Main Street. A feeling of dread formed in her chest, and Ava said a silent prayer.

"Let's head back home," Ava said aloud to her four-legged companion. Once Sophie led them back into their cozy house, Ava glanced at her watch. She still had plenty of time to take a leisurely shower and make it to Ruby Park Senior Living by eight o'clock sharp.

When she pressed the start button that brought her car alive, the 80s radio station her mother had selected earlier in the week was playing. Ava turned up the volume and sang at the top of her lungs to "It's Raining Men" by the Weather Girls.

As she reached a stop sign, Ava was startled to see the flashing lights of emergency vehicles parked in front of the Ruby Lake Community Center. She turned off Main Street and drove slowly past. Yellow crime scene tape blocked the main entrance to the parking lot. Her cell phone buzzed, and she jumped.

Ava parked her car parallel to the curb and checked her phone. She had missed a couple of text messages. One from Lauren said *call me ASAP*. The other from Shannon read *did you hear what happened?*

Ava called Lauren first, who picked up immediately.

"Where are you?" Lauren asked, foregoing a greeting.

"I'm at the community center," Ava said.

"Really? Were you there when it happened?" Lauren sounded shocked.

"I just parked on the street to see what's going on. When what happened?"

"You haven't heard, then. Brooke Sweetwater was shot. They found her at the community center this morning."

Ava gasped. "No, that can't be. I just saw her the other night. Dear Lord, what's going on?"

"I'm so sorry. One of the seniors in the Silver Sneakers club told me. They all came over here to get coffee and hang out since the center is closed until further notice. The manager and a custodian found her early this morning when they were setting up for the Jazzercise class. She was outside the equipment room."

"Is she alive? Is she going to be all right?"

"She was alive when they found her, but she's in critical condition. We haven't heard any updates yet."

"She's an amazing person. Who could do such an awful thing?" Ava tried to push the memory of Pete holding Brooke by the wrist out of her mind. "Poor Zoe, I can't imagine potentially losing her mom. She's just a kid."

"I know. I'm feeling horrible for Cody too."

"Cody who?" Ava asked.

"Cody Meyers, your nutrition manager. I heard he's been seeing Brooke."

"I can't believe what I'm hearing. She's married to Dave, right? I need to take a minute to pull myself together, and then I'll circle back and stop in. I'll talk to you soon."

Moments later, Ava held the front door of the coffee shop open for a weary-looking woman attempting to push a stroller through the entryway with one hand. The young mother was holding a bag of goodies in the other. Ava looked around and noticed several people were set up to work on their laptops while sipping a fresh brew of coffee. Two college-aged baristas were quickly taking and filling coffee orders.

"Who knew there were so many people out and about in the morning rather than hiding out in an office building?" Ava sidled up to her sister and their friends, Shannon and Rosie, who were huddled around a high-top table, each with a white ceramic coffee cup in hand.

"You should take more time to see how the other half lives," Lauren teased. "And here comes trouble now… Good morning, Randy."

"Morning, ladies. I thought I'd grab a cup and an earful. Des just told me about Brooke." He adjusted his cap. "Damn. I can't wrap my head around it."

"We're all stunned. Everyone here has been speculating about what happened. What's your opinion?" Shannon removed her glasses. Her dark curly hair rested on her shoulders.

"We've all heard there's a feud between Pete and the Sweetwaters, though I don't know what he'd stand to gain by hurting Brooke," Randy said.

"That's a frightening thought," said Rosie. She owned the floral shop across the square and was Shannon's mother. "I think I'd feel more comfortable if it was some random act. I don't know if it's safe to go out."

"What's their dispute about anyway?" Ava asked.

"It goes back to the days when Pete was a CPA in town. There was some fallout, and they stopped working together," Shannon said.

Ava checked her watch. She had a meeting that morning. "I'm a bit freaked out by all this, but I'd better get into work. Please let me know as soon as you hear any updates on Brooke."

Matt joined the table and asked Ava, "Were you able to follow my directions for your security system?"

"Yeah, it's pretty easy. I really appreciate it, and I feel so much better. Especially now… Let me know the cost, and I'll pay you on Venmo."

"No problem. I was glad to have a project outside of the restaurant."

Ava waved on her way out. "You're the best. See you guys soon."

⌁

"Hi everyone," Ava murmured as she approached her team at Ruby Park. Her employees were standing in the entrance to the Human Resources offices talking about the community center's yoga instructor. "I know this is going to be a challenging day. The news about Brooke Sweetwater is a complete shock."

"We heard she's in the ICU. We got her a card from our gift shop. Feel free to sign it," said May.

"You guys are amazing. I was thinking about visiting her at the hospital tomorrow afternoon."

"If you go, can I tag along with you?" asked Jenny through her tears.

"Of course, I don't know if they'll allow visitors, but we can drop off a card and flowers."

Des said, "I can't believe this. Who could possibly want to hurt Brooke? She's such a caring soul."

Ava wiped the tears forming in her own eyes. "I can't imagine why this happened, and I hope they find whoever did this soon. Thank goodness she survived, but the next day or two will be critical."

"We'll support her anyway we can," Noelle, the volunteer coordinator, said.

"I know you will."

Ava retreated to her desk and gathered her notebook and pen. *Eat the Frog First*, she thought. The expression, inspired by Mark Twain, meant it was best to get the most difficult task completed early.

She made her way down to the first floor to speak with Cheryl. Ava was impressed with their Chief Financial Officer and hoped they'd become friends. Cheryl was sensible and intelligent. She was much more outgoing than most accountants she had met in the past, and her easy manner made her approachable. Cheryl waved her in.

"Did you hear the news about Brooke? She was shot while prepping for yoga class," Cheryl said. She was wearing a beige pant suit which contrasted her dark hair and complexion.

Ava nodded. "Yeah. I stopped at the coffee shop this morning. I think I'm still in shock."

"It's unbelievable. Speaking of which, let's talk about Pete. Dang, what was he thinking?"

"We'll have to ask him." Ava filled in the remaining details regarding the complaint she received the day before. "I'm sure you understand what this means if the accusations are true."

Cheryl shook her head. "We can't keep Pete on board."

"Well, it's quite possible he'll deny it. If he shares a very different account of Lindsey's visit, I'll continue the investigation."

"I'll follow your lead."

"By the way, I saw a note in Pete's file from last year. He had an angry outburst at staff meeting and was swearing. Has anything like that happened since?"

"Nothing serious. Pete's a glass half empty kind of guy. He's been particularly irritable recently, but I attribute that to the auditors being on site the past few weeks."

Cheryl called Pete and invited him to her office. It took him ten minutes to make the one-minute walk down the hall to her office. He shot Ava a look of disgust when her saw her sitting at the conference table in Cheryl's office.

"Am I in trouble?" Pete looked worried, and his hair was disheveled.

"Please have a seat," said Ava. "We asked you to meet with us because we received a complaint, and we want to hear your account of what happened."

"Okay. What's this all about?" Pete's scratchy voice sounded like he was eating sandpaper.

"I understand that you met with a sales representative from A to Z Medical Supplies last Friday. Is that correct?"

"Yes, Lindsey came by. She stops in monthly and asks for feedback on the quality of their products, and she tries to sell me on new items. I have sales people from different companies coming and going all the time."

"Did you ask Lindsey to show you an adult diaper last week?"

"Yes, she brought in a package from a new product line."

"Did you ask her to put one on?" asked Ava.

"Yeah… why is that a problem?" Pete's eyes darted between the two women.

"Do you not see that it's inappropriate to ask a woman to wear a diaper in your office?" demanded Cheryl.

"How else would I know if the new design provided the coverage needed by our residents?" Pete responded in an equally negative tone.

Cheryl said, "It's incredibly demeaning. You are aware of our sexual harassment policy?"

"You're not serious?" Pete tugged at his shirt collar.

Ava ended this line of questioning. "Pete, this is a violation of our Code of Conduct policy. We have zero tolerance for harassment of any kind. We no longer need your services, and your employment with Ruby Park is terminated effective immediately."

Pete groaned and said, "Lindsey complained to you. Christ, why didn't she say anything to me? Don't I deserve a second chance?"

"We expect our leaders to behave in a professional manner at all times," Ava said.

"That's cold. You are going to regret this." His hands squeezed into fists.

"Our decision has been made."

"Are you kidding me? What are my options?"

"Your employment is terminated effective immediately." Ava handed him the written separation notice she had prepared in advance in the event they determined Lindsey's complaint was true. She continued, "You may elect to resign if you wish. Please hand me your badge and your corporate credit card." Pete took off his ID badge and dug through his wallet to find the card.

"What if I want to resign?"

"If that's your choice, we'll accept, but I'll need it in writing. Please leave your laptop computer on your desk before you go. If you decide to resign, give your notice to Cheryl."

"All you women are so uptight," he seethed as his face reddened.

"Cheryl will walk you to your desk to collect your keys and any necessary personal items. We'll schedule a time for you to collect your larger belongings after business hours. Thank you for your service. I wish you well in the future." Ava got up and left the room as planned. Cheryl would walk Pete out of the building.

Ava returned to her office and dialed the phone. She planned to wrap up this case and complete her investigation report while it was all fresh in her mind.

"John Carlson speaking."

"Hi John, this is Ava Andrews from Ruby Park Senior Living. We spoke yesterday regarding a complaint from one of your company's employees, Lindsey Green."

"Yes, hello Ava."

"I wanted to let you know that Pete Reinholtz no longer works for Ruby Park. We deeply regret how Lindsey was treated during her last visit. Please extend our apologies, and let her know she's welcome to visit our center at any time."

"I've got to admit that I am grateful to hear from you so quickly. I will extend this message to Lindsey. Thank you," said John. Ava detected much more energy in John's voice than during yesterday's conversation.

"I appreciate you too, John. Have a good day."

"You too."

Next, Ava stopped by Jenny's desk. "Good morning, Jen. Pete Reinholtz no longer works with us. I'd like you to call the Facilities Management Department immediately to disable his building and computer accesses, and then ask May to prepare his final paycheck. He'll be paid through today plus any accrued paid time off."

"Sorry about the rough start," Jenny said, "but your day can only get better from here." Jenny had said before that she didn't aspire to become a Human Resources Director like Ava. She definitely preferred onboarding employees over offboarding. Most of her interactions were with new employees excited to start their careers at Ruby Park.

"Thanks for always pointing out the bright side," responded

Ava as she walked to her desk to document her conversations with Cheryl, Pete, and John.

๑

It was late-afternoon when Ava returned from her shift serving up-side-down cake and coffee at the resident's reception. She barely had a chance to talk to her grandpa but took comfort that he was joyfully preoccupied discussing politics and current events with his companions. Though the Rose Dining Room had buzzed with chatter and speculation about the violent attack at the community center, she didn't learn anything new about Brooke or the shooter.

Ava brushed lingering cake crumbs off her jacket and closed her eyes, grateful to have a moment to meditate. She whirled around in her chair when she heard a slight tap at her office door.

Nellie, a petite woman wearing a housekeeping uniform, popped her head into Ava's doorway and asked if she could dust the office furniture.

"It's good to see you, Nellie. How are you doing?" asked Ava.

"You know, same old same old," Nellie replied in a cheerful voice. "My little one kept me up all night. My fiancé, Hayden, is working the night shift these days, so I didn't get any help."

"I'm sorry to hear that. I hope you catch up on your rest tonight. I'd love to see a picture of your daughter. Do you have one you can share?"

Nellie beamed. "Not on me, but I'll bring one next time. She's such a cutie. She loves playing dress up. You should see all the clothes she has. Her grandma brings over dozens of outfits every time she visits."

"I'm sure your mom is very proud of you and your family," Ava replied.

"Oh, she sure is." Nellie carried her feather duster from the bookcase to the credenza.

Ava walked around and checked in on her team. She waved at Jenny who was on the phone. May was answering payroll questions for an employee seated beside her. Ava watched Nellie push her cart back down the hallway.

The roar of the county's tornado siren made Ava jump. *Is it the first Wednesday of the month? Yes, it is. And it's one p.m.?* Ava confirmed the time with the clock. She followed this routine monthly when the test sirens sounded. Fortunately, the loud noise ceased after a minute.

Des sat behind her desk staring at her computer screen. Ava entered the tidy office, adjacent to her own, and took a seat in front of Des.

"Nellie is a sweetheart," said Ava. "You know she's never shared a picture of her daughter with me. It seems strange since mothers typically have hundreds of photos on hand. Maybe she's not allowed to carry her cell phone with her."

"Oh, you don't know." Des covered her mouth to suppress a laugh. "Nellie doesn't actually have a daughter."

"What?"

"She lives with her mother across town. I don't think she's ever been engaged, and she definitely doesn't have children. I've worked here longer than she has, so I would know. I believe she invented her family to have something to talk about."

"Are you serious? Whenever I run into her, she mentions Hayden and their daughter."

"I don't think she's ever given her daughter a name," said Des. "Her 'little one' as she calls her has been two years old for several years. She tells everyone that she's dating a guy named Hayden. I think that's the name of a popular character from a soap opera she follows."

"Really?" Ava rested her chin on her hand.

"Yeah, she's been planning their wedding for well over a year, and if you ask about her wedding gown, she'll show you a picture. Nellie keeps it in her uniform pocket. She cut a photo out of a bridal magazine. It's the exact dress that Meghan Markle wore when she married Prince Harry."

"Well, this just got more interesting. Is she okay? I mean does Nellie believe this, or does she just like to tell stories?"

"I believe she's perfectly fine. She comes to work on time and does her job. She seems to like the attention she receives. We've never gotten a complaint about her work performance or her stories."

"Thanks for filling me in. I feel a bit embarrassed about it," Ava said. "I'm sure I've talked to Nellie about her family with other coworkers nearby. Guess I was out of the loop. Now that I know, I won't steer our conversations toward family. Keep me posted if this causes a problem."

"Nellie is part of the fabric of this organization. Everyone just goes along with it since she's harmless."

"Good to know."

Chapter Six

AVA STEERED HER Bronco into town with her four-legged companion in tow and pulled into the parking lot alongside Woodcrest. As Sophie bounded out of the vehicle, she pulled on her leash with full force, knocking Ava off balance.

"Whoa! Take it easy, girl. Let's walk around to the deck in the back." Ava spotted Lauren on the covered patio, setting small pails of napkins and utensils on tables.

"I was just looking for you," Lauren said. "I'm so glad you brought my favorite puppy." Lauren had set out a bowl of water on the wood planks. "I wish we could get a dog, but it would be too much with running this place day and night."

"I still find it hard to believe you opened a coffee shop. The brewery part I get, but a morning person you are not," joked Ava. She took a seat at a rectangular table and plopped her bag down on the chair next to hers.

"Hey, that's what the coffee's for!" Lauren said.

"You should've started drinking coffee in high school. That might have kept you from getting so many tardy slips."

"Ha, ha. You're probably right. What can I get you? I know

you like our sweeter brews. We have a new IPA with a hint of blackberry. Do you want to try that along with a cheeseburger?"

"You've read my mind." Ava enjoyed tasting the different varieties of craft beers Matt served. Inventing new brews was a creative process in its own right. She surveyed the brewery menu. The list of twenty options on tap included Farmyard Crawl, Beach a Go-Go, Vampire Daze, and Top Dogg among others. This made her smile.

"Great, coming right up!"

Lauren quickly returned with two tall glasses of beer. "I put your order in at the front of the line. It should be out in a few minutes."

"It's good to know people." Ava smiled. "Do you have any news about Brooke? Last I heard, she was in surgery."

"Just that she's in critical condition. The next forty-eight hours should determine whether she'll pull through."

Ava shook her head. "Last time I saw her was at Yoga class. She wasn't her usual self the other night. I feel terrible for her."

"There's a rumor going around that Dave and Brooke are having financial problems."

"That's unfortunate. And you said they've split up too?"

"It appears that way."

"You seem to know everything that's going on around here. There's no privacy in Ruby Lake, is there?" Ava asked.

"It's small-town living. If you want privacy, you'll need to drive at least fifteen miles out of town. It was confining for us as kids—we wanted to see the real world—but now I find it a comfort. Everyone is just looking out for one another. Besides, I'm both a barista and a bartender now. I listen to people all day long."

Ava nodded. "We share that in common."

"So, how's work? Any juicy gossip?"

"You know I can't afford to add to the town rumor mill. I have my reputation to uphold."

"I was kidding. Don't be so serious all the time."

"I'm sorry. I regressed into my big-city mode. I really love working at Ruby Park. Appreciation week has been a blast… Dang, no pun intended."

"Remember, I'm here for you anytime you need me. I'm also available to puppy sit." Lauren reached down and scratched Sophie's ears.

"Thanks, Sis."

"Now we just have to find you a man," Lauren added with a hint of a grin.

"Oh, brother." Ava shook her head, then smiled at the sight of Des who was approaching her table while carrying a beer and a burger plate.

"Your dinner is served, madame." Des placed the plate neatly in front of Ava and took a seat across from her.

"I didn't know we hired extra help." Lauren grinned.

"Matt told me Ava was out here, so I offered to deliver."

"Thank you! It's getting rather busy. I'm going to check inside." Lauren touched Ava's shoulder and left the two women alone at the table.

Ava said, "I didn't know you were going to stop by tonight."

"Me neither. Harper and I picked up her cap and gown for graduation and then stopped by the Chic Boutique for a party dress. Wait until you see her in it—she looks so sophisticated. Anyway, Randy said he was meeting a friend for a beer, and we decided to join him for dinner. We just placed our order. The guys are inside playing darts."

"I'm so glad you did. Tell Harper and Randy to join us out

here. Looks like the last table on the patio was just taken." The unusually warm June evening was bringing everyone outside.

"It's gorgeous out here, and I'll take you up on the offer. What a week it's been so far. We deserve some downtime."

"Cheers to that! Tell me about Harper's graduation party. How many kids are coming?"

"You know how it is. I think she invited the entire senior class. With all the open houses scheduled, that crowd will be moving from one house to another over the next few weekends."

"Harper must be thrilled."

"So am I. I'm fortunate she still wants to spend time with me, and I'll take every minute I can get. It won't be long before we're moving her up to Duluth to start college. She's a great kid. It's Will who I have to keep my eye on. He turns fifteen next month, and he's all testosterone."

"What the hell is your problem?" bellowed a male voice. Ava and Des snapped their heads toward the open windows connecting the patio to the indoor dining area. Pete Reinholtz was sitting next to Harper with his arm around her shoulders. The voice belonged to him, and he was glaring at Randy.

"Keep your sleezy hands off of her," Randy commanded. He was standing over Pete as Pete was moving to stand up. Randy stepped back allowing Pete to take to his feet.

"Relax man. I didn't know she's your lady."

"She's my daughter, you idiot." Randy's voice was intense.

"Looks like she's a full-grown woman to me. If she's eighteen, she's legal." Pete drawled.

"You're a moron. She's in high school. Listen up Pete, if you come near her again, I'll freaking kill you."

"Yeah, you're not man enough."

"I'm serious. I'll destroy you."

Pete cackled and then stumbled as he nearly missed the back step while making his way onto the patio. "You're a pussy," Pete slurred.

"Go home and sleep it off, Pete," advised Matt. "How did you get here? I can call you a ride."

"Nah man, I walked over. What do you care, anyway?"

Pete approached Ava and Des on his way to the sidewalk. "Well, if it isn't Miss Perfect," he remarked slowly. "Bet you think you're something special."

Sophie instantly stood at attention while uttering a low growl. It was the same sound she made during the lightning storm earlier in the week. Ava took her by the collar and leaned toward Des, trying to create more space away from Pete.

Pete pointed at Ava. "You better watch out. I'm coming for you next."

"Get the hell out of here," called Randy.

"What an ass," said the attractive stranger who was approaching Randy.

"You've got that right," replied Matt. The crowd on the patio had quieted to a dull roar. "Sorry, for the disturbance, folks. The next round of beer is on me."

Matt's declaration was met with applause and cheers. The three friends stepped toward Ava and Des. Des waved to her daughter, Harper, gesturing her to come outdoors and join them.

"Ava, this is our friend Jack Lindstrom." Matt made the introduction. "Ava is Lauren's sister."

"Hello, Jack. Welcome to Ruby Lake." Ava raised her glass.

Jack replied, "That guy is nuts. What's he babbling about?"

"It appears Pete is lashing out tonight. Ava fired him this morning," supplied Lauren.

"Who did you hear that from?" Ava asked.

"His mother-in-law, Karen. She was here telling a group of women over lunch."

Randy studied Harper's face. "Are you okay, honey?"

"Yeah, Dad."

"I didn't even see him move in on Harper," Randy said. "When I turned around, he was at our table leaning toward her. She asked him to leave, and I just sped that process along."

Des said, "I'm glad you were there Randy, but Harper is going to be out on her own soon. She'll need to learn to manage these things."

"Geez, you guys. I can handle it," Harper declared.

Randy clasped his hands. "I can't stand that there are vultures around like that guy."

Ava pushed her plate aside. It held a half-eaten burger. A cheerful waiter arrived with three dinner plates for the Sparks family. He asked Ava, "What are you drinking? I'll get you a refill."

"I think it's called Black Sabbath," Ava replied.

"That's a heavy metal band—the beer is called Blackberry Mammoth."

"Yeah, I'll have that one." She nodded with a wide grin, and everyone at the table laughed.

"Coming right up!"

"Would you like to play a game of darts while these folks enjoy their dinner?" Jack asked Ava.

"I'd like that." Ava raised a brow at Des.

Des caught her unspoken request. "Go ahead. We'll keep an eye on Sophie."

Ava glanced around as they headed indoors. She loved the warehouse-chic vibe of the restaurant. She and Jack took turns throwing darts, and she was every bit as accurate as he was.

"You didn't tell me you're a dart shark!" Jack said.

"You didn't ask."

"How did you learn to play like this?"

"Small-town living. I grew up here. There's not much to do as a teenager except throw darts, bowl, and hang out at the lake during the summer. How about you?"

"Same. I grew up in Roberts, Wisconsin," Jack said. "My folks had a hobby farm so I had a lot of chores, but I managed to find myself a fair share of trouble too."

"How did you end up here in Ruby Lake?"

"I attended college at the University of North Dakota. That's where I met Matt. He saw my recent Facebook post about restoring my dad's car, and he recommended Randy for the engine work. Randy is an expert with classic cars."

"So, you're the guy with the Mustang. My mom ran into you at Sparks Auto this week."

"Grace? She's a hoot. She was trying to get me to enter the Fourth of July car show."

"You seem to have time on your hands," Ava said.

"Oh that. I work as a commercial pilot now. I'm based in Minneapolis. I rotate a few days on and a few days off."

"How do you like flying for the airlines?"

"It has its ups and downs."

Ava snorted as she tried to hold down the beer she'd just sipped. Jack grinned back at her, obviously pleased that she appreciated his joke.

"What do you do when you're not firing people?" Jack's blue-green eyes twinkled. Ava found his five o'clock shadow alarmingly attractive. He rubbed his hand along his square jaw as though he knew Ava was checking him out.

"I don't... oh, you're teasing me. I recently joined Ruby

Park Senior Living as their HR Director. Most of the time I'm hiring staff, delivering training, and trying to improve benefits and the work culture. It's usually pretty tame, but there are some crazy days. So, are you going to enter the car show?"

"Will you be there?"

"Are you kidding me? The whole town will be there. We live for that stuff. Every business will be shut down that day."

Jack gazed intently into Ava's eyes. "I don't know yet if I'll enter the show. I'm not scheduled to work on the fourth, but I'm not sure the car's engine will be ready in time. Will you put in a good word for me with Randy? Maybe he'll speed things up."

"Sure thing," Ava responded lightly, though she felt her heart had just skipped a beat. She found herself hoping Jack would make the summer festival.

❦

"You like him," Lauren chirped to her older sister after Ava approached the bar.

"Oh, grow up, Lauren," Ava replied cooly though she knew she was blushing. The evening rush had died down, and she and Des offered to help Lauren prep the coffee station for the next morning.

Lauren grinned at Ava, "You *like* him, like him. You have to admit you think he's hot."

Ava rolled her eyes.

"I think he's hot," added Des. "I may be married, but I'm not blind." She glanced at Ava.

Lauren rested a hand on her hip. "Come on, Ava. We saw the way Jack looked at you. I definitely observed major chemistry going on there."

"You know he's not my type, Lauren."

"Not all serious and buttoned up you mean."

Ava reflected briefly. "I guess I tend to go for mature businessmen."

"And how's that been working out for you?" Lauren nudged Ava in the shoulder.

"Good grief. Let it go, woman."

Chapter Seven

BELLS JINGLED AS Ava swung open the door to Rosie's Floral. The shop didn't open until eight a.m. on weekdays, but Shannon told her that Rosie would leave the door open. "I'll be right out," chirped a tender female voice.

"It's me, Ava."

"Come join me in the back, dear."

Ava browsed the fresh blooms and silk flowers of nearly every possible color. The air in the bright flower shop was filled with sweet and fruity fragrances. She peeked into the back room and discovered Rosie was leaning over an industrial sink with her clippers in hand. The work space smelled musky in contrast to the front showroom. "Hi Rosie… Ma. I don't know what to call you these days."

"Either is fine with me. I enjoyed when you called me 'Ma' while you and Shannon were in school. You girls sure were joined at the hip. We're both overjoyed that you're back in town for good."

Ava and Rosie's daughter, Shannon, bonded in the fifth grade over their mutual infatuation with the Backstreet Boys. After spending one afternoon in Shannon's room listening to

CD's, Ava knew she had a second home. They had danced and sung the hit song "I Want it That Way" into their hairbrushes for hours. Shannon was an only child who had entered her parents' lives when Rosie was nearly forty years old. She loved doting on both girls, and they ate up the attention.

Rosie wore her silver-gray hair in a short bob. Sometimes she added a shocking touch of color. Today, she showed off frosted pink tips. She had rounded out her look with pink floral leggings, a gray sweatshirt with the words 'flower power' written in purple, and aqua jelly sandals.

"I think you should keep the pink highlights. They complement your face as well as your name perfectly," Ava said.

"You're so sweet. You know I don't like to commit to one choice. It's the same with flowers. There are just so many options that I couldn't possibly choose a favorite. That's probably why I became a florist," Rosie said, and Ava smiled in acknowledgment.

"Shannon isn't here yet," Rosie continued. "The gift shop opens at ten o'clock, but you already know that. I assume you're here to pick up the sunflowers, snapdragons, and daisies you ordered. They make a lovely combination. You have a great eye for harmonious colors. Do you need help carrying them out to your car?"

"Once I put them into shopping bags, I think I can manage it."

"I included strips of burlap and raffia ribbon for you to experiment with."

"You're the best." Ava gently opened two of the flower packages and grasped a couple snapdragon stems and a daisy. She placed the simple arrangement in a bud vase and set it down next to Rosie. She recalled Rosie used to say to the girls,

I don't want people to send flowers to my funeral; I want to enjoy them while I'm living.

"For you, Ma. I hope you have a super day!" Ava gave Rosie a side hug because the older woman's gloved hands were dank from leaves and floral debris.

Anthony, the short, hefty gentleman who ran the pizzeria on the square, held the door for Ava as she made her way to the entrance.

"Thanks, Anthony. I don't think the shop will officially be open for another hour," she said.

He held up a container with two cups of coffee in his other hand. "I know. I offered to bring Rosie coffee this morning."

Ava couldn't help wondering if he used hair dye. For a man well over sixty, his hair was surprisingly jet black. Rosie had become a widow several years earlier, and Ava was pleased she had a male companion.

Ava managed to wrangle her car door open without dropping her packages and felt relieved. She was parked on the street in front of Rosie's shop. Lauren's place was directly across the square, beyond the original town hall which occupied the center block. The old stone building currently housed a library and the history museum where her mother volunteered on a part-time basis.

Ava strolled down the sidewalk, passing the sign etched in the window that signaled she'd reached Woodcrest. Her brother-in-law, Matt, had bought his uncle's old bar when he retired and had converted it into the trendy hangout that brought in customers from morning to nighttime.

While studying ag-business in North Dakota, Matt had worked at a brewery part-time to support himself. Once he got this craft brewery up and running, he hired Lauren to run the front of the house. Ava was proud of what they had accomplished and admired how the couple worked so well together.

As she swung open the door, the smell of fresh grounds instantly greeted her. "Good morning, Matt. Do you mind if I help myself to a cup of hot cocoa? I think I could use a good sugar rush this morning."

"Help yourself," he said and laughed. "Expecting a long day?"

"You could say that, but it's got to be much better than yesterday." Ava said as she added a heaping serving of whipped cream to cool down her drink. While she'd given up coffee years ago, she felt it was only fair to be able to indulge in an occasional cup of hot chocolate. After all, the amount of caffeine was a fraction of that in a serving of coffee, and a woman should treat herself from time to time.

Matt continued to set up a display of muffins, cinnamon rolls, and their famous rhubarb Danishes. Ava was tempted to grab one but reminded herself of the afternoon cake auction. She stuffed a few bills into the tip jar not wanting to take advantage of her sister and brother-in-law's generosity.

She went outside and hopped into her vehicle once again, amazed by how quickly she could run errands on the square before work. She settled comfortably into her driver's seat and relaxed for a moment. Soon she was headed to Ruby Park.

❧

Ava darted toward her desk to grab the ringing phone, dropping her bags of flowers in the process.

"Good morning, Yvonne. How are you?" she asked, slightly out of breath.

"Hi Ava. I wanted to follow up about the physical therapist we talked about the other day. The one with the pattern of absenteeism. I'm really concerned. I think she has a serious problem."

Ava asked, "What did you learn?"

"She came in today with a split lip, and her face is swollen. A couple of her co-workers told me they believe this is a domestic issue," reported Yvonne.

"That's awful. Did you ask her about it?"

"Yes. She made a lame excuse about running into a door. I don't know what to do."

"I'll walk over there now to take a look," said Ava. "What's her name?"

"It's Natalie Reinholtz."

Ava paused for a second. "Any relation to Pete Reinholtz?"

"Pete's her husband."

Struck with dismay, Ava simply said, "I see. I'll come right over."

Even though Ava had seen Pete when he was angry, she found it difficult to believe that the man could harm his wife. However, she had spoken to victims of domestic violence before and was aware it was more common than most people knew.

"See you in a few minutes," Yvonne said.

Ava headed straight to the physical therapy gym at the back of the skilled nursing wing. It wasn't hard to spot Natalie. While her auburn bangs were draped over her eyes, her hair and heavy makeup didn't hide the purple bruises on her cheekbone. She also had a scab on her swollen lower lip. Ava waved hello to the therapists and residents and then stepped into Yvonne's office.

"Hey, I saw Natalie. She looks like she was in a boxing

match. Of course, a major accident of some sort could cause that too. I'd like to speak with her alone, if you don't mind."

"Good," Yvonne said. "That'll make me feel much better."

"When is she finished with her current patient?"

"Within the next ten minutes. I'll take Natalie's next appointment."

Ava cautioned, "This might take a while. Do you have coverage if she needs to leave for the day?"

"Yes, I can arrange that or cover myself." Yvonne assured her.

"Thank you. Can we use your office?"

"Of course."

Ava asked, "After you introduce us, would you mind walking over to Social Services? Ask Pam if she has time to come over here to speak with an employee about potential domestic abuse. Please don't share Natalie's name at this time. I'll ask Natalie whether she's ready to speak with a social worker before I invite her into your office to join us."

"I'll do that. I really appreciate you being here. I didn't know what to do. I feel terrible for her."

Ava eyed a box of tissues on a bookcase and moved it to the center of the table. Yvonne had turned her institutional space into a homey environment. There were framed pictures of her kids, a few plants, and a table lamp. Ava sat in one of the two chairs in front of the desk. Several minutes later, Yvonne introduced Natalie to Ava then she closed the office door behind her.

"Thank you for joining me, Natalie. Please have a seat. Your coworkers and I are deeply concerned about your safety. I noticed the bruises and cuts on your face. Can you tell me what happened?"

Natalie bowed her head and folded her hands in her lap. "Oh, this is so embarrassing. I am such a klutz. I ran into a door when I was getting ready this morning."

"I'm not a medical provider, but it looks like your injuries have occurred over a period of time. Some of the bruises might be from earlier than today. It also looks like somebody or something hit you recently."

Natalie shrugged. "I know, I'm so stupid."

"Did this happen at home?" Ava asked gently.

Natalie gave an almost imperceptible nod, and Ava waited for a verbal response. "It's all my fault. I was asking Pete why he was home from work early yesterday, and I pressed him for answers to why he lost his job. I should have known better. I set him off."

Ava paused and then asked, "Has he hit you before?"

"Yeah." Natalie shuddered slightly.

"And you've been making excuses for your husband to cover for him?"

Natalie only nodded.

"That's a huge burden to carry," Ava said in a soft tone.

Small tears welled in Natalie's eyes and slowly crept onto her cheeks. Ava understood the art of talking versus listening. There was a time for each, and she remained quiet. Ava pulled a couple facial tissues out of the box that was waiting on the round table and handed them to the petite woman crying silently next to her.

"Thank you," Natalie whimpered. "Pete had been drinking. I shouldn't have nagged him for an answer about his job. I deserved it."

"No, you did not deserve this. Pete is responsible for his own actions. May I give you a hug?"

"Okay."

Ava wrapped her arms around Natalie whose thin frame quivered as she began sobbing in Ava's arms. Ava held onto her more firmly now and allowed her to cry. After this continued for a couple of minutes, her tears slowed to heavy breathing. Natalie spoke first. "You're not going to report him or anything are you? I started the argument. It's my fault."

"This is not your fault. Is his behavior the reason you've missed a few Monday shifts recently?"

Natalie nodded. "Since he's no longer working here, I guess I can tell you. Pete started drinking again several months ago. He gets a bit out of hand over the weekend."

"Most importantly, I want you to be safe. There are a number of resources available for you and your family. I heard you have children, is that correct?"

"Yes, two. My son, Tyler, is sixteen, and Tess is twelve."

"Perhaps there's someone you can stay with, a family member or a friend while you're working through this. We have an employee assistance program that offers free and confidential counseling and referral services."

Ava opened an envelope and took out two brochures. "I highlighted their toll-free number on the front. Counseling can be very helpful. Our program also includes free legal service. You might consider getting a restraining order. If you choose to do that, please give me a copy, and I'll notify our security team. I'll put this back in the envelope, so you can keep it confidential."

Ava heard the footfalls of high heeled shoes reverberating on the tile floor. It sounded like someone was walking toward them and then slowed to a stop. She assumed the social worker must be nearby. A pair of blue eyes peeked into the office door window. Ava held up her index finger, asking for one minute. Pam nodded.

"I'm sorry I'm crying like this." Natalie sniffled.

"Never be sorry for sharing your emotions. I can tell you're a very capable woman. We all need support sometimes." Ava tilted her head toward the door. "Yvonne asked Pam from Social Services to stop by to see you. If it's okay with you, I'll invite her in."

"Yes, I know Pam. I'll speak with her."

Ava opened the door and invited Pam inside. Pam gave a dismayed look and said, "Oh, look at you Natalie. What happened?"

"I know—it looks worse than it is. My husband got mad at me." She gazed at her hands and picked at the tissues she'd scrunched into one of her palms.

Pam turned toward Ava, seeking direction.

Ava said, "I'll give you two your privacy. Yvonne is covering Natalie's appointments for the rest of the day. Take all the time that you need here."

Ava patted Natalie's hand. "You may leave whenever you wish. Please call Yvonne if you need additional time off. We all want you to feel better soon. Call me if there's anything I can do for you. I wrote my personal cell phone number on my business card. It's with the other materials I gave you."

Natalie looked up. "I can't thank you enough."

"Please take care of yourself."

Ava entered a private restroom provided for visitors. She promptly locked the door as tears formed in her eyes. She had remained calm for Natalie's sake, but now she needed to let go of the emotion she had bottled up inside.

Why did some people think they had the right to hurt others? And how could a man beat his wife?

Ava knew she would never comprehend this. She had spoken with victims of domestic abuse before. It wasn't unusual for a woman to say she wanted to give her partner another chance. She had also learned in counseling courses that some people blamed themselves and protected their abusers. Ava peered in the mirror. Thank goodness, Natalie had been receptive today, but they would see what tomorrow would bring.

Damn, this is hard. Ava had heard Natalie's story, but she couldn't fix it. Ava briefly imagined a utopia where everyone was kind and respected one another. She washed her face, practiced a smile, and stepped back into the real world.

❦

Ava checked her watch. The morning was slipping away from her, and she needed to set up for Ruby Park's first ever charity dessert auction. An hour later, she glanced around the community dining room for the twentieth time checking to make sure every detail matched her exacting standards and couldn't stop the impulse to move a flawless floral arrangement just three inches over to her left. *Now that's perfect.*

Jenny approached Ava. "These sunflower displays are a gorgeous touch. It all looks so festive but casual, in a good way. You definitely have a flair for decorating."

"Thanks, I was going for the relaxed feel of our gardens. Since this is a charity fund raiser, I want the desserts to steal the show."

"You nailed it. Speaking of desserts, the prep kitchen refrigerators are full of the donations that employees dropped off prior to their shifts. What time should we set them out?"

"Let's wait another half hour, so they'll be as fresh as possible at showtime. That reminds me, I need to stop in the kitchen. Be back in a minute."

Ava approached the prep kitchen and stopped when she heard voices.

"My cousin knows the custodian who found her, and he said he heard the office safe was unlocked. Maybe the guy tried to rob the place," a female voice said.

A masculine voice asked, "Who says is was a man?"

"Poor Brooke. She shows early up for work, and gets caught off guard," said another person.

"I don't think she's all that innocent. Apparently, she and Cody are as thick as thieves. Candace saw them eating lunch together at that small Mexican place outside of town," Renee from facilities explained while filling her water jug. Ava saw her as she opened the swinging door.

"Hi everyone," Ava said. "I need to grab a roll of paper towels."

Renee turned her back and walked out.

"I assume you're talking about Brooke Sweetwater? Everyone's pretty upset about what happened," Ava said as she turned toward Gloria, a nutrition supervisor.

"I've never seen Cody this unhappy. He's been hiding out in his office," she said.

"I'm sure all of her friends are very sad. Hang in there. They'll get to the bottom of this." Ava tried to reassure them. "I'll see you soon."

Ava returned to the dining room. "I think I was just snubbed by Renee."

"I heard she's ticked off that Pete got fired. I'm sure she doesn't know the real reason, or she'd get it," Des said.

Ava shook her head. "Jenny is going to take pictures of our bakers with their donations. We can highlight each contributor in the upcoming employee newsletter."

"Perfect. Everyone likes to see their name in print. Plus, it'll encourage even more participation in future events."

"Exactly!" Ava agreed.

A thrum of excitement circulated as employees began arriving to set up their cakes, pies, and cookies on their assigned trays and cake platers. In front of each dish, a place card listed the name of the dessert and the name of the employee who baked it along with a form for auction bidders to write their name and their bids.

Just minutes before noon, Jeff strolled into the room. He was dressed in a blue suit with a silver tie. "Wow, this is incredible. This room has never looked better. How did you pull this off on our budget?"

Ava said, "My team found a stash of decorations in Latisha's activity storage, and I prepared the flower arrangements myself. They're my donation to the auction."

"It doesn't get any cheaper than that," said the CEO.

"We're awarding a small bonus to the employees whose cakes raise the top three highest bids. I included this in the campaign announcement to encourage donations."

"I'm very impressed. There's a line of excited folks waiting to get in to take a look. Should we get this show on the road?" Jeff asked. Ava took this as a high compliment. While Jeff was typically all business, she could tell from the look on his face that he was sincere.

Ava nodded and ushered Jeff just outside the main entrance to the dining room. A small crowd of senior living residents and employees were gathered in the lobby, awaiting permission to enter. After briefly sharing his thoughts on the value of community and thanking everyone involved, Jeff handed the microphone back to Ava.

"I'd like to echo Jeff's words on how greatly we appreciate the spirit of teamwork here. Ruby Park's success is a reflection of the pride and service each one of you provides to our residents. Now, the first annual silent dessert auction is officially open."

Ava and Des served as hosts, welcoming everyone and answering questions about the desserts and the bidding process. During a quiet moment, Des asked, "Which dessert do you think will bring in the highest bid?"

"I'm not sure. You know I'm partial to chocolate. Ginny's red velvet marshmallow crème delight is gorgeous with those red roses on top, but I'm telling you right now, I'm not leaving the building without Dorene's Death by Chocolate Cake."

Des laughed. "I'll stay out of your way on that one. I think I'll bid on several others right now to raise the stakes."

"You'd better be careful. You may end up going home with five cakes tonight."

"They'll freeze, won't they? But, you're right, I think I should diversify. I'll bid on the Funfetti cake for the kids, Stacey's key lime pie, and how about the new and improved See's Candies chocolate tower gift basket?"

"Now you're talking. We could share it with the team." Ava giggled and shook her head. "We'll never live that down!"

At one-thirty, Ava rang a bell signaling the auction had concluded. Des announced the winners to the small group that lingered in the dining room. These were the die-hard dessert lovers who strategically planned to be the last and highest bidders.

In the end, all twenty-eight desserts were sold. The top earner was a lavender cake with fondant icing topped with macarons and blackberries. It was purchased for $250 by the

Center's Medical Director. Ava scored the Death by Chocolate with her generous donation. A few others also collected higher donations while the remaining sold for an average of $20 each.

"I'm glad everyone who really wanted a dessert was able to get it for a reasonable price." Des stacked up the action bidding cards.

"Me too," said Ava. "I think this was a huge success. We raised money for a great cause, and morale was very positive. Let's notifying the winners right away, and I'll follow up with a congratulations email announcement to all employees."

Chapter Eight

"WHY ARE YOU working at your computer with one eye closed?" Des asked when she and Jenny poked their heads in Ava's office. Ava was attempting to proof-read the Employee Handbook she had created over the past few months. Focusing on this task proved challenging that afternoon.

"Oh, was I? I hadn't noticed," Ava responded. "It's an old habit since childhood. I concentrate better this way. I once read an article that said blocking out half of your vision gives your mind more power to focus. I don't know if it's true or not, but it does reduce the amount of glare while I'm reading."

"We just stopped by to check on you," said Jenny. "Do you need anything?"

"Not right now, but thanks for offering. I'm planning to leave in an hour to visit Brooke. Are you still interested in coming along?"

"Absolutely. Just let me know when you're ready."

"Des, how about you?" Ava asked.

"It's the last day of school so I was hoping to leave early

to take the kids for ice cream if you don't mind. It's a silly tradition, but it's the last time I'll get to do this with Harper."

"That's right—I almost forgot with everything else going on. Of course you can leave. In fact, I insist."

Ava's phone rang. "Just a sec, let me get this call," she said and then grabbed the receiver.

"Hi, this is Barb from Independent Living. Does Ruby Park pay for employee relocation costs?"

"Yes, we provide relocation assistance for specialized nursing and technical positions."

Barb said, "I'm interested in moving to Mankato to be near my sister. How much of my moving expenses would you pay?"

"We only pay moving expenses to new hires that are joining Ruby Park. We don't offer them to employees who leave to work somewhere else." Ava smiled, and Jenny's eyebrows raised in shock.

"Well, do you have a list of job openings at senior living centers or hospitals in Mankato?" asked the nurse on the line.

Ava replied, "No, I'm afraid not. We only advertise Ruby Park positions. Good luck in your search, and have a good evening." Ava returned the receiver to its holder.

"Ha, that's hysterical," Jenny said. "An employee wants us to pay moving expenses for them to leave!"

Des laughed. "I can think of a few employees we might make that investment for."

Ava smiled and shook her head. "It's time for you to head out, Des. Go celebrate with your kids!"

≪

Ava and Jenny entered the lobby of the Garrett County Hospital where they were directed to the Intensive Care Unit. Ava pressed the call button for the nursing station. After providing identification, the doors unlocked allowing them to enter. Ava was impressed with the security at this small facility.

The unit was arranged in a L-shape. Each patient room had glass windows facing the nursing station allowing staff to view all six of the beds at once. Brooke was the only patient. The privacy curtain was open slightly, providing a brief view of Brooke as they proceeded toward the waiting room.

Brooke appeared to be attached to a dozen wires, and the monitors were beeping. Dave Sweetwater, who was sitting by his wife's side holding her hand, appeared absolutely crushed. He did not look at all like a man who was separated from his wife.

A uniformed deputy from the Garrett County Sheriff's Department was seated in the waiting room. Jenny whispered to Ava, "Where should we sit?"

"Let's take a seat in the lounge and wait to speak with Dave. If the deputy wants to talk to us, remember, it's best to stick to facts."

"I'd rather not say anything."

The waiting area was quite small. It held a sofa and four chairs along with a small television. Ava sat across from Deputy Bob Hildebrand, who was bald and overweight. He was likely the oldest deputy at the department.

Ava greeted him. "Hello, we just stopped by for a short visit. I see Dave and the nurse are with Brooke now."

"I'm also here to speak with him. How are you ladies?" Bob asked kindly.

"Honestly, I've been better. This is very disturbing. To the whole community. This is Jenny—we work together at Ruby Park Senior Living. Jenny, this is Deputy Hildebrand."

"It's good to see you again, Ava. I heard you were back in town. The sheriff's department will do everything we can to locate the person responsible for this crime. I understand you two attend Brooke's classes. Can you answer a few questions for me?"

"I can try," Ava answered.

Bob nodded and pulled out a small notepad. "When was the last time you saw Brooke?"

"Monday evening. I attended her yoga class at the community center, and I left right after class. That was around six-thirty."

"How about you, Jenny?"

"The same. Ava and I walked out to the parking lot together," responded Jenny.

"Were there any new members in your class or someone who seemed out of place?"

Ava imagined the gym full of attendees. "No. I don't believe so."

"Me either."

"Do you have knowledge of who or why someone might want to harm Brooke?"

Ava shook her head, "Not in the slightest. Brooke is always very easy going and friendly. She's one of the kindest people I know. Everyone in the class adores her."

"I agree." Jenny nodded.

"But I heard it might have been an attempted robbery," Ava said, hoping to gain more information.

"Where did you get that?" Bob asked.

"A group of people were talking about it at work."

Bob scratched his nose. "There's no shortage of gossip…

We're reviewing all possible angles. Did you see anything out of the ordinary at the community center recently?"

Ava sighed. "Honestly, I don't know if this is important. Just before the five-thirty class, I saw Brooke and Pete Reinholtz talking in the center office. She appeared to be upset. Pete was holding onto her wrist, and she pulled it away. I couldn't hear what they were saying. Brooke joined everyone in the gym a couple of minutes after that."

"Thank you." Bob leaned forward. "Here's my business card. If you think of anything else, call me, okay?"

"Of course." Ava accepted the cards and passed one of them to Jenny. "I see Dave is coming out of Brooke's room. Please give us five minutes, Bob." Ava gave him an imploring look. "I promise we'll be quick."

"He's all yours, ladies." Deputy Hildebrand gave a slight smile and nodded.

Ava turned to Dave. "Hi, I'm Ava Andrews. I don't know if you remember me, but I'm a friend of Brooke's. This is my co-worker, Jenny. Both of us attend Brooke's yoga classes."

Dave's brow was furrowed and his eyelids were heavy. "Yes, it's been a long time. Nice to meet you, Jenny. Thanks for visiting."

"How is Brooke doing?" Jenny asked.

"She's a fighter. She was shot in the right side of her chest. Thank God, the bullet missed a major artery. She made it through surgery like a champion. Her surgeon said the next twenty-four hours will determine whether she makes it through." Dave shook his head and added, "After that, we will see what type of rehabilitation is required."

Ava felt crestfallen. "I'm so sorry. I assume she's unconscious?"

"Yes, she may be for several days. What we need most now is time and prayers."

Both women nodded. Ava handed him an envelope and said, "We brought a card from her friends at Ruby Park Senior Living. There's also a gift card enclosed to Woodcrest Coffee House and Brewery. We thought you might prefer take-out meals over hospital food. If we can help you and Zoe in any way, just reach out."

"That's very kind. Zoe is staying with Brooke's folks tonight, so I can stay here. Today was the last day of school."

"Poor kid, what a way to start summer vacation," Jenny said.

"We'd planned to go camping in Grand Marais this weekend," said Dave. "I can't make any sense of this. I really appreciate your visit—It's been too quiet this afternoon. If you'll excuse me, I need to touch base with Deputy Hildebrand."

"Of course. Can I give you a hug?" Ava offered.

Dave replied, "I'll take all the hugs I can get."

After they said their goodbyes, the two ladies left the facility.

Climbing into Ava's vehicle, Jenny said, "I hope the sheriff's department can send additional deputies to help. Deputy Hildebrand seems nice enough, but I didn't get the vibe that he has the energy to get to the bottom of this quickly."

"I agree with you one hundred percent."

"Dave looked so sad." Jenny frowned sourly.

"And I bet he didn't sleep a wink last night."

Jenny said, "I didn't realize you saw Pete fighting with Brooke. You know, I've never liked that guy. He's so condescending like he thinks he's too good for everyone else."

After dropping Jenny off at her car, Ava headed straight

home. She quickly flipped through her mail, which included an advertisement for a local dental office, her utility bill, the June/July issue of *Architectural Digest*, and a clothing catalogue. With fresh reading material in hand, Ava poured herself a glass of chardonnay and padded out to her patio to relax. Sophie occupied herself by running along the fence, stopping occasionally to smell the lilac and peony shrubs.

She stretched out her legs in front of her and smiled, thinking about her previous night out. She enjoyed recalling every moment, except for her brief interaction with that jerk, Pete. Now, Jack Lindstrom was a breath of fresh air—he was easy on the eyes too.

An hour later, Ava cuddled with Sophie on her leather sofa to watch a popular dating reality show she'd recorded earlier in the week. It was one of Ava's guilty pleasures, a mindless escape from listening to the more serious struggles of everyday lives. Ava munched on tortilla chips and flipped through her design magazine, seeking inspiration for a new rug.

"Oh, for Heaven's sake," she groaned at the television. "Why did you give that guy a rose? Anyone can see he's using you to further his career. There's a reason he doesn't get along with anyone else on the show!"

Ava realized this activity was not giving her the relaxation she was seeking, so she switched off the TV and ran a hot bath. She added bath salt and bubbles before slipping into the lavender-scented water.

Instead of relaxing, Ava felt a sense of impending doom, as though things were about to get a whole lot worse before they got better. She tried to shrug this off as sadness from visiting Brooke and Dave. However, Ava was driven by intuition, and there was no denying that she had a gift of perceiving things that most people didn't notice.

Ava didn't believe she was clairvoyant, but sometimes visions just came to her at random. Like the time she received a jigsaw puzzle as a kid and told her mother before opening it that the pieces would not replicate the photo pictured on the box. It was true. The family struggled to put the puzzle together. At the last conference she attended, she entered a prize drawing and knew the instant she dropped her business card in the box that her name would be called to pick up the grand prize. A couple of months ago, she imagined a rock flying up and cracking her windshield, and it actually happened the following day.

It didn't happen often, and sometimes she was too busy to pay attention. But Ava was on full alert now.

Was someone trying to murder Brooke, or had this been a burglary gone awry? Had she gotten into a conflict that upset someone to that extreme? Hopefully, a law enforcement officer was guarding her at the hospital. Ava wished she'd asked. Was Pete Reinholtz capable of murder? If so, what was the reason? Was Brooke having an affair with Cody? How did he fit into all this?

Chapter Nine

"GOOD MORNING, EVERYONE," Ava said. Her teammates were wearing jeans and their Ruby Park Employee Appreciation Week T-shirts, identical to the one Ava was wearing.

"Hey, TGIF." Jenny raised her hand slightly and looked up from her computer screen.

"You're actually wearing jeans today—that's a first." Des gave Ava the once over and nodded. "Cute jacket too."

"You never know who might stop by today. I didn't want to be too casual." Ava was keenly aware she appeared to be much younger than she was. In jeans and tennis shoes, she looked like a co-ed. She regularly wore blazers and dress pumps at work to convey that she should be taken seriously.

"You're prepared for a natural disaster," said Noelle. "Don't you have like three jackets and a half dozen pairs of shoes in your office closet?"

"True. I prefer comfortable shoes, and it's convenient to store them here. I'll switch to a pair of flats before the picnic." Ava never gave it a second thought. In Minneapolis, it was common to change shoes before walking though the skyway system.

"Let's get to it. We've got a busy day." Ava smiled as she tapped a large cardboard shipping box. "These recruitment postcards need to be labeled and ready for postage this afternoon." Ava quickly glanced out the window and was pleased the blue sky was perfect for serving a barbeque luncheon.

"I'll be in my office conducting phone screening interviews for the Memory Care nursing manager vacancy," Ava continued. "May, please let me know if you need help completing the federal equal opportunity report. I know it's due next week."

It was late morning when Ava checked her watch. She stretched and flexed her hands to prepare herself to flip burgers and chicken patties outdoors on the grills. The leadership team would also be serving side dishes and a choice of dessert. Cody said it would take two hours to complete lunch service.

Ava popped her head in Des's office and reported, "I'm headed downstairs. See you guys soon."

"Okay. How did the interviews go? Any strong candidates?"

"I'm excited about a couple of possibilities. The nursing supervisor from Buffalo and two nurse managers from the western suburbs all seem to be strong candidates. The key will be whether they can manage the commute or are willing to relocate."

"That could provide more business to your mom."

"That reminds me. We should create relocation packets for our out-of-town candidates. Let's include brochures for local business, healthcare providers, veterinarians, and real estate agents."

"Great idea. You know, Grace only has one competitor who's actually based here in town, and Barbara Harris is no comparison to your mother. Those city firms just can't offer her personalized service."

"I agree, but I have to remain impartial." Ava pointed in the direction of the rear gardens. "I'll see you at the picnic."

"Have fun out there, and say hello to Grandpa Charles for me."

On her way, Ava walked past the hair salon and the gift shop. She stopped when she saw a group of residents in the craft room. "What are you creating today?" Ava asked Latisha, the activities manager.

"We'll be painting on canvas. We're attaching stencils to create designs on burlap shopping bags. Truly, any durable cotton or denim fabric will do, but I picked these up at the dollar store."

"Looks like a fun activity to do with friends. Could I use any acrylic paint?"

"Sure, we're using these smaller tubes I found at the hardware store. I dilute the paint with textile paint thinner first. That allows the paint to dry slower and also prevents it from cracking." Latisha held up a pair of canvas sneakers and a couple of denim jackets she had completed as inspiration.

The seniors responded with delight followed by multiple questions. Ava leaned in and commended Latisha for her patience before continuing on her journey.

She found her grandpa in the oversized media room facing the big screen. The classic hit movie, *Cocoon,* was playing. Being careful not to block anyone's view, Ava crept up to Charles from the side. "Hi Grandpa," she whispered.

"What?" responded Charles. "I can't hear a word you're saying."

"Shh," came from the rear.

"I'm sorry. Enjoy the show." Ava gave him a kiss on the cheek before departing.

On her way out the door, Ava heard one of the seniors say, "That's the new bigwig from Minneapolis. I heard she's shaking things up."

Ava crossed the main lobby and exited through the large public doors at the rear of the complex. Employees were attaching vinyl tablecloths to the picnic tables. Three large grills were smoking on the patio. A long line of tables filled with food containers ran end-to-end. Two huge plastic pails were filled with ice, water bottles, and a variety of soft drinks.

"What can I do to help?" Ava asked Cody.

"You're exactly the person I wanted to see this morning. Can I talk to you privately for a minute?" Cody inclined his head in the direction of the garden. When Ava nodded, Cody led her down a short path, and he sat on a bench next to the water fountain.

"What's going on? Everything ready for the picnic?" Ava inquired as she joined him on the bench.

"I got a message from the sheriff's office. They want me to call back today to schedule a meeting about Brooke. I don't know what to do. What are my rights?"

"First, you're not required to speak with the authorities. But if you choose to, you can have an attorney with you while you're being questioned. I'm sure they're reaching out to everyone who saw Brooke this past week. They're not going to arrest you or anyone unless they have probable cause. If you have nothing to hide, you should relax."

"Does this mean I'm a suspect?" Cody asked nervously. "Why me?"

"Honestly Cody, I hate to say this out loud, but I want to be transparent. I've heard rumors that you've been spending a lot of time with Brooke. Maybe someone pointed that out." Ava provided a sympathetic smile.

"What is it with folks in this town? Can't a man and a woman just be friends?" Cody ran a hand along the back of his neck. "It's ridiculous that people think we're having an affair. Is that what they're saying?"

"You're right. People shouldn't speculate, but you're both wonderful and attractive people."

Cody glanced around them before saying, "First of all, Brooke is completely devoted to Dave. And… I'm just not that into women. Brooke's a dear friend. We were both theater kids in school. Geez, we've been rehearsing together to try out for the Starlight Community Theater. That's it, end of story."

"Do you have an alibi for Wednesday morning? That would certainly help."

"As a matter of fact, I do. I was having an early breakfast with Ian Valencourt."

Ava smiled. "The high school English teacher who manages the drama club?"

"One and the same." Cody lowered his voice. "We've been seeing each other for a few months."

"Good for you guys. I don't see that you have anything to be worried about… other than hoping for Brooke's recovery, that is."

"Would you mind keeping this between you and me? I prefer to keep my private life out of work, and this relationship is still fairly new."

"Absolutely. You have my word."

"You're the best. I think we should get back to the food prep before a hungry mob arrives." Cody jutted a thumb toward the serving line.

Once they returned to the patio, Cody said, "You could help by emptying a dozen bags of buns into this tub. Then open all the condiments at the other end of the table."

"Happy to help!"

"Thanks for volunteering." Cody leaned toward Ava and whispered, "It's not often that the nutrition staff members see you executives rolling up your sleeves."

Ava observed Cody interacting with his team. As they worked side-by-side, they followed his instructions and jokingly responded with *yes, chef* after each instruction. She didn't sense anything inappropriate, despite what Stacey had suggested the other day.

Before long, Cheryl, Stacey, Yvonne, and Jeff joined Ava and Cody on the food line. The men gravitated toward the grills and kept the hamburger and chicken patties coming. Dozens of employees made their way through the service line, while chatting.

"We're going to serve roast beef and chicken plus New York Strip because that's Hayden's favorite," Nellie from Housekeeping said to her co-workers while they collected their meals. They were discussing the menu for her wedding reception.

Another employee in scrubs said, "My sister had chicken and salmon at her wedding because some people don't eat beef."

"Yep, we're going to have salmon too," Nellie said.

"You'll invite everyone in Housekeeping to the wedding, right?"

"You bet! I'm going to invite everyone from Ruby Park. It's going to be the biggest wedding of the year," Nellie replied proudly.

When the line of employees came to an end, Yvonne asked the other leaders how they were holding up. Cheryl responded first. "I have to admit that standing for this length of time is tiring, but I'm glad to be outdoors."

"Welcome to my world," Stacey said. "We nurses spend most of the day on our feet."

After helping herself to a plateful of food, Ava joined a long table where a group of human resources, accounting, and information technology employees were gathered. The other leaders spread out to mingle.

"This is so much fun," Ava said. "What a great way to get to know our co-workers."

Noelle smiled. "You're a natural. You could have a future in the food industry."

"Serving a crowd this size a couple of times a year is good enough for me," Ava said. "Seriously, I need to work out a bit more, and I could definitely use a massage." She rotated her shoulder cuff. "When I drove to the Wooddale Mall the other day, I passed a place called Magnificent Massage. I should give them a call."

"No!" cried several people at once.

Des said, "That spa was raided a few months ago due to sexual activity. I believe they were shut down temporarily."

"Well, I guess there's no such thing as a happy ending," Ava replied in a deadpan manner.

After a moment of silence, the table erupted in laughter. "Good one," said Dean with a big grin.

❧

Ava arrived in the CEO's outer office promptly for her last-minute meeting with her boss, Jeff. His assistant, Ginny, waved her back to his conference table. Ava was curious to learn the reason for the urgent request as Ginny had called her only fifteen minutes prior.

She browsed the CEO's décor which reflected his love for fishing. Several stuffed prize-winning fish hung on a long wall along with an original Big Mouth Billy Bass. The plastic fish flapped its tail while it played songs, including "Take Me to the River." Jeff had explained this classic was a gag gift from his buddies. The family photo on his desk featured his smiling sons holding up their prize catches at a local tournament.

Jeff joined her. "I'm sure this is one week we won't soon forget."

"You can say that again, but I'd hoped it would be the result of the astounding success of Appreciation Week." Ava offered a half smile.

"You and your team are doing a wonderful job." Jeff made a steeple with his fingers. "I heard a lot of positive feedback while serving lunch today. Also, Cheryl was pleased with the way you handled Pete's exit. Thank you. His behavior was very disappointing."

"Yes, it was."

"You were at the hospital yesterday, right? How is the Sweetwater family?"

Ava replied, "Dave was distraught, as you can imagine. Worried whether Brooke would make it through the night. By the way, I heard she was still unconscious this morning but stable. I sure hope she can identify the attacker or give some insight as to what happened. Everyone is on edge."

Jeff shuffled in his seat. "Right, people are scared. We're all wondering if this was an isolated incident, or if there's a lunatic running around town."

"Exactly."

"Being the second largest employer in town, this will no doubt impact some of our employees. I've heard some are being contacted by the sheriff's office to provide statements."

"That's true. In fact, Jenny and I spoke with Deputy Hildebrand last evening," Ava offered.

"If anyone is implicated from Ruby Park, this could have a major impact on our reputation which you know affects our resident occupancy rate. Since you have experience conducting investigations, could you do some digging around to see what you might find? It's not that I don't trust the authorities, but Bob Hildebrand isn't the sharpest tool in the shed. Anything we can do to speed up the process to prove there's no link to Ruby Park would be appreciated."

"Of course. I'll do my best." Ava certainly didn't want to let him down.

"I know you will. Also, I'm sorry I forgot to give this to you sooner. I received an official looking notice from the Minnesota Department of Human Rights. It's in regard to a former employee, Dawn Barone. She was our Nutrition Services Manager before I hired Cody last fall. I had to let her go due to performance issues. I received far too many complaints about the menus and food quality."

"May I open it?"

Jeff handed her an envelope, and she removed the letter to examine its contents. Having seen similar documents in the past, Ava knew exactly where to locate the information she was seeking. "She's citing discrimination in the workplace based on age and gender. They're requiring an initial response next week."

"Dawn is fairly young. Early 40s maybe. And why would she sue Ruby Park after this long?"

"Well, the statute of limitations for filing an employment discrimination complaint to Human Rights is one year. Anyone over the age of forty has the right to claim age discrimination."

"I see."

"I'll check whether she's still receiving unemployment

benefits. If the six months have passed, she may be seeking financial assistance. It's also possible she's taking a stand on what she feels is the right thing to do, especially if she has female friends still working here."

Jeff shook his head. "That could be. I was working with Stacey on this initially. She was against letting Dawn go. There's a strong bond there that I missed, so Des sat in the meeting when I informed Dawn of her dismissal. Do you think we should involve an attorney on this matter?"

"That's my recommendation given the limited timeframe. An attorney will request an extension and prepare a formal response to the agency. I'll gather Dawn's personnel file and any investigation notes we have. The Human Rights Office will also request extensive data regarding our employee demographics and policies."

Jeff removed his reading glasses and put them in his shirt pocket. "I'm sorry to add this to your plate with your friend's recent tragedy."

"It's what I do. I imagine Des has documentation of Dawn's dismissal, and she can assist."

Jeff nodded. "Do you know where can we find a good employment attorney on short notice?"

"Yes, but, full disclosure—he's my ex."

"If you can work with him, I'm fine with that. Please keep me updated."

Ava returned to her office. She took several deep breaths while working up the courage to make the phone call. When she was ready, she used her office phone to dial a number she knew by memory.

"Grant Foley speaking."

"Hey, this is Ava. I could really use your help."

Chapter Ten

"WHAT IS IT, Ava?" Grant asked.

Is that concern or irritation I'm detecting? Ava wondered. She pictured him wearing a suit and tie, his standard work attire when they were dating.

"Did I catch you at a bad time?"

"I'm preparing for a mediation, but I have about a half hour."

"This is going to sound a bit crazy," Ava said. "I've been up to my elbows with employee issues while also trying to throw the best employee recognition week Ruby Park Senior Living has ever seen. Plus, a friend of mine was shot in the chest on Wednesday morning. Today, I received a discrimination claim to respond to. I would really appreciate your assistance."

"Somebody was shot? Was this an accident or an attempted murder?"

"It's under investigation. No one's been arrested as far as I know. The shooting happened at the Ruby Lake Community Center. Brooke Sweetwater, my yoga instructor, in the ICU at the local hospital. I stopped by yesterday… It's really bad. A couple of employees here are being questioned by local authorities."

"I have a contact at the Garrett County Sheriff's Department. I'll give him a call about Brooke. Tell me more about the discrimination complaint and what you know about the former employee."

"Yes… her name is Dawn Barone." Ava held back tears now realizing she needed a shoulder to cry on, but knowing Grant wasn't that guy. "I'll have Desiree Sparks on my team email you all the information. Please call me after you've had time to read it, and I can answer any questions."

"I can do one better than that. I'm golfing with my dad and a client at the Pine Ridge Golf Course tomorrow. Text me your address, and I'll pick you up for an early dinner there tomorrow night."

"Since this is a business meeting, how about I meet you there?" Ava asked politely. She felt slightly annoyed that Grant assumed she would be available for dinner on a Saturday night, but she was the one who reached out for his help. She also wanted to remain friends, so she reined in her emotions.

"Sure, does six o'clock work for you?" he asked.

"That's perfect. I really appreciate this." After disconnecting the call, Ava leaned back in her desk chair and rubbed her temples in attempt to thwart an oncoming headache.

She certainly hadn't imagined her first conversation with Grant after their breakup being a call for help. Had she ever expected to call him again? She'd thought they might bump into each other at a mutual friend's wedding or at a law seminar.

And now she'd agreed to have dinner with him tomorrow night. What was the appropriate attire for a business dinner with an ex-boyfriend, anyway? *Ugh*, she needed to take something for her headache.

Ava washed down her pain medication with ice water,

but she was craving a cola. She couldn't believe she had to give up caffeine for these darn headaches. Coffee and cola had gotten her through graduate school while working full-time. She thought about the first time she saw Grant. He'd been the teaching assistant in her employment law class. He had been so confident… or had he been cocky? Well, he'd been very handsome in that clean-cut, preppy style of his.

Pull yourself together, Ava. You are so over Grant Foley!

Ava walked over to Des' office and peeked in. "Do you have a few minutes?"

Des glanced up from her computer screen and said, "What can I do for you?"

"I have a project for you. You'll need to write some of this down." Ava gave Des a photocopy of the discrimination complaint and explained the next steps.

Des stacked a few documents she had been working on, moved them to the side of her desktop, and took out a pad of paper from a drawer.

"I also wrote down the contact information for the attorney we'll be working with, Grant Foley. He's with Foley and Schmidt in Edina. You can email him those documents once we've gathered everything. I'm meeting with him tomorrow."

Looking at Ava's handwriting, Des asked, "Why does this name look familiar?"

"Probably because he's my ex-boyfriend. I mentioned him before. He's the guy I broke up with before I moved here."

Des froze, and her eyes widened. "Wow, Ava. How are you feeling about seeing him?"

"I must be ready. When Jeff asked if I had a contact, I instantly thought of Grant. I'm sure he'll be a tremendous resource for us.

Des grinned broadly.

"What? I'm not going to date him again. When Mr. Right comes into my life, I want to be focused only on him. You know what I mean?" Ava shook her head and sat down.

"You don't want to settle just because you were comfortable with Grant."

"Exactly. I want a love like you and Randy have. You two have each other's backs, you're raising three kids, and anyone can see you two are still crazy about each other."

"Crazy is one word to describe us. We've been through some rough times over the years. When his dad died and Randy decided to take over the auto shop, I didn't know if we were going to make it. I was about your age, working and raising a daughter and two boys while he was at the shop eighty hours a week paying off debt to turn the business around. Then my mother needed me when she fractured her hip."

"That's what I mean. You got through it—together. That takes commitment."

"You'll find it. I know you will."

Ava massaged her hands. "By the way, Grant said he'd call the sheriff's department to see if they'll give him any information about Brooke's attack. Have you heard anything new?"

"No, but I've been praying for Brooke, Dave, and little Zoe."

✍

Ava prepared a salmon filet and a small salad for herself in her bright kitchen. She was eager to spend a Friday night at home for a change. Shannon texted her earlier to see if she was interested in joining a group of friends to hear a live band, but Ava declined. She explained she had a migraine and was still reeling from the crazy week. After her dinner, she picked up a novel and climbed into bed to snuggle with her puppy. On her plush new mattress, she felt as if she were floating on a cloud.

Around nine o'clock, Ava awoke. Sophie had stretched out across the bed, and Ava's legs were pinned under the covers. Her bedside lamp glowed brightly, and the forgotten book had fallen off the bed. She picked up her phone to check the time and saw she had missed a call from her best friend. She heard Shannon's voice as she played back her message. *Hey there, I hope you're feeling better. There's a huge crowd at the bar tonight. We're moving on to the bowling alley. If you change your mind, stop by and join us. Bye.*

Her headache was gone, yet Ava was in no mood to socialize. She turned off the light and fell back to sleep. Soon she would learn that going out that night would have saved her some major hassle, however, in that moment, she desperately needed a good night's rest.

Chapter Eleven

AVA GREETED THE first rays of sunlight. She reached both arms up in the air to stretch and realized her muscles were becoming stiff. With the community center closed, she would miss out on another yoga class this morning. Ava knew what she needed to do.

She dressed in workout attire and called out, "Want to take a walk?" Sophie skidded across the wood floor nearly plowing into the front door. "Of course you do, Sophie."

While she preferred to follow the nature trail, she quickly decided that a woman shouldn't be wandering along heavily wooded paths alone until Brooke's assailant was behind bars. She elected to jog down her neighborhood street and connect to the paved path around the Pine Ridge Golf Course community. Golfers would be hitting the course soon.

Huge pine trees lined its fairways and obscured traffic from the main road that winded through the neighborhood and up to the country club. The eighteen-hole course was dotted with ponds and sand traps as well as oak, elm, and maple trees. Ava didn't see any golf carts on the path yet, so she detached Sophie's leash and allowed her to roam free.

Ava could see the clubhouse coming into full view, but Sophie had run ahead and was no longer visible. Other than the occasional vehicle driving down the neighborhood street, there was no one nearby.

"Sophie, come!" Ava commanded. Her dog came out from behind a cluster of large pine trees and stood still.

"Sophie, come!" Ava repeated. Sophie ran to her side and then darted back toward the trees.

"I'm not playing." Her dog sat in the distance. "You're in big trouble. I'm going to put you back on leash." As Ava approached, Sophie sprinted behind the trees. "Get over here right now!" Sophie only barked.

"What are you doing? What is it, girl? I should've enrolled you in obedience school."

Ava rounded the clump of trees and saw her dog standing next to a man. He was lying on the ground face down with his head turned to one side. Sophie's tail hung low between her hind legs.

"Who's there?" Ava asked as she walked closer. "Are you okay? Oh my God—is that you Pete?" Ava's voice quivered. The back of his head was covered in blood. "Pete, do you need help?" Ava bent down and looked at his face. His eyes were wide open, but she knew he was dead. Ava placed her fingertips to her throat. "No, I can't believe this."

Sophie nuzzled her snout into Ava. "Good girl, good girl," Ava said. Her body was frozen in disbelief. She trembled as she stood up, began crying, and regained her balance. Then, she attached the dog's leash and led her about thirty feet away from the body.

Struggling to catch her breath, she doubled over and touched her hands to her knees. Ava reached into the back pocket of her jogging shorts, grabbed her cell phone, and barely managed to dial 911 with her shaky hands.

"This is Ava Andrews, and I… I'm at the Pine Ridge Golf course. There's, there's a man. I believe he's dead. We were walking and found him on the ground. I'm… I can see the driving range. By a little bridge where the golf cart trail crosses the creek."

❧

"Mitch? Thank God it's you." Ava stood as the burly man in a tan uniform drew nearer. He had a short, military style haircut and a familiar boyish face despite his large size. He had served in the Marine Corps police force before joining the Garrett County Sherrif's Department.

Detective Mitchell Sullivan was also Ava's older cousin. He asked, "Ava, what happened here?"

"I really have no idea," she moaned. "I mean we were taking a walk, me and my dog, and we found his body lying there. His head is covered in blood." Tears streamed down her cheeks once again.

"Do you recognize him?"

"Yes, his name is Pete Reinholtz. We used to work together at Ruby Park Senior Living."

"Are you okay?"

"No… no, I'm not, and I might throw up." She placed one hand on her stomach. "Who would do such a horrible thing?"

Mitch shifted his weight from one foot to the other. "Did you see anybody on your walk? Was there anyone else around when you found his body?

"No one that I noticed."

"Did you touch the body or anything on him?" Mitch asked.

"Seriously? Of course not. I saw him lying there and thought he might need help. Like maybe he'd fallen or had a heart attack. I didn't know who it was until I walked around and saw his face. Once I realized Pete was dead, I came over here and called for help." She couldn't get the terrifying image out of her mind. His eyes… it had been like he was staring at her.

"Hey—you're going to be okay." Mitch gently squeezed her shoulder. "I'm sure this was quite a shock."

"Yeah, can't imagine anything worse. But I'm relieved you're here… Why are you here? Mom told me you were working in Lakeway."

"The department asked for backup in Ruby Lake after the shooting on Wednesday morning. I'm thinking about transferring after Deputy Hildebrand retires, so I offered to work here temporarily."

"Thank goodness. We really need your expertise."

Mitch held up his index finger and made a swirling motion. "I'm going to request additional resources to search the area."

He stepped away, made a quick call, and returned. "The coroner is sending someone to pick up Mr. Reinholtz. I need you to sit tight and catch your breath. Then we're going to start from the beginning, and you can tell me how you know the victim and how you found him here."

After listening to his cousin's story, Detective Sullivan attempted to summarize. "Ava, let me make sure I've got this right. You were taking a walk alone at the crack of dawn and found the victim's body. The last time you saw the deceased alive was Wednesday night at Woodcrest. You were with Lauren and Matt, who can confirm that Pete threatened you for firing him the day prior. He also made a pass at your employee's daughter and made a scene during his exit.'

"I didn't say I fired him. I communicated the employment separation, but his manager made the decision to end his employment."

"When was the last time that you saw Brooke Sweetwater?"

"At her yoga class on Monday evening, and I visited her at the hospital the other day. I provided that statement to Deputy Hildebrand."

"Yeah, I read it. You were at the community center the same time your friend Brooke Sweetwater and Pete Reinholtz were arguing. Correct?"

"Mitch, I need to go home now. Please contact my attorney if you have further questions. I know you've met Grant Foley."

"Oh, come on, Ava."

"I've told you everything I can recall. You're making it sound like I'm involved."

"You must understand how this sounds. I'm worried about you. Just keep a low profile, okay?"

"You know I'm telling you the truth. There are several folks in town who had contempt for Pete Reinholtz, and I'm really counting on you to find his murderer."

⁕

Ava sat on a counter stool at her kitchen island for several minutes trying to calm herself. Her heart was racing, so she took several deep breaths. Then she picked up her phone. *I hope he answers.*

"Grant speaking."

Despite feeling breathless, she managed to talk. "Grant, I know I'll see you this afternoon, but I have to give you an urgent update." Ava continued to explain what she had just discovered at the Pine Ridge Golf Course.

"Jesus Ava, what have you gotten yourself into? You found a dead man's body?" Ava discerned Grant's frustration through the phone.

"Actually, it was Sophie. We were taking a walk early this morning, and she found him."

"Who's Sophie?"

"She's my dog. We walked along the path between Lake Boulevard and the Pine Ridge Course. I was heading toward Edgewater Park, but we didn't quite make it that far. Sophie was off leash and sniffed out his scent."

"Wow, you bought a house and a dog. You've really moved on with your life."

"Focus, Grant."

"Right. Do they think he was murdered?"

"It looks that way. He likely died late last night, and the sheriff's department suspects foul play. We'll have to wait to hear results of the autopsy."

"That could take days."

"Listen. Pete Reinholtz worked for Ruby Park as an Accounting Manager in the Finance Department. That is until Wednesday when we fired him for harassment. Do you think they'll request details of my harassment investigation?"

"They might, but I doubt it. They'll focus on any obvious suspects based on evidence first. Remember you don't need to offer any information."

"As far as I am concerned, that employee investigation is confidential, and the report itself is not part of the personnel file anyway. The poor woman who Pete mistreated should not have to be subject to police questioning."

"I agree. If they request it, ask for a subpoena. In fact, if the department contacts you again, tell them I'm representing you."

"Yeah, I already did. Thank you, I'll see you this evening."

"I'll be at the golf course this afternoon, and I'll ask around. We can determine the next steps tonight. Please stay home and out of harm's way until then," Grant said with an air of authority.

"Not a chance. I know how rumors get started, and this does not look good for me. I found Pete's body after firing him earlier in the week and was seen in public where he was threatening me. I have to find out who did this to clear myself as a suspect."

Chapter Twelve

AVA PHONED HER sister next. She hoped to catch her before the news got out. "Lauren, do you have a minute?"

"Sure, are you going to stop by this morning?"

"I'd like to. I need to talk. Are you at home or at the Coffee House?" Ava drummed her fingers on her granite countertop.

"Matt opened this morning, and I'll join him within the hour. What's up? You sound a bit panicked or something."

"Pete Reinholtz is dead. I found him by the golf course when I was jogging with Sophie."

"Oh my God, that's awful. Tell me… was he shot, or was it a heart attack?"

"Neither. He was bleeding from his skull. Mitch said it could be an accident, but he suspects foul play."

"Our cousin, Mitch?"

"Yes, they sent him in response to my call. We were running along the path, and Pete was lying behind a group of pine trees. I thought he needed help, but it was too late." Ava cupped her right hand on her forehead.

"This is crazy. Geez, I wish you didn't see that. How are you holding up?"

"I'm not gonna lie—I'm pretty shaken. I need a hot shower and a fresh change of clothes."

"Of course, take your time. Text me when you're on your way, and I'll have a warm breakfast waiting for you."

Ava turned up her stereo and relished the steaming shower. She washed away her tears and wished she could erase her memory. After shutting off the faucet, she could hear Coldplay singing her favorite crying song "Fix You" which warmed her heart. *Talk about perfect timing.*

Less than an hour later, she circled the town square twice before finding a parking space on the east side of the building. Woodcrest's designated parking lot was completely full, and the order line extended to the door. Lauren spotted Ava and led her to the front counter.

"I'm glad you're both here. I don't feel like being alone today," Ava said to Lauren and Matt.

"Of course not. Everyone is shocked that Pete died. Geez, it's horrible."

"I see you're drawing a crowd this morning," Ava said. All eyes had turned to her when she walked through the vast dining space. She squeezed into the last remaining seat at the bar which was shaped in a curved design to maximize seating. Ava thought it resembled the arch of a boomerang. A large chalkboard menu hung overhead.

"News travels quickly. Pete's death is bringing the whole town in here. Are you okay, Ava?" asked Matt.

"I think I'm still in shock."

Lauren set her palms down flat on the counter. "We're all so worried about you. Dad called and is on his way. Do you want to eat breakfast with me in the kitchen? We can catch up when he gets here."

"That's a nice gesture, but I'll have to face everyone's questions soon enough. They might as well hear it straight from the horse's mouth," Ava said.

Matt stepped closer and placed a hand on her shoulder. "You're a brave woman. Sounds like Pete was murdered. That's the second violent crime in a week. Damn, everyone is freaked out."

"You heard he was murdered then?" Ava asked.

Des came up from behind. "Deputy Hildebrand told Rosie that the coroner is conducting an autopsy, but they think he was murdered. What if it's true, Ava? Will Randy be a suspect? A lot of people heard him threaten Pete the other night."

"Randy wouldn't hurt anyone," Lauren said. "Oh no— Matt kicked him out. Do you think a deputy will stop by and question him?"

"If the sheriff's department investigates Pete's death as a murder, they'll probably ask to speak with you both since he was here the other night. We're getting ahead of ourselves. Let's take it one step at a time. Perhaps he fell and hit his head."

Matt splayed his hands. "I hope you're right, but a lot of people hated that guy."

"Enough to murder him?" Ava asked.

Randy placed a hand at Des' waist. "He was an all-around jackass. I was at the high school baseball game the other night, and I couldn't believe the language he was yelling from the stands. Some of the parents changed seats to get away from him. His son Tyler was pitching, and Pete ridiculed him. My heart was breaking for the poor kid."

Ava said, "I wonder how Natalie is taking the news."

"Maybe she snapped and killed him," Lauren said. "I heard Natalie finally moved out. Apparently, that monster has been hitting her for years. Karen, that's her mother, was here yesterday afternoon pacing around while on a call with Natalie. She invited Natalie and the kids to stay with her as long as they needed. After that, I heard Karen tell her friends that she's been suspicious of violent behavior for some time."

"How awful, but I bet Natalie is somewhat relieved," Des said, receiving surprised looks in response. "Well, I mean, no one will benefit from his death more than she will. Afterall, he was abusive, and she no longer has to deal with him."

Randy leaned in and said, "Ruby Lake will be safer without him. At least his family will be."

Shannon joined the expanding group and put an arm around Ava. Her burgundy glasses created a striking contrast to her green eyes. "I saw Pete at the Lady Luck last night. It was an older crowd, so we went over to the bowling alley before nine o'clock. My mom said Pete got so drunk that he was even hitting on senior citizens."

"That's right," said Des. "Rosie told me a Beatles cover band was playing until midnight. There were plenty of folks hanging around downtown. Especially on the square."

"There's no need for us to stand up here. I see a few seats open at the two long tables occupied by the Silver Sneakers." Matt extended his arm, pointing them out. "I'll grab another pot of coffee."

The Silver Sneakers was a fitness group organized by the community center for retirees and adults over the age of sixty. There must have been a dozen people wearing jogging suites along with gray or silver sneakers.

As the group approached the tables, Rosie called out, "There's a few chairs next to me."

Heather, the community center's manager, was regaling a story to her tablemates. "That's when I overheard them arguing. Pete grabbed Brooke, and she yelled 'Let go of me or I'll call the cops.' Then he yelled back, 'You wouldn't dare.'"

"You don't say." Rosie leaned in.

"When I tell you Brooke had an angry look in her eye, I mean I've never seen that side of her. She pointed at him and said, 'Oh, wouldn't I? You picked a fight with the wrong person. I'm on to you, Punky.'"

Ava asked Heather, "Was this before yoga class early in the week?"

"Yeah. How did you know?"

"I walked by but couldn't hear their conversation. Do you have any idea what they were arguing about?"

"No," Heather said, "but those two have some sort of history. A few weeks back, Pete asked me if he could teach classes over the summer. But you know, everyone's going to be hanging out at the lake and taking vacations with their families. I don't think anyone is thinking of taking finance and investing classes in July. Anyway, Brooke approached me later and practically begged me to say no to his request."

"Was the community center robbed the morning Brooke was shot?"

"No, the safe was unlocked, which was strange, but nothing was missing. We only keep petty cash on hand anyway."

Ingrid, who owned the antique shop, said, "I attended one of his financial investment courses a couple years back. It felt like he was soliciting participants to take out loans backed by him."

"Have you heard him called Punky before?" Ava inquired.

"Not me," Heather said. The collective group at the table shook their heads.

Shannon said, "I can think of much more descriptive words than that to describe Pete Reinholtz."

Ingrid furrowed her brows. "Now ladies, let's not speak ill of the dead."

"It's all true, and talking about it may help us find the killer. Right, Ava?" Lauren asked.

Ava tucked a lock of hair behind her ear. "Absolutely. Sharing memories and facts can help piece together what happened, and maybe we'll uncover the murderer's motive."

Rosie sat back and cross her arms. "Well, Brooke's mother, her name is Bonnie… she told me that Pete is suing Sweetwater Farms."

"Really? What for?" Shannon asked her mother.

"Can't imagine. Dave and his dad are good people. Hard workers. Would be a damn shame if they had to close the family farm. They've been working that land for generations. Bonnie said the legal bills alone are wiping out their bank account."

Shannon asked Ava, "What happens when a plaintiff dies?"

"I believe the lawsuit is placed on hold for input from heirs to the estate." Ava pulled a small ring-bound notebook and pen from her tote.

"I hope that Natalie doesn't pursue this. I bet it's bogus," Heather said.

Ava turned her head to the group. "Did anyone see Pete after ten o'clock last night?"

Rosie answered, "I saw Pete at the Lady Luck. He was trying to get attention on the dance floor, but everyone was ignoring him because he was drunk. Let's see… Karen was there, and Anthony was too. He got up from his barstool and pulled Pete aside. They're neighbors you know. He was probably advising him to stay out of trouble. Pete stayed away from the dance floor after that. Last I saw him, Pete tried to order a whiskey at the bar. Zeke, the bartender, told him he had enough and showed him to the door."

"Do you remember what time that was?" Ava asked.

"It must have been half past ten by then because the band was taking a break before their last set."

"Oh geez, that must have been something! What was the name of the band, Rosie?" Ingrid asked.

"They're called the Sixties All-stars. They played mostly Beatles and 60s songs mixed with some classic dance music. I hope they bring that group back. A few of us retirees strutted our stuff on the dance floor until close to midnight. That was a better workout than my shine dance fitness class."

"Don't you mean line dance, Rosie?" asked Ingrid.

"No, Brooke calls it shine dance. You should come. She instructs it every Tuesday at two o'clock. I mean she used to. It's supposed to improve your cardio while dancing to hit music. Everyone does their own thing mostly, but Brooke demonstrates some steps to encourage a workout."

Ava glanced at Rosie. "What about Natalie's mom? Did you notice when Karen left?"

"Not exactly. But I remember she left the dance floor when Pete got out of hand. It was well before the last break."

Ava took down some notes, then she raised her head again. "Who here plays golf at Pine Ridge?" When a number of hands went up, she asked, "Was Pete a good golfer?"

Hazel, a stylist from the salon, spoke up. "Ha, he fancied himself a pro, but he played an average round. Why do you ask?"

"I was wondering if he played last night," Ava said.

Ingrid shook her head. "He was two sheets to the wind. I don't know how he'd have managed to play."

"Anthony here said he saw him at the course yesterday. Didn't you?" asked Phil Ferguson, a local farmer and feed supplier. He was sitting with Anthony at a high-top table, an arm's length from where Ava was seated.

"Yeah," Anthony replied. "He was carrying on about his new Mercedes to a couple of guys. I didn't recognize who he was golfing with. From out of town, probably."

"Now that you mention it, I did see a golf cart in the Lady Luck parking lot," Rosie said. "Thought that was strange, but it could have belonged to anyone. Practically half of our town folk are golfers."

Hazel pressed her index finger to her chin. "You know, I saw a golf cart weaving down Maple toward Lake Boulevard when I drove home. It was dark by then, and I didn't look closely at the driver... You sure are asking a lot of questions, Ava. Do you have an opinion about who did this?"

"Not yet, but we'll all breathe easier once the sheriff's department gets to the bottom of this."

Lauren said, "Ava has investigated employment issues for years. Theft, threats, workplace violence, and stuff like that."

"Of course, a murder investigation is much more complicated," Ava gave an awkward smile though she appreciated Lauren's sisterly pride.

"Well, this is a huge mystery," declared Lauren. "The sheriff's department will need all the help they can get."

Rosie pointed up at the TV where a broadcaster was delivering the news. "They're saying that Sheriff Donahue said the department added extra investigators. I'm sure that's why Mitch responded this morning."

"The Minneapolis news station must have young reporters in vans driving all around the state just waiting for a big story like this to break out," Hazel said. "How else did they arrive in Ruby Lake this quickly. Now they're saying that the mayor is going to speak in a half hour."

Phil removed his baseball cap and ran his right hand through his blonde hair. He had a large build. His hat displayed a fish with a hook in its mouth with the caption *Don't be a Dumb Bass.*

"I should hope so," he grumbled. "This town is scared half to death. There's a shooter and potential murderer on the loose. How are we supposed to ensure our kids are safe now that they are out of school? We can't allow them to play without constant supervision. Our town's about to triple in size with the invasion of the summer cabin owners and tourists coming in from the five-state area."

"Yes, fishing season is well underway. I wonder if this is going to scare people off. Our local businesses need the revenue. We depend on it to survive the rest of the year," Anthony said. He owned and operated the pizzeria on Main Street.

"The graduation ceremony is being held at the high school in a couple of hours," Phil said loudly. "Hope that they've called in reinforcements to provide screening and security. Otherwise, this could be the lowest attended graduation in Ruby Lake history."

Heather crossed her arms in front of her. "Think about all the teenagers attending graduation open houses this afternoon and throughout the month. As a parent, I need to know that our kids are going to be safe."

"The senior class is holding a lock-in party tonight at the high school," Hazel explained. "Most of the parents have signed up for shifts. We all need to be on high alert. The plan is to have students and parents enter the building at the front entrance. All other doorways will be emergency exits only."

"Good grief, who would've imagined this would happen up here in rural Minnesota?" Ingrid asked. "Matt, please turn up the TV. They said a special news briefing will be held shortly. We'd all like to hear what Mayor Thompson and Sheriff Donahue have to say about Brooke's shooting and Pete's death this morning."

Ava felt a sense of warmth surrounded by this community that gathered together to support one another. There was something truly special about knowing your neighbors. She could ask for help at any time, knowing that someone would have her back.

Ava's father, Doug Andrews, hurried into the building and scanned the crowded dining space. He was slightly over-dressed, wearing tan chinos and a pressed button-down shirt. The tall, distinguished man found his daughters and gave each a hug.

"Thank goodness you're safe, Ava."

"I'm so glad to see you." Ava managed to lift one side of her mouth in a lopsided smile. His strong presence was comforting.

"We've been worried sick." Doug shook his head. "Why were you out jogging around the golf course so early this morning?"

"I couldn't sleep, and I needed to burn off some anxious energy."

"Honey, you could have asked anyone one of us to join you."

"I figured there'd be golfers out there earlier. Little did I know it was the most dangerous place to be this morning."

Doug shook his full head of black and silver hair. "I'm glad Mitch responded. And we're lucky to have him working on these cases. I'm sure he took good care of you."

Ava turned her head away. She had no intention of sharing Mitch's subtle accusation in front of this crowd.

Doug looked around then spoke louder, "I'm curious what the sheriff has to say about all this. Did I miss the news briefing?"

"No, but we're expecting it to start shortly," Lauren answered.

Ava stood and leaned close to her dad. "Mitch told me Pete's time of death was several hours prior based on his initial review of the body. The medical examiner will be able to provide a narrower timeline."

"Did he believe Pete was murdered?" Doug whispered.

Ava nodded.

A couple of ladies seated at the long table scooted their chairs down to make room for Ava's father. "Here's a chair for you, Dad," said Matt.

Doug placed his hand on Ava's once they sat down. "I wish I had been there instead of you. Anything to spare you from this nightmare."

Ava choked back a tear. "I spoke to Grant briefly once I got home, and I'm meeting him for dinner this evening."

"Are you sure you're ready for that given all the stress you're going through?" Lauren asked with sisterly concern.

"He is my attorney. Plus, I'm hoping he'll get the inside scoop. It's all so surreal. I never imagined anything like this happening here."

Doug nodded. "We'll work together to get to the bottom

of this. We can't allow fear to keep us from living, but we need to be vigilant."

Randy was looking at the big screen television, reading the captions aloud. "Now they claim the sheriff is talking to a person of interest. Does anyone have a guess as to who that is?"

"Hell, that could be anybody," Phil called out. "We're all interested citizens. I think he's just blowing smoke up our skirts. Sheriff Donahue will say just about anything to get voters. That man is all politics and no action."

"At least we have Deputy Hildebrand to patrol our streets daily," said Ingrid.

Phil had pulled the bass cap back on his head. "What good is he? Bob may still be able to drive, but he's not fit to catch anyone. But then, there's been nothing to see here before this week. Pete's murder is the most excitement Ruby Lake has seen since the Labor Day incident of 2002. You know, when all the statues in town were vandalized while everyone was down at Memorial Park. Those boys were suspended from their first week of school senior year and had to do community service for months."

"Let me think… wasn't Pete involved with that pack?" Ingrid asked.

"You're right," Anthony said, "and his parents never recovered from their embarrassment. The Reinholtz family relocated to Minneapolis when Pete graduated from high school. Why he moved back here, I'll never understand."

"Because he's a narcissist, that's why," Ingrid scowled. "He wanted to prove he was a big man with a business degree so he started a CPA firm in town. When he couldn't keep enough business, he got a job with the senior living center."

Rosie responded, "I think he came back for Natalie. I

imagine none of those city girls would put up with his crap. Natalie always stuck by his side. Well, until she left him the other day. She should have done that a long time ago, I tell you. Poor girl… she's been through the wringer with that jerk."

"You've got that right," Anthony said. Everyone nodded their agreement.

"I've been wondering how we can increase local support for the county women's and children's shelters. I hope all of this media attention raises awareness about domestic violence. Would you all be interested in participating in a fundraiser?" Ava asked the group.

"You betcha!" declared Ingrid.

"That's a wonderful idea, Ava. Let's show Ruby Lake's community spirit," added Rosie.

"Great, I'll present a few ideas to the Chamber of Commerce. Perhaps we can do something for the July 4th Jubilee." Ava was pleased to turn something bad into positive action.

Doug said, "I'll be glad to assist you, honey. Since your mom serves on the Chamber, I'm sure she'd be happy to submit this for consideration for the Jubilee."

"I'd love to create the proposal with you."

"Ava, can you come here for a minute?" asked Matt.

"What is it?" Ava approached the counter. "Let me just squeeze right past you," she said to the two women blocking the passageway that led behind the coffee bar.

"We just received a call from Dave Sweetwater requesting a take-out order. A good samaritan gave him a gift card." Lauren winked. "That was very generous of you, by the way. I'd hate to see him thrown to the wolves. He won't be able to get out of here with all their nosy questions." She tilted her head toward the packed dining area.

Ava had an idea. "Matt, why don't you call Dave back and tell him I can deliver his order to the hospital?"

"Terrific—I'm texting him right now. Wait… says he's at the farm picking up some things while Brooke's parents are at the hospital. I can tell him you'll run out there, if that's okay." Matt looked up at Ava.

"Of course. I haven't been out to Sweetwater Farms in years. Plus, it's the perfect opportunity to ask questions and take a good look around."

"Did I hear you say you're heading out to the Sweetwater place?" Shannon approached with an empty coffee cup, likely seeking a refill.

"Yeah, I'm delivering food to Dave. Want to ride along?"

"I'd love to." Shannon set her cup on the counter. "I'm free all day now that I hired a new sales clerk. I haven't had a full Saturday off in months."

"That's awesome. We can hang out like old times."

"You two go on ahead." Lauren smiled. "The lunch crowd will probably be even crazier. News and speculation are bringing people out in droves."

"Will I see you tomorrow for my ladies' luncheon?" Ava asked.

"Absolutely! Mid-afternoon at your place."

"Good, we have to get running." Ava grabbed Shannon's elbow and started for the door, stopping momentarily near Doug. "Talk to you soon, dad… and let me know if you learn anything new from the news briefing."

Chapter Thirteen

AFTER HEADING WEST through the picturesque countryside along the edge of town, Ava drove into the visitor's lot at Sweetwater Farms with Shannon serving as her navigator.

"Wow, this property is much bigger than I recall. Last time I visited, I was with my dad picking up our Christmas tree," Ava exclaimed. She felt a bit guilty that she hadn't been part of her family's holiday preparations in recent years. Sure, she came home for celebrations, but she hadn't fully participated since she was in college. She'd been working diligently, taking a long weekend off here and there and saving up her vacation time like it was a bank account.

"Dave and Brooke are investing back into the farm, adding new crops to their fields every year. They're the family's next generation of farmers since Dave's older brother wasn't interested in farm work. I heard he lives in St. Paul."

Ava followed Shannon along the crushed pebble path up to the clapboard-sided farmhouse. She was enchanted by the impressive two-story structure built for a large family back in the 1940's. Stone pillars greeted them at the entrance. The wrap-around porch must've provided a lovely respite after working a long day in the fields. It was in need of a fresh coat of paint which was not uncommon following a punishing winter. The farm and its buildings were a major undertaking.

Dave was standing in his doorway awaiting his guests. His wavy hair was tousled, and his jaw reflected the early growth of a beard.

"Hi Dave, it's good to see you. How's Brooke doing?" Shannon asked as they reached his front porch.

"She's a fighter. It's truly remarkable. How's your mom?"

"Doing quite well, thanks," Shannon responded.

Ava lifted a delivery bag in the air. "We've brought your food order. Matt added a growler of beer plus dinner as well."

"Please come in. Let's set these bags down in the kitchen. Looks like you brought enough food for a week. I can't thank you enough for your generosity." Dave smiled politely.

Ava marveled at the large rock fireplace in the adjoining living room. Oversized plush furniture gave the space a relaxed and lived-in feel. She noticed the hardwood floors were inlayed with mahogany, the same species as the wooden staircase.

"We're all happy to help," she replied. "Say, I understand you were friends with Pete Reinholtz. I'm sorry for your loss."

"Some friend." Dave raked his sandy hair with one hand. "We were colleagues years back, but we had a falling out."

"Oh?" Ava practiced restraint, hoping for an explanation.

"I hired Pete to set up my accounting records a few years ago. Pete's fees kept escalating, and to be completely honest, I suspected he was stealing from my profits. Anyway, I replaced him and ended our business relationship. That set him off."

"He held a grudge?"

"I'll say. Pete accused me of ruining his reputation and

sued me for defamation. He also claimed he came up with ideas to grow my farm business."

"Really? How could he do that?" Shannon asked.

"After Dad passed the farm down to me, I added the retail operation, corn maze, and the fall festival. We're bringing in food trucks and bands throughout the summer too. Sure, Pete and I discussed some thoughts over beers. But I implemented my own ideas. And even if I had used one of his hair-brained suggestions—which I didn't—why would he expect financial compensation? Friends help each other, right?"

"Absolutely."

"Now, he thinks he's got some right to a percentage of my profits. Or, he did that is. It's all bullshit. I'm up to my neck in legal fees."

Ava shook her head. "That's too bad. Do you think he was in some financial trouble and needed extra money?"

"That's a good question." Dave scratched his trim beard. "He was into buying the latest gadgets and computers. Liked to show off new cars and fancy watches. I don't really know if he could afford it or not."

"Did you ever play golf with Pete? We heard he played often."

"Nah, golf isn't my sport. I take part in the summer softball league just for fun. Watching football is more my speed."

"Were you at the hospital all night on Friday?"

"Yes, I was right by Brooke's side all day and night." He looked at Ava. "Why? You don't think I had anything to do with Pete's murder, do you?"

"Not at all," Ava replied. "I assumed you were with her or at home resting. We're just trying to find out who all was in town and if anyone saw something that will help with the sheriff's investigation."

Shannon said, "Ava is also investigating the crime."

Dave appeared to ponder that for a moment. "Good luck to you. I really mean it."

"At Woodcrest this morning, a lot of people expressed their concern about Brooke. You both have tons of emotional support," Ava said.

Dave nodded, and Ava half grimaced before continuing, "Also, I hate to mention this, but a few were speculating that you two are separated?"

"That's just ridiculous," Dave said in a raised voice. "Sure, we've been going through some hard times… like all couples do." He shook his head.

"Sorry Dave, you don't need this gossip. I was there too and heard someone saying Brooke has been hanging out with Cody Myers quite frequently," Shannon added.

One side of Dave's mouth turned up slightly. "Well, that's pretty funny actually. Let's just say Cody is harmless. They're old high school friends. I thought you were going to say Pete. Brooke hated that man more than I did."

"Why is that?"

"It's rather personal. Brooke and I want to have a second child… Zoe just turned seven. Been planning to try infertility treatments, but that's on the back burner due to our temporary financial challenges, which she blames on Pete." Dave glanced at both Ava and Shannon. "I'm counting on you both to keep this confidential."

"Yes, of course," Ava said. "Do you think Pete could've shot Brooke after an argument?"

"That thought crossed my mind. I shared my concern with the authorities."

"I guess we should leave you to enjoy your lunch. I apologize if I upset you in any way."

"It's okay, really. I prefer to know what's going on. Hope you get to the bottom of this. Deputy Hildebrand hasn't come up with any leads yet, as far as I know."

Shannon said, "While we're here, we'd love to do a little berry picking. I saw a sign advertising juneberries as we drove in. Can you direct us to the vines?"

"Sure, right this way." Dave led them to the entrance of his retail barn before turning back to his home.

Ava and Shannon toured the refurbished building which housed a retail area selling wicker baskets, barbecue and picnic sets, and logo apparel. Crates of fresh produce nestled on shelves alongside a beverage counter where a student helper was selling flavored lemonade iced teas and apple cider. Picnic tables were arranged around a small stage, and a large chalkboard listed the produce for sale and the harvest dates for fresh berry picking.

"This barn is beautiful!" Ava spun around. "They must use the stage for bands. Dave mentioned they host live music here. Don't you think this place would be an awesome wedding venue? Imagine hanging huge chandeliers from these beams and an arbor just inside this doorway. Ceremonies could be held indoors during bad weather. They're certainly set up to cater food."

"You have a great eye. I always thought you'd be an excellent interior designer. If you ever grow tired of managing other people's problems, you could have another career."

Ava smiled in return. "That could be fun."

The two friends proceeded outdoors and plucked purple berries from a row of shrubby juneberry trees which they had all to themselves. Shannon set her basket on the ground and stretched. "So, do you believe Dave?"

Ava turned her head to Shannon. "About being with Brooke at the hospital all night?"

Shannon nodded.

"Of course. That'll be easy to verify. Talk about rough patches though… between the lawsuit, fertility challenges, and now dealing with Brooke's recovery. Must be overwhelming."

Shannon sighed. "I can't imagine. It gives him a motive to murder Pete though."

"That's what I was just thinking."

After twenty minutes of harvesting berries, Shannon interrupted Ava's thoughts again. "Should we check out? My arms are beginning to freckle." Shannon's fair skin burned easily in the sun. Her dark brown hair glinted a hint of red, and its natural curl had sprung into ringlets due to the humidity.

"Yes, I'm ready." Ava glanced at her watch. "Let's head straight back to your place. You can show me your ideas on remodeling your studio."

Ava paid cash for their berries. "I ate a few of mine," she confessed to the teenager working the cash register. "Charge me extra for at least a fistful. I couldn't resist. They'll be amazing with the chocolate cake I'm serving tomorrow."

Shannon and Ava strolled toward the gravel parking lot where Detective Sullivan was exiting his vehicle. Mitch tipped his hat and nodded at the two women. "Looks like you're one step ahead of me again. Ava, can I talk to you for a moment… privately?"

"Sure." She handed her car key to Shannon. "Go ahead and start the engine to get the AC running."

Shannon saluted Mitch and turned toward Ava's car.

Ava and Mitch walked to the far side of the parking lot. "What's up, Mitch?"

"What are you doing here?"

"Delivering food to Dave. He placed an order while we were at Woodcrest earlier, and I offered to bring it to him."

"Are you sure you're not here to investigate?" He placed his hands on his hips. "I'm worried about you. You could be in very serious danger. A murderer who doesn't want you nosing into their business may still be wandering around town. Additionally, Sheriff Donahue is very eager to arrest someone in this case. This is not doing you any favors."

"Are you saying that I'm a suspect?"

"Yes, you're currently on a short list. I know there's no way that you did this, Ava, but you should lay low."

"That's ridiculous. What's gotten into the sheriff?"

"You did fire the guy last week. There's a group of witnesses who saw Pete threaten you last Wednesday night, and then you were alone when you found his body this morning."

"Why would I have called in his death if I was the murderer? The guilty party just left his body and high tailed it out of there, right? Were there any tracks or footprints?"

"You mean other than Pete's, yours, Sophie's, and dozens of golfers? It's a public area. There are numerous footprints along with bike treads, golf carts, and scooters. To answer your first question—there are neurotic murderers who do it for the attention. One theory is that you want to be the town hero, the center of attention. You're viewed as an outsider since you moved away from town."

"That's a terrible thing to say. And I hate being the center of attention. You know that. Who else is on this short list of yours?"

"Natalie, of course and her father. Randy Sparks though I

don't believe he did it either, but he doesn't have proof of his whereabouts late Friday night."

"There's no way Randy is involved. Is Dave's alibi solid? Was he at the hospital all night?"

"Yes, he was. The nursing staff saw him there."

"There has to be something that links Brooke's shooting to Pete's murder, don't you think?" Ava asked.

"If they're not, it's a strange coincidence. However, we don't have any solid evidence. Brooke was shot and Pete was struck in the head. It would be odd for a serial killer to use different murder weapons."

"Pete seemed to have a lot of enemies. You ought to focus on real motives for his murder rather than Donahue's weak theory about me. I returned to Ruby Lake for my job, and I have a lot of family here. Spend some time at the coffee shop like I did this morning, and you'll find a whole lot of folks with stories about Pete."

"My investigation is well underway," Mitch said.

"Also, I wasn't going to say anything about this because I don't think it's really a credible threat, but last Tuesday morning after midnight, I saw a man on the hiking path behind my house. It had just started thundering, and I briefly spotted him during a lighting flash. I couldn't tell who it was. After Brooke was shot, I started to think that maybe it was Pete coming after me."

"You said this was Tuesday morning?" Mitch withdrew a small notebook from his shirt pocket.

"That's correct."

"I thought you fired Pete on Wednesday. Why would he try to harm you on Tuesday morning?

"Because I also issued disciplinary action to Pete on

Monday. Then a second incident was reported on Tuesday that resulted in his job termination."

"All right, I'll add this to the report. I wish you would've said something sooner."

"Like I said, I didn't really believe anyone was trying to break in at the time."

Mitch looked up from his notepad. "Someone may suggest that you invented this so we would sympathize with you."

"You can check it out with Lauren and Matt. I spoke with them that morning, and then Matt came over and installed a security system for me. I have the receipts."

"I'm glad you did that. Does your system include cameras?"

"Yes, door cameras."

"If anything like that happens again, I'll view the video. Make sure you lock your doors and set your alarm system every time you come into the house, not just at night. Call if you need anything at all. I'm sorry, Ava... but please stay out of trouble. I want to rule you out as a suspect almost as badly as you want me to."

"Will do," replied Ava. She trudged toward her Bronco where Shannon was sitting with the door open.

Shannon climbed out of the driver's seat. "What was that about? You look really upset."

"I am—I can't believe him. Mitch just told me that I'm a suspect. He's also worried that the killer is roaming around."

"He is?" Shannon crossed her arms.

"I'm not willing to hide because some creep is wreaking havoc on our town. I need to get to the bottom of this to clear my name."

"Oh sweetie, I'll help you any way I can. Mitch can't possibly believe that you'd have anything to do with Brooke's shooting or Pete's murder."

"He doesn't. It's Sheriff Donahue and Mayor Thompson's desire to arrest someone to calm everyone down."

"You know that Sheriff Donahue couldn't find a criminal if one slapped him across his face. He's just a figurehead. Between you and me, I hope there's a really strong contender during the next election, so we can vote him out."

"I can't believe what a horrible day this is. Would you mind driving us back to town? I'm too distracted," Ava said.

"Sure, hop in. Let's go find some peppermint bonbon ice cream. That always lifted our spirits as kids."

"Now you're talking."

The ice cream parlor was located around the corner from Rosie's Floral. Three young children pressed their noses to the display freezer while pointing out their favorite flavors to their mother. Once Shannon and Ava had finally purchased their sugar cones, they went into the floral shop, crossed through the gift shop, and headed back to Shannon's art studio in the adjoining suite.

Shannon tilted her head toward the faded leather sofa. "Let's consider this our hideout where no one can find us," Shannon joked.

Ava smiled at the thought. She and Shannon loved to build forts as kids. "This old couch is still really comfortable. We hung out on it for hours in your basement."

"This is cathartic, isn't it? Reminds me of when my dad used to read to me on this old couch. I couldn't let Mom throw it out when she moved into the apartment above her shop." Shannon ran a hand along the tiny imperfections of her sofa. "You know, I was thinking about having that old fireplace restored."

"Are you thinking wood burning or gas?"

"Either would be fine. Gas would be cleaner. I imagine adding two or three large tables in front of it with easels along the window wall. I'd like to offer arts and crafts classes, and I could hold special events to prepare for the holidays. I also plan to add craft supplies to the gift shop inventory, which could increase retail sales."

"I love it. I bet you'll find plenty of people who are interested. Plus, you have so many possible mediums to choose from. That reminds me, Latisha was showing off some cute painted fabric jackets and shoes to the seniors the other day," Ava said. "I bet that would be a fun class. If you provided some patterns and examples, participants could complete a simple project in one evening."

"You're right. Fabric painting is very popular now. I'd have to bring this room up to building code. I really don't know how much it would all cost. Do you think I'd need to close up the ceilings and add sheetrock to the back wall?" Shannon asked.

"I really like the original brick. Keep as much of it as you can. I don't know anything about building code, but some of the other businesses around here are using original materials in their décor."

"I'll need to keep it cost efficient so proper insulation would be important. I'll have to put together a business plan and go to the bank. I hope I can get a loan. Do you know any contractors?"

"I don't, but Matt worked with someone a few years ago. We could ask him for a recommendation. This is so exciting. I love watching your dreams come true," Ava said.

"Heather from the community center told me that Pete was looking for investment opportunities. He approached business owners and offered loans at exorbitant interest rates. I wonder if anyone else in town has recently done business with him."

"Good point. We can ask around." Ava wrapped her arms around her knees. "You told me you've been adding to your savings. If you keep the scope of your renovation small, you might be able to cover the cost yourself."

"I hope so, but what I hear from other store owners is that renovation costs easily go well beyond budget. Plus, I haven't had a chance to tell you this yet—I'm planning a big surprise for my mom."

"For her birthday?" Ava asked.

Shannon smiled broadly. "You know her seventieth is coming up... I'm taking her on a tour of Ireland. She and dad always talked about visiting their parents' homeland. After Dad's heart attack, she never brought it up again. I can't wait to tell her now that I've hired additional help."

"I'm excited for you! Rosie's going to freak out. Speaking of extra help, I'll be glad to pitch in. I can work the cash register on the weekends and even a couple evenings if you'd like."

"You're an amazing friend. I'm thinking about reducing our store hours while we're on vacation, but I'll let you know, okay?" Shannon was glowing. "I've read lots of books about Ireland over the years, and I finally get to see if for myself. I hope it's as green as I imagine."

"That could actually be a perfect time for you to have your remodeling done," Ava pointed out.

"You're right! I didn't even think of that. I'd like to go ahead and purchase the plane tickets and tour vouchers, but that's going to take a hit to my savings account."

"That's such a heartfelt gift," Ava said. "She'll be so thrilled to spend that quality time with you."

"I was also thinking we could take one of those DNA tests to get some more information about our ancestry before we go. You know, we may feel more connected to the towns we visit."

"You should do that right after you share the news, so you'll have enough time to get the results back. That is so cool. I'm jealous. Now, tell me every detail about your itinerary."

Chapter Fourteen

"TAKE YOUR TIME," Shannon said, lying sprawled across Avas's bed, propped on one elbow. She scratched Sophie's ears and flipped through a fashion magazine as she watched Ava pop in and out of her bedroom, modeling various outfits for her dinner that night. Ava wouldn't have time to change between Harper's graduation open house and dinner with Grant, so her selection would have to do double duty.

"I don't know why I'm having such difficulty making decisions today," she called out from her closet.

"I wish I didn't have to remind you that you discovered a corpse just this morning, and you're going to be meeting up with your ex-boyfriend tonight. I'd say that's a whole lot of excitement for one day."

Ava reappeared in a pair of black pants and a sleeveless silk blouse. Its sapphire sheen complimented her doe brown eyes. "How's this?"

"Too corporate for Harper's open house."

"You're right. Back to the drawing board. Ugh, you know, I really thought my life had slowed down when I moved back here."

"People are people everywhere you go, Ava. You can't escape conflict."

"I didn't expect to avoid it. I just thought it would decrease due to the smaller population. It's a simple statistical equation. Percentages and probability."

"It's hard to believe that we have evil citizens living among us in Ruby Lake, but you know you're surrounded by your family, friends, and neighbors who care."

"I wish Sheriff Donahue was one of those people."

"Good will prevail. Mark my words," declared Shannon. Ava returned in an athletic skirt and polo shirt top. Shannon shook her head and said, "Sorry, too casual, hon."

Ava headed back to her dressing space. "Hopefully, Grant will have some clout to help move this along. He said he would call the sheriff's department and the hospital. I expect to get some good updates this evening."

"And how are you feeling about seeing him after all these months?"

"I admit I'm a little anxious. Not because I want him back or anything like that. I hope our conversation isn't too awkward. I'm curious how he's doing, and I think a bit of closure will be good for both of us."

"I understand. You were together for a long time," Shannon said.

"He told me it was up to me to reach out to him… I just thought it would be regarding a much more positive circumstance instead of over work conflict and murder suspects. I can't believe this is my life right now. Grant might not have been my lifetime partner, but I respect him. And he's one hell of an attorney. I'm glad to have him by my side."

"You're going to get through this even stronger."

Ava returned wearing a navy and white halter dress.

Shannon sat up. "Wow, perfect choice. You're going to knock him dead tonight. Whoops, no pun intended. You can carry a cute little blue cardigan in case the air conditioning is too cold during dinner."

Turning her attention to her bathroom mirror, Ava quickly played with a few different hairstyles. She grabbed her hair in one hand and held it up first high in back, then dropped it into a ponytail, and let it back down. In the end, she left her long mane down and added some anti-frizz cream to keep her loose waves in check. Ava never wore more than minimal makeup, but she added a little lip balm.

"Which earrings do you suggest?" Ava held up two options.

"Try the hammered gold ones. They're classy but understated."

Ava slid her feet into her new espadrilles rather than her usual flats. "It's only dinner. I don't have to stand in them for hours, right?"

Shannon nodded in response and pushed on the bridge of her glasses that had slid down her nose. Her high cheek bones gave her a regal quality.

"You know, I can't even think about eating dinner right now. It seems like we've been eating all day. First at the coffee shop... and can you believe we finished off those huge sugar cones?" Ava said. "I've had so much fun with you the past few hours. You really do know how to make me feel better."

"I'm glad. I've enjoyed catching up with you too."

"Well, I'm ready to go," said Ava. "We'd better get moving so I can make a respectable appearance at Harper's open house before I have to cut out. I'm really glad you get to stay later to enjoy all the fun."

❧

The Sparks' residence was located a few blocks from Randy's auto shop in one of Ruby Park's original neighborhoods. Its streets were neatly lined in tidy rows, and most of the quarter-acre lots were hugged by white wooden fences. The sidewalks were shaded by enormous white oak trees that hosted hopscotch games, lemonade stands, and afternoon strolls.

Ava parked her car two blocks away from Des and Randy's house while Shannon snagged a much closer spot. The long line of cars parked along the curbs promised that Harper's graduation party was well attended. She soon spotted the guest of honor in her backyard playing volleyball with a mob of teens. The tangy aroma of chilidogs and bratwursts with sauerkraut filled the air. Randy waved to her from his post at the grill.

While she tried to dodge questions from nosey but well-meaning guests, Ava quickly became exhausted from making polite conversation. Seeking shade, she found Ian, the high school drama director under a canopy tent.

"Hi," Ava said as she approached him. "Guess you're celebrating the end of the school year, too."

"Absolutely, but I'll miss my kids. Join me." Ian patted the folding lawn chair next to him. "You look delicious in that halter dress. Are we trying to impress someone?"

Ava accepted his invitation and responded, "Why thank you. I do have dinner plans… Speaking of dates, have you seen any good movies lately?"

"As a matter of fact, I was just at the Wooddale movie theater on Tuesday night. They're featuring classics all summer long during their ten o'clock late show. We saw *Gladiator*. Russell Crowe is spectacular."

"And, did your date enjoy it too?"

"Did Cody tell you? I guess that's a good sign."

"I didn't say that." Ava smiled. "But I'll keep that tidbit to myself. Thanks for the tip about the movies. I'll definitely head over there on the weekend. I don't like to be out late on week nights—I have to show up early for work."

Ian said, "They're featuring a different movie each week to keep us coming back."

"Good strategy, and I heard you've been holding tryouts at the community theater. That must keep you busy during summer break. What show are you producing?"

"You're catching up quickly after being back in town just a few short months. We're presenting *Legally Blonde* at the end of August."

"I love that movie. Can't tell you the number of times I've seen it. I'll definitely buy tickets to your live show."

"With a date, I'm assuming?"

"We'll have to see about that." Ava raised her eyebrows and shrugged.

Shannon ambled toward the white tent. "Here you are, Ava. I thought you'd be leaving by now."

"Is it that time already?" Ava glanced at her cell phone to check. "Oh, you're right. I should say my goodbyes. Here Shannon—take my seat." Ava stood up and looked at Ian. "I really enjoyed catching up with you, and it was nice not talking about the murder."

"You bet. Take care, honey," replied Ian as he gave her a wink.

Although Ava had been mingling for less than an hour, she was already yearning for a quiet evening. She found the party's honoree. "Harper, you're an exquisite hostess, and I swear you could pass for twenty-five. You look absolutely gorgeous."

"Thanks, Ava!"

"Don't go giving her any ideas," Des said with a grin. Her pride for her daughter was radiant. "I told you it's her dress. She'll change into her Duluth Bulldogs sweatshirt before the school party tonight."

"It's more than the dress," Ava said to Harper. "You're a confident woman, and I know you'll be successful in any career field you choose." Ava gave Harper a big hug before walking toward the front yard.

As Ava searched for her Bronco Sport, the song "I Did It All" by Vince Myers was still playing in her head. She had heard it multiple times during the open house. Randy had produced a heartfelt video montage of his daughter's school years that he played on a loop. She was humming the tune which lifted her spirits. A squad car cruised slowly down the street. It stopped alongside Ava, and Mitch rolled down his window.

"Just in case you're following me Mitch, I'll save you the suspense. I'm heading over to the Pine Ridge Golf Course where I'll be having dinner with my attorney."

Mitch smiled and saluted Ava. "Drive carefully, and don't talk to strangers," he said with a sly grin before continuing on to patrol the streets of Ruby Lake.

Chapter Fifteen

G RANT WAS SITTING at the bar holding a cocktail and chatting with a bartender when Ava arrived at the Pine Ridge Country Club. Her eyes instantly gravitated toward him as she approached. He appeared more handsome than she remembered. He could be on the cover of *GQ*, or perhaps more appropriately, Young Attorney's Quarterly, if there was such a thing.

Grant stood up as soon as he saw her walk in the doorway and gave her a quick hug. "You look sensational, Ava." Ava gave him a polite smile. At 5'9", she was a tall woman, but she felt overpowered next to his lean, 6' 4" stature. Grant was several years older than Ava, and his dark hair was sprinkled with gray flecks at his temples which made him look distinguished.

"I like this casual look of yours. You must admit a polo is much more comfortable than wearing a suit and tie every day." Ava gave a genuine smile to her former boyfriend.

"That's true. Are you ready for dinner? I reserved us a table."

Ava followed him to the dining room where the hostess nodded and led them across the room. They were soon seated alongside a floor to ceiling window that offered them an amazing view of the golf course. "I love this place, Grant. I'm glad you suggested it."

An attractive waitress stopped by to request their drink order. "I'd like a Pinot Grigio, please," replied Ava.

"And for you sir?" Their server batted her full eyelash extensions toward Grant.

"I'd like a Jameson with a water back," Grant responded easily. Then he returned his full attention to Ava. "I was so relieved to hear your voice. I was beginning to wonder if I'd hear from you again. You didn't have to cut me completely out of your life when we broke up."

"It was the only way I could move forward at the time. I committed to my new job, and I couldn't second guess my decision. I'm sorry if that hurt you. These past few months have been such a healing process for me. I hope it's been the same for you."

"I don't know. I was such an insensitive jerk. I should have known you were expecting a proposal that night."

"It's not your fault that I had my hopes up."

"I invited you to the most romantic restaurant in town and promised you a surprise."

"You did surprise me by telling me about your promotion and suggesting I move in to your townhouse in Minnetonka."

"My dad thinks that I'm a dumbass."

"You told him about it?"

"Not the details… The look on your face showed me I really screwed things up. I was selfishly focused on my own needs. I won't make that same mistake twice. Could we try again?" Grant asked hopefully.

"I believe this is the way it was meant to be. There's no

need to rehash things, but as I said, I didn't feel right moving further from my work if you didn't envision a future for us. Living with you would have been very comfortable, but I needed a commitment and a change of lifestyle first. I don't want to sound contrite, but I do want to keep our friendship. I really enjoy your company, and we speak the same language."

"We can be more than that if you give me another chance."

"You and I both know we'd come back to this in a few months. We've been on this ride. We aren't on the same time-table, and we have different goals now."

"I know I want you in my life." Grant looked at Ava with an intense sadness that she had not seen from him since his mother's funeral.

"I want a family, Grant." Ava spoke gently, and Grant's eyes widened. "Not immediately but soon. I see that clearly now. I'm proud of my career like you are of yours, but for me, it has to come after family and friends. You've always been more ambitious than I am. I could never ask you to slow down."

"I'm not sure about that. I wonder if my mom had survived her cancer battle, whether she would have influenced me differently. My dad's quest to have me join his firm fueled my drive."

"That may be, but I can't see you being happy without the challenge of putting out fifty fires at once. By the way, I heard a rumor from my Grandpa Charles that you're running for mayor?"

"Wow, gossip does travel fast. Dad suggested it, but I haven't given it much serious thought. Of course, he sees it as a first step for a future run for State Attorney General or Governor."

Ava borrowed an expression from her grandpa. "You're as honest as the day is long. We all could use a respectable guy like you in office."

"Thank you, Ava. Your opinion means the world to me."

"Your mom would be so proud of you."

"I miss her. She'd think I was an idiot for losing you."

"You haven't lost me." Ava touched his hand. "Friends for life?"

Grant nodded. "You betcha!" They both burst out laughing. Grant rarely used the Scandinavian expressions that their older relatives used, and Ava appreciated his rare attempt to be funny.

The waitress returned with their drinks and took their dinner orders. Ava selected the almond crusted walleye, and Grant requested the sea bass.

Ava knew it was time to discuss business. "Do you have any news about Pete Reinholtz?"

"Yes, the autopsy concluded his cause of death was blunt force trauma to his skull. Pete didn't die from a fall. He must've been hit with some force. He also had bruising on the right side of his face which means he might have been punched during a struggle, or he hit something when he fell. The coroner believes the bruises coincide with being struck by a left-handed fist."

"I've been trying to determine who would be angry enough to do this. You don't think our decision to terminate his employment led to his murder?"

"It seems far-fetched that a woman he harassed would retaliate by committing murder. You responded immediately and let him go. No one could expect more from his employer. Besides, you said there were plenty of other people who disliked Pete. He was an abusive person."

Ava dabbed at a tear forming in her eye.

"Don't over think it, Ava. You know as well as I do that this is a no-fault state. Either party can terminate employment for any reason or no reason. You had good reason. Pete damaged his employer's trust and reputation. This situation stinks, but you have nothing to feel bad about."

"What about the three employees that he kissed earlier in the week? I wonder if one of them might be harboring some resentment."

Grant shook his head. "Pete was quite a character—No, they expressed how they felt and wanted to keep working with him." Grant touched Ava's hand and consoled her. "Hey, stop wrestling with your conscience. This is not your responsibility."

Ava appreciated his kind attempt to calm her nerves. "I feel bad for my friends, Des and Randy. Several people overheard Randy threatening Pete Wednesday evening when Pete made a pass at his daughter. I hope he's not a suspect."

"I doubt it, though he may be questioned. You have a big heart, but you can't fix this mess. The investigation will take a while. Ruby Park doesn't have its own police force, as you know, so the Garrett County Sheriff's Department will investigate. Their resources are spread thin, and Mitch is likely the only investigator assigned to the case. Let him do his job."

Ava nodded. "That guy over there keeps glancing at our table. Look over your shoulder."

"Sure. I talked to him earlier on the golf course. His name is John Carlson, and he works in human resources too. I've bumped into him at a couple conferences. They do business with our firm."

"You're kidding me. He works for the same company as the sales rep that Pete harassed. He was the one who called me with the complaint. Isn't this a coincidence? I spoke to him on the phone a couple times."

"Our order will take a while. Let's walk over there, and I'll introduce you."

John stood when Grant greeted him. Ava thought he appeared agitated or nervous, perhaps because his pale complexion was turning pink. The men shook hands, and Grant introduced Ava. John was quite a bit shorter than Grant, and he had reddish-blonde hair.

Ava said, "I'm so glad to meet you in person, John. What a surprise. Do you get to Ruby Lake often?"

"Unfortunately, no. I had the opportunity to visit my grandfather today at Ruby Park. I don't get to see him as often as I'd like, but I was invited to golf this afternoon, so here I am."

"I hope you're pleased with the care he's receiving."

"We are. My parents chose it because it's one of the top senior communities in the state. The nursing staff are caring and very friendly. By the way, I was surprised to learn that Pete Reinholtz died. I heard from some other golfers that he had a heart attack on the golf course."

"Actually no, Pete was murdered," Ava said. John's face flushed, and he nervously strummed his fingers on the table.

"That's horrible. Have they caught the person that did this?"

"Not that I'm aware of. It just happened early this morning," Ava said. She looked around wondering if John was expecting someone to join him. "By the way, how is your co-worker doing? I hope she's well."

"Yes, thanks for asking. Lindsey's been out of town in Brainerd for a state medical supply chain conference." John said to Grant, "I hope you enjoyed a good round of golf."

"I did. Dad and I try to get out to this course a couple times each season. Good to run into you again," Grant said before turning toward Ava. "We should head back to our table before our meal arrives. Enjoy your dinner, John."

"You too, and it was a pleasure meeting you in person, Ava."

"Have a good night." Ava smiled, and she and Grant returned to their table.

"That was strange, don't you think?" Ava whispered to Grant as they sat down again.

"How do you mean?"

"The way John was fidgeting. Why was he so nervous?"

"I didn't notice. That's probably his normal disposition. Maybe he's waiting for someone to join him."

"He seemed very uncomfortable when I shared the news that Pete was murdered. Do you think he knows something?" she asked.

"It's a shock to learn of a murder out here in rural Minnesota."

"It was more than that."

"You're reading too much into your hunches," Grant said.

Ava had a revelation. Grant was objective to a T. Give him the facts, and he could defend any case. But he wasn't good at reading feelings.

If only he could be more sensitive. She was sure if they both completed one of those personality questionnaires corporate trainers used for team-building, that Grant would score high in using his thinking skills rather than his feelings. She was the complete opposite. Ava leaned on her feelings and intuition when making decisions.

Ava was now aware that this disconnect prevented them from achieving greater intimacy. Grant had discounted her intuition. Why couldn't he at least hear her out? It was like she had to present concrete evidence on a silver platter.

When their main dishes arrived, they stuck to the less

controversial discussions of their fish dishes, the weather, and Grant's round of golf that afternoon.

"Can I get you anything else?" asked the young waitress. Her bright eyes focused on Grant.

"Yes, two slices of key lime pie and another round of drinks please."

"You've got it." She shot Grant a sexy smile and turned on her heel.

"You remembered my favorite dessert."

"Of course, and I know it's only featured here in the summer. Better enjoy it while you can."

"Well, thank you again. I haven't eaten this much since Easter brunch," replied Ava. "Do you mind if we talk about the human rights claim?"

"I believe you have a really strong case. Dawn's only claim for gender discrimination is that she was replaced by a man. Your employment demographics illustrate that the management team is female dominated. The compensation data you provided shows no indication of higher wages given to male employees, and the new manager is earning less that she was."

Ava nodded.

"As far as age discrimination goes, her former manager, Stacey, is much older than Dawn was when she departed. Plus, you have a couple supervisors near retirement age," Grant said. "There's a high likelihood this will be dismissed by the department. At that point, Dawn will need to determine if she wants to file a lawsuit. Though I can't imagine she can afford an attorney if she's unemployed, and the chances of winning are much too low for an attorney to take the case pro bono."

Ava exhaled. She hadn't realized she had been holding her breath. "I checked our accounting records. Dawn's state unemployment compensation ran out at the end of March. She could be seeking a quick settlement to have funds on hand."

"That's plausible. You're aware that most discrimination claims are resolved through mediation and end in a cash settlement rather than going to trial. Perhaps she has a friend or family member giving her advice. The other possible motive is vengeance."

"I imagine she was angry or embarrassed after her losing her job, but does anyone seek revenge after this period of time?"

"People are complicated, Ava. You know that as well as I do."

The pretty blonde waitress returned and said, "Here's your bill. Is there anything else I can do for you?"

Ava attempted to hold back a grin. She could tell that Grant had no clue the waitress was flirting with him.

"No, thank you," replied Grant. Ava reached for her pocket book. "I've got this," Grant said. "I appreciate you sending your business our way."

"There's no one I trust more."

Grant took Ava's elbow as they left the dining room. "It's such an amazing night. We should take a walk."

Ava pointed to the heels on her sandals. "If we keep it a short one."

"How about we walk across the street to Edgewater Park and enjoy the lake instead?"

"I'd like that. Thanks for dinner and for picking this restaurant. I'm always amazed by the view."

Grant held his gaze on Ava. "I was just thinking the same thing."

They crossed the street and passed a small parking lot to their left. A map of the Ruby Lake city trail system was posted near the rubbish and recycling bins. After several more steps, they entered Edgewater Park. Two young boys sped by on their scooters. The younger of the two challenged the older to race. They couldn't have been older than ten. Their delighted laughs reminded Ava of summer breaks, of being young and free with a season full of surprises waiting to be discovered.

They turned to their right and followed the path to the fishing pier. A father was helping his daughter and son bait their fishing rods. Ava found an open space and leaned forward, resting her arms on the railing. Facing the lake, Ava could feel the sun's warmth on her face and bare shoulders. Grant joined alongside her, and she looked up at him.

Grant was born with classic good looks. He owed his perfect smile to his parent's wise investment in orthodontia during his formative years. This decision had paid off handsomely. His nearly black mane was kept neatly in place thanks to his trusted barber who he visited religiously every three weeks. This meant his hair never touched his shirt collar. She studied Grant's strong profile. He was a politician in the making. Ava knew she wasn't the right woman for him, but that didn't stop her from feeling nostalgic.

They stood for a while enjoying the sound of the waves crashing against the shoreline. Grant pointed to a couple sail boats in the distance and voiced his surprise, "Doesn't it seem a bit quiet out here tonight? Ruby Lake is usually swarming with speed boats on a Saturday night."

"The high school graduation ceremony was held earlier today. Half of the community is celebrating at various open houses, and the senior graduation party at the high school begins at eight tonight. We're enjoying the one and only quiet Saturday evening at the lake this summer. I'm sure things will start picking back up tomorrow afternoon, and this town will soon be crawling with summer tourists."

While the sun wouldn't set for a couple more hours, its rays streamed through colorful clouds that sparkled across the waves. "Look, that cloud formation reminds me of a dragon. With the sun coming through from behind… I see fire coming out of its mouth."

"Where? I don't see it." Grant squinted as he peered above the horizon.

Ava threw a glance at the sky, then back at him. "What do you see when you look at the clouds?"

"I'm not sure. Cotton balls or popcorn."

"Huh," Ava replied.

When Grant started to move away, Ava followed him and asked, "Before we head back, would you like to walk past the wildflower field by the fountains?"

"Anything you like."

A young couple joined them on the pier. The suntanned woman held a frisbee in one hand and a dog leash in the other. Their German Shepherd stood still with his head buried under a guard rail. The young man had curly blonde hair. He called out, "Hey Skipper. Come here, boy." The dog wasn't listening.

"What did you find, big guy?" Grant asked the large dog. He turned to Ava. "I see a metal object along the shore. I'll take a closer look."

The woman was not much older than a teenager. She came forward and retrieved her dog by the collar. "Come on Skip! Sorry, you guys. I'll keep him on his leash."

"No worries." Ava joined Grant, and she knelt down to get a better look. "I think it's a golf club. Who would throw a club in the lake?"

"A man having the worst game of his life." Grant pulled a handkerchief from his pocket, lifted the club from the sand and examined it closer. The end was coated in a brownish, red muck. "Or possibly a murderer." He turned to her. "This is a three wood. I don't like what I'm seeing on the head. I don't think it's mud."

"You think it's blood?"

"It might be. I'm calling the sheriff's department," Grant said.

Within a few minutes, an official cruiser parked nearby, and a uniformed deputy sauntered over. "Hello again, Mitch," exclaimed Ava. "Grant, you remember my cousin, Detective Mitch Sullivan."

Grant extended his arm for a handshake. "That's right. We met at Lauren and Matt's wedding a couple years ago."

"Hey, Ava. Nice to see you again, Grant. What do you have here?"

Grant held out the golf club. "Do you think this is related?'

"It could be. I'll submit this to the crime lab. If this is blood, we could be looking at the murder weapon in the Reinholtz case. You're having quite a day, Ava. First you found Pete's body and now this. Perhaps you two should consider careers in law enforcement." Looking at Grant, he continued, "Ava discovered Pete's body not too far from here, just across the street. I'm sure Ava told you about it."

Grant pointed to the pier. "Actually, the dog belonging to the couple over there found this club. I just called it in."

"Got it. Did either of you touch this club with your hands?"

"No." Grant said. "I used a handkerchief."

"Good thinking. Please show me exactly where you found this."

Ava stood frozen in place as a chill rushed down her back. Grant and Mitch peered into the lake and the surrounding shrubbery.

Mitch took out his phone. "Hopefully, this will be the evidence we need to identify the murderer. The coroner said Pete was hit in the back of his head at great force. I'd appreciate it if neither of you discuss finding this golf club. This is an active investigation."

"We understand," Grant said. Ava responded with a nod.

"Did that fall injure his face too?" Ava asked.

"Perhaps, but he was struck in the face at some point. Possibly a struggle with the perpetrator, or he could have gotten into a fight earlier in the evening. Folks say he caused a ruckus everywhere he went on Friday."

"Either of you witness anything out of the ordinary this evening?"

"No, we've been walking through the park for the past half hour. I've watched folks pass by along the trail and a couple of boats across the lake," Grant said. "What was the time of death, Detective Sullivan?"

"You can call me Mitch. Pete was last seen alive at approximately ten-thirty p.m. Several folks spotted him around the town square Friday night which narrows the possible time of the murder. I should see a final report tomorrow, but the coroner believes Pete died between eleven p.m. and one a.m."

"Have you determined how he arrived here last night? We heard he was at a bar earlier."

Mitch said, "We found his car right here in this parking lot. He left a set of clubs in it. We don't know if he was meeting someone or practicing his putt."

"How's Pete's wife, Natalie?" Ava asked.

"She's cooperating in the investigation. Still in shock as you can imagine." Mitch turned and scanned the lakeshore. "Say, I have more work to do here searching this area. I'll be in touch if I have further questions."

"Okay," said Ava. Then she turned to Grant. "I'm ready to call it a night."

"I'll walk you back to your car. Are you alright?"

"Not exactly. It's hard to believe there may be a murderer still wandering around my hometown."

"I could drive you home?"

"I really appreciate the offer, but I'll be fine." Ava took a deep breath. "Lauren convinced me to install a security system."

"Remember, it only works if you use it." Grant stated the obvious fact.

"You don't have to tell me twice." Ava smiled and opened her vehicle.

Chapter Sixteen

AVA POURED HERSELF a glass of lemonade, carried it out back, and reclined on a patio chair. Her faithful companion was guarding her back yard when her phone buzzed with a text from Des.

Is it okay if we share your cell phone number with Jack Lindstrom? He requested it.

She responded *Sure, thanks for checking in first.*

Ava's phone rang shortly afterward, and she pressed the answer button on her cell at the second ring.

"Hello, this is Ava."

"Hi, this is Jack Lindstrom. Randy just told me what happened this morning. How are you doing?"

"It's nice to hear from you." The timbre of Jack's masculine voice made her feel warm. "What am I hearing in the background?"

"I'm in Honolulu for an overnight. I'm hanging out on the boardwalk, and it's pretty windy. You're probably picking up on that or listening to the waves."

"That's amazing. Are you by Waikiki Beach?"

"I am."

"Shouldn't you be on a surfboard or out on the beach on your day off?"

"Oh, you're picturing me wearing a speedo, are you?" Jack chuckled. "Say, I can't imagine finding that guy on your morning run. I feel terrible for you. What's going on in that small town of yours?"

"I wish I knew."

"Do you think it's related to your friend who was shot?"

"There's a lot of speculation, but it's too soon to know. The good news is that Brooke made it through surgery. She's still in critical condition, and I'm hoping she wakes up soon. Maybe she can shed some light on this."

"I'm wondering if there's someone out there who doesn't want her to pull through. I know that's a horrible thought."

Ava said, "A scary possibility, for sure, but security at the hospital is tight."

"Have you been keeping your mind occupied?" Jack asked.

"I got home a little bit ago. To say it's been hectic would be an understatement. I just had dinner with my attorney."

"Oh… is that your ex?"

"You heard about that did you? From a little birdie named Desiree perhaps?"

"Actually, Randy mentioned it when he told me about Pete's death. It's really none of my business," Jack said. "I apologize for bringing it up."

"That's all right. I had arranged a dinner meeting to discuss an employment matter at the senior living center. And then this all happened. His firm will be representing us," Ava explained.

"I'm glad you have people close by looking out for you."

"Support comes in many ways. I really appreciate you reaching out."

"I'll be back in town on Monday. Randy invited me to a high school baseball game that evening. Will I see you there?" Jack asked.

"Yes, it's the final game of the section tournament. If the Royals win, we'll play in the State Championships next weekend. I'm going with Lauren and Matt before a family dinner with my folks. I'll look for you in the stands."

"Great, save me a seat."

"I'll do that. Goodnight, Jack." Ava disconnected the call and briefly closed her eyes. Jack's deep voice brought up an image of his strong, handsome face.

Sophie set her head on Ava's lap. "Okay, let's head back in the house and find a snack."

Ava double checked the locks on her doors. She climbed into bed but couldn't fall asleep. After tossing and turning for over an hour, she got up and grabbed her notebook. Because her head was spinning with suspects and motives, she decided to write them down to avoid ruminating for hours just to recall the same information in the morning.

She divided her paper into three columns to list suspects, possible motives, and known alibis. First, there was Natalie who had been struck by Pete this week. Anyone would assume she was angry. Second, was Randy Sparks. Ava was certain he wasn't responsible for this, but he had threatened Pete, so he had to be listed. She'd cross his name out when she solidified his alibi.

Next, was Lindsey Green, who submitted the harassment complaint. Ava had never met her, but she didn't think a woman would file a formal complaint and then commit a violent murder. She wondered why John Carlson was acting strangely. Perhaps he knew more than he shared. Ava made a note to follow up regarding Lindsey's alibi of attending a conference over the weekend.

She added Natalie's mother, Karen. Lauren claimed she was angry and gossiped about Pete's behavior around town last week. Ava witnessed how strongly Randy protected his daughter Harper against Pete. She considered how much hatred Natalie's father must be harboring toward his daughter's abusive husband. She heard his name was Malcom. She'd look up Natalie's maiden name at the office or ask someone tomorrow.

And then there was Pete's son, Tyler. Randy said Pete embarrassed the teen at his baseball game last week. Of course, Mitch said the family all claimed they'd been together the night he was killed.

Ava laid awake for hours before she finally succumbed to the calming sound of rain pattering on her roof.

Chapter Seventeen

*D*RIVING DOWN A *mountain pass, Ava caught a glimpse of the pristine, crystal lake at the bottom of the steep ravine to her right. She applied the brakes as she approached a curve in the narrow road, but they didn't respond. Fortunately, there were no oncoming cars in the opposite lane, so she swerved over to hug the mountainside and made the turn. Whew!*

Her car was picking up speed now. She tried pumping her brakes, but nothing changed. She pressed the brake pedal to the floor and… nothing.

Ava pulled the emergency brake. The car slowed slightly, but she sensed it was not going to slow enough to navigate an upcoming hairpin turn. She brushed alongside the guard-rail, hoping the friction and the gravel on the shoulder below her tires would help her come to a stop. The guard rail snapped. She was headed into a tree—the crash was inevitable—

Ava bolted upright. Her pajamas were soaked, and her pulse was racing.

To avoid her anxiety getting the best of her, she pulled herself out of bed in search of physical exercise. Not quite ready to go jogging again, she brought her yoga mat out to her patio and practiced her poses while Sophie enjoyed rolling in the lush, damp grass. Her mind and body finally relaxed. Her next thought didn't occur until the ring of her cell phone startled her.

She picked it up. "Ava speaking."

"Good morning, this is Natalie Reinholtz. I apologize for disturbing you on a Sunday."

"I said you could call me anytime and I meant that. I am so sorry for your loss… I don't know if I have the words to express this. What can I do for you?"

"I know. I still can't believe it." Natalie sounded much calmer than she had last week. "I have a question about taking time off. The policy allows three days off work for bereavement leave. I feel bad asking because I already took off last Wednesday through Friday, but I need at least another week to get things in order. Do you think I can take all of this week off work?"

"Certainly. Take all the time you need. I'll let Yvonne know. You're welcome to request a leave of absence if you need more time. I can't imagine what you and your kids are going through. Remember, our counseling program is available to them as well."

"I'll keep that in mind. They're both so confused by their feelings… We all are. I'm glad we've been staying with my parents. The change of scenery has been a distraction. Summer break just started for the kids, and my mom can stay with Tess when I return to work."

"That's so nice. Were you staying with your folks when Pete died?"

"Yes, I haven't left their place since I packed our bags and came over around lunchtime on Wednesday. I was afraid to run into him, you know?"

"I can understand that. Do your parents live here in town?" asked Ava.

"Yes, they actually live in the Pine Ridge Golf Course community."

"That's such a beautiful neighborhood. Is there anything else I can help you with today?"

"Not that I can think of," Natalie said. "You've already done so much. I can't thank you enough."

"Glad if I can help even a little. I'll talk to you soon."

"Bye, Ava."

⌁

Ava passed Detective Sullivan's vehicle as she drove into the Pine Ridge Clubhouse entrance, and she gave her cousin and Deputy Hildebrand a quick wave. She'd been in a hurry when she met Grant for dinner the previous night. This time, she meandered toward the front entrance and took in the beautiful clubhouse. It was an impressive stone building reminiscent of a mountain lodge. The front lawn was perfectly manicured, and large planters adorned the entrance. Once inside, the tavern was visible across the lobby just as she recalled, and the main dining room was off to her left.

A hostess greeted Ava. "Good morning, are you visiting us for brunch?"

"Not today. Actually, I left my sweater behind when I was here for dinner last night. Do you have a lost and found?"

"Yes, the general manager keeps all items left behind locked in her office for safe keeping. Please wait here just a minute, and I'll get her."

A woman wearing a floral dress soon appeared. "I heard you lost something. What will I be searching for?"

"I left a royal-blue cardigan in the dining room. It has faux pearl buttons."

"Please follow me." Once inside her office, Ava was greeted by an expansive view of the course.

"Is this your sweater?"

"Yes, thank you so much. Is this a private club?"

"Pine Ridge is a public golf course. Everyone is welcome, and you can make reservations to pay per round. We also offer club memberships to those who play frequently which provides a discount along with invitations to special events during the season and initial preference to play in tournaments."

"There are so many lovely homes on the course. Do home-owners play golf for free?"

"No, though we have a special membership offering for our neighbors. They're also able to come out and practice their putting during closing hours. We see neighbors doing that early in the morning and just before sunset. The path sur-rounds the entire course."

"It's truly amazing. Thank you for your time." Ava left the manager's office and slowly wandered through the clubhouse, appreciating its wooden beams, paneling, and archways. Huge brass and glass light fixtures added a modern elegance to the otherwise masculine building. She descended the wide stair-case and discovered locker rooms, a spa, private offices, and the pro shop. Glancing through the store windows, her eyes landed on a large sign advertising clothing on sale. Ava loved picking up a bargain almost as much as she enjoyed receiving gifts.

She sorted through a rack of ladies' polo shirts with a 60% markdown and selected one in her size. She pulled on the hidden price tag to reveal its cost. *Ouch.* Who could afford the full price? The store attendant was preoccupied showing a set of clubs to an older gentleman. He reminded Ava of her dad; there was an air of confidence about him. The man wore a club member's jacket and explained he was purchasing a new set of clubs for his wife's birthday. *That's an impressive gift.*

"I'll be right with you," the salesman promised Ava.

"Take your time. I'm just browsing." Ava walked around the perimeter of the shop.

"Thank you, Mr. Montgomery. We hope to see you and your wife soon," the salesman said to his customer.

"That's a guarantee. Have a good one, Aaron."

"Is there anything I can help you with?" Aaron approached Ava. She was looking at golf clubs.

Ava took advantage of this opening. "Is this a good brand? I believe the gentleman before me just purchased a set."

"Yes, the top of the line."

"I'm just starting out and have a basic set of clubs already. Which woods do you recommend I upgrade?"

"Here, let me show you a couple in our median-priced selection."

"I appreciate that." Ava glanced at the selection and asked, "Do you recommend I get a three and a five wood?"

"Huh, that's interesting. A couple of deputies were here this morning asking if anyone had purchased a three wood in the past month."

"Oh?" Ava waited for him to continue. Practicing silence was a technique she often used to encourage candidates to share more information during job interviews.

"I've sold several single drivers and putters, but no individual woods. Lately, I've been selling full sets. Everyone is enthusiastic at the beginning of summer. June is our top selling month. If you just want to upgrade one or two clubs for now,

I recommend you start with this putter to see if you like the feel of this brand."

"I appreciate your advice. Do you offer golf lessons?"

"Yes. I'm Aaron, by the way. Here's my card." Aaron's business card highlighted his occupation as Pine Ridge's golf pro. "I provide group and individual lessons. Give me a call or email me if you'd like to proceed."

"Wonderful, I'll definitely give that some thought since I'll have more free time next month. I think I'll just buy this polo for now." She opened her wallet, deciding it was best to pay cash for her purchase.

Chapter Eighteen

SHANNON WAS THE first to arrive to Ava's Sunday afternoon luncheon which she had scheduled two months prior. Ava had considered cancelling it the previous night but had decided the company of her close friends would be healing. Shannon set a couple of bags filled with craft supplies on the dining table, then returned to open the front door for Des who quickened her steps to get indoors. Sophie greeted both women, her tail wagging uncontrollably.

"Hi, big girl," Des said to Sophie. "I think she's grown, Ava." Des was holding a large serving tray up and out of the dog's reach.

No doubt sensing the puppy had energy to burn, Shannon opened the back door for Sophie to run outside. A gale of humidity blew in. "Feels like we're in for another storm tonight. Have you seen the forecast?"

Ava smiled. "No, but I predict this afternoon is going to be mostly sunny with a high probability of sangrias."

"Now you're talking," replied Des. "Let's test the sangria, and I'll uncover this veggie tray. You would not believe the leftovers I have from the open house. This platter wasn't even touched."

"Lucky for us." Ava took a glass pitcher out of her refrigerator.

"Your sangria looks beautiful," Shannon said to Ava. "Did you prepare this last night?"

"I did. I used the juneberries and strawberries we picked at Sweetwater and added orange slices for more flavor." Ava reached into a cabinet and selected a set of stemware.

"Let's cover the dining table before setting up." Ava pointed to the vinyl table cloth sitting on the counter. While Ava didn't have a formal dining room, her breakfast nook was large enough to seat eight people.

"Oh, I'm jealous of your view." Shannon said with a sigh while straightening the table cloth. She set out card stock, stamps, ink, glue, and various other card making supplies.

"What do you mean?" Ava asked. "You get to see the lake every day from your shop."

"I guess you're right. I'm so use to it that I take it for granted. Perhaps it's because cars are always passing by. Plus, you're up on a hill."

The doorbell rang. "Come in," Ava yelled. "The door is open." Suni and Heather walked in together. "Have you two met?"

Heather waved. "We just introduced ourselves outside."

"Terrific, you're already friends. How was the drive, Suni?"

"It took me about an hour and fifteen minutes. But it's such a peaceful drive. Wonderful to see the countryside."

Lauren walked in. "Look who I brought along. Mom was at the coffee shop."

Grace spoke brightly, "I hope you don't mind me joining you for a bit. I can't stay long though, girls. I have a meeting with a potential client in little over an hour."

Ava took her mom's purse and sweater, and set them on a bench. "You're always welcome. You know that."

"Suni, I haven't seen you in years," Grace said. "Ava told me you joined a medical practice in Edina. I heard you're engaged too. Let's see your ring." The women gathered in a tight circle admiring Suni's engagement ring. "You'll have to tell us all about your wedding plans, dear."

"Okay Mom, let's give Suni a minute to catch her breath. She drove a long way. Everyone, come on into the kitchen. I have sangria, lemonade, and iced tea. I abandoned my original plan to make my salmon and wild rice hot dish because I didn't have time to stop at the grocery store. Hope you don't mind that I'm going to order pizza from Anthony's."

"Perfectly understandable with everything that's been going on with you." Suni poured herself a glass of iced tea. "I'm actually surprised you didn't cancel."

"Pizza is wonderful, but you really should've let us cook for you today," Shannon said.

"No… I invited you. It's my treat. It's hard enough for us to find time to get together. I didn't dare attempt to reschedule. Plus, having you all here makes me feel one hundred times better."

Ava selected a music station on her television while Shannon shared the craft supplies she brought. She offered ideas for creative card making. The women chatted about summer plans and wedding traditions for the next sixty minutes while decorating greeting cards.

"Let's see how they turned out," Shannon said encouraging the women to share their creations.

"They all look so good," said Lauren. "Shannon, you could sell yours at your store."

"Do you think anyone would buy them?"

"Absolutely. Not from me, but yours are beautiful," replied Suni.

"I'll make a few more this week after I think up new designs."

Suni told everyone that she and Raj moved up their wedding ceremony to October because it was the only time they could both take a full week off. "Since we don't have the time to plan a large wedding here, we'll have a second reception in India next year with Raj's family. I'm excited and a bit overwhelmed, to be honest."

"A wedding celebration in India will be an incredible experience. You'll have to take lots of pictures to share." Grace stood and checked her watch. "Look at the time. I have to be going now. Enjoy your dinner."

"I'll walk you out." Ava opened the front door and held Sophie by her collar. "Who is your potential client, Mom?"

"Natalie's mother called and asked me to give her a valuation on Pete and Natalie's home in town. She said they're considering all of their options. Please don't say anything yet."

"No worries. Drive carefully."

Ava walked back into her kitchen and announced, "Okay, ladies. Our pizza should arrive soon, and I've prepared a salad. Please help yourselves to another drink or anything else you'd like. Remember, we've got cake for dessert."

"This chocolate cake is beautiful. Did you bake this?" Heather asked.

Ava shook her head. "I got it from a charity auction at work. This is Doreen Becker's creation."

Lauren asked, "Do you mind if I turn on the local news? It's about to start."

Six sets of eyes were glued to the television—seven if you counted the golden furball laying at Ava's feet. "It's so strange to see the words 'Murder in Ruby Lake' written across the television screen on the local eyewitness news," Des said breaking the silence in the room.

"Oh look." Lauren pointed at the screen. "There's Mitch with Sheriff Donahue and Mayor Thompson. Our sheriff is pretty cocky. He's certainly playing up to the camera."

"He sounds confident they're going to solve this murder quickly. I wonder who their person of interest is," Suni mused.

"The whole town was talking about it today," Heather said. "The TV station might be running the same news story that was broadcast this morning. With all this media attention, I imagine they'll have to add resources to solve this case quickly. Sheriff Donahue has a big ego, and he'll want to save face. This is an election year, after all."

When the doorbell rang, Ava called out, "I'll get the door. Lauren, can you please set out the plates?" Lauren knew her way around her sister's kitchen and quickly opened the white cabinet doors and selected blue ceramic dishes.

Ava returned to the kitchen with three pizza boxes and set them on the center island. You'll never guess who delivered these."

"Okay, don't waste our time," Lauren said with a smirk. "Who was it?"

"It was Dawn Barone."

"No, way."

"She's working with her dad at Anthony's until something else turns up. They were short drivers today."

Heather added, "Dawn also has a part-time job at the community center. She started working in the office on Tuesdays and Thursdays, which are the days I teach Jazzercise. She handles administrative tasks around the office which is a big help."

"Good for her," Shannon said. "Who knows? She might

discover she really likes office work. Some people change their careers after a job loss."

"She's certainly going to meet a lot of people. And if a new opportunity pops up, somebody there is going to let her know. We have a super group of senior members, and they are really friendly to all of the staff," Heather said. "By the way, I am going to fill in for Brooke this summer and will teach yoga classes on Monday and Wednesday evenings. I'm still looking for someone else to cover the Saturday sessions as well as Brooke's Shine Dance classes."

Lauren turned away from the television. "How's Brooke doing? Has anyone visited the hospital lately?"

Heather said, "Dave reported she would be in a medically induced coma for approximately seventy-two hours following her surgery. I believe that ends tonight. Then it can take many hours before she can communicate clearly depending on how she handled the anesthesia."

"Bless her heart. I sure hope whoever did this is far from town by now." Shannon shook her head.

Lauren said, "I'm willing to bet my teacup collection it was Pete—and he got what he deserved in the end."

"Do any of you think Dave is responsible?" asked Suni. "I mean, it's possible Brooke and Pete were having an affair, and he did this in a jealous rage. If that's the case, Brooke is safer in the hospital."

"Dave told us she hates Pete," Shannon said.

"Or is that what he wants everyone to believe?" Suni asked.

Shannon sighed. "You guys, there is so much speculation about Brooke having an affair. Some people are even suggesting that she was sleeping with Cody Myers. I mean, how far out of the park is that?"

"I thought that at first," Lauren said and was met with smiles. "Well, I didn't know that he's gay, and they were hanging out together a lot."

"Where has Dave been spending most of his time these days?" asked Des.

"Probably working at the farm. That place is a huge undertaking. Marriage isn't always sunshine and roses, ladies. My ex-husband couldn't handle the demands of my job," Heather said. "But I think they're a solid couple. Plus, a health crisis can bring people even closer together."

"You're speaking from experience. I really hope that Brooke can make a full recovery. I can't wait to see her instructing the evening yoga class again… I'm sure you're going to do an amazing job as well. You know what I mean," said Lauren.

Heather nodded. "I'm happy to help out as long as she needs me, but I already have a full-time job as general manager. Spencer has custody of the kids for the first half of the summer vacation, and then my mom can help with them if Brooke doesn't return by late next month."

"What day is the community center reopening?" Ava asked.

"We'll be open to the public on Tuesday morning. The sheriff's department completed their search of the building, and we have a sanitation crew thoroughly cleaning the building this weekend."

Lauren winced. "Eww… I don't even want to think about that."

"If Dave didn't kill Pete, who do you think did?" Heather asked.

Des said, "I hate to say it, but the spouse is usually the first one they focus on. Given the history of abuse, it's not out of the imagination to think Natalie could have finally gotten the strength to fight back."

Shannon poured herself a glass of sangria. "I heard she's got an alibi though."

Lauren said, "Well, she and her family are all vouching for each other. They have strength in numbers, but how do we know they're telling the truth? Karen's been talking smack about Pete for months, and she was so thrilled when Natalie and the kids moved in with them. She announced to the whole town that Natalie finally left that jerk. And how about her dad? There's nothing like the bond between father and his daughter."

"I get it." Des stood and walked toward the kitchen. "Look how angry Randy got when Pete made that pass at Harper? Fathers have a natural instinct to protect their daughters."

"Too bad Pete didn't have that same instinct for taking care of his own wife. He was a poor excuse for a husband." Lauren shook her head. "What's your theory, Ava?"

Ava furrowed her brows. "I can see why all eyes are on Natalie; however, I don't think she possibly could have done it. Hitting somebody that hard in the head is brazen. It was a brutal crime. She might have been angry, but I don't think she would hunt him down and kill him. You have to wonder, why that night and not during a previous fight?"

Shannon touched Ava's elbow. "Do you think he was fighting with someone on the golf course, or did someone dump him there?"

"Good question. But, if you're going to the trouble of moving a body, why not dump him in the lake?" Ava asked.

Suni rubbed her hands together. "Perhaps Pete was having an affair with someone who believed he was involved with Brooke. It could have been a case of mistaken identity. Then the unidentified woman killed Pete after a fight."

"Interesting... though that doesn't explain why Pete was

running around town drunk and alone." Lauren leaned over the counter while selecting another slice of pizza. "Once Natalie left, he was free do whatever he pleased. Not that he didn't already, but I haven't heard anyone say they saw him with another woman."

"There are plenty of other people who disliked Pete. I don't know if disrespecting the guy is enough for murder though," Heather said. "That gets me wondering about Dave again since they used to have a business relationship."

Ava said, "Until they find the weapons used in these two crimes, Brooke is the best source of information."

Heather raised her glass, "I'd like to propose a toast to Brooke. May she recover quickly and regain the peace she deserves."

Lauren raised her glass and the others followed. "To Brooke," the ladies said in unison.

"This has been a fun afternoon, but I really should get going," Suni announced as she bussed her plate to the kitchen sink.

"It feels like you just got here. Can't you stay for dessert?" asked Ava.

"I wish I could, but it's a long drive, and I have patient appointments first thing in the morning."

"Okay, give me a hug." Ava gave Suni a side hug while arranging pizza slices. "Let me send some pizza home with you."

"That's not necessary. Please don't go to the trouble."

"I'll never eat it all. I insist." Ava opened the refrigerator. "I'm adding two slices of death by chocolate cake so you can share it with Raj."

Moments later, she handed Suni a paper grocery bag

loaded with full Tupperware containers. "Here you go. There's a container of juneberries in there too."

"Thank you, but I don't know when I can return your Tupperware," Suni said.

"Don't worry, I have a whole cabinet full of containers. Wait—don't forget your artwork." Ava held up the greeting cards Suni had created with intricate paisley designs.

"Where's my head? Thanks for reminding me. Do you have a minute to walk outside with me?"

"Of course I do." Ava opened her front door and escorted Suni to her car.

"Ava, I wanted to ask you in person. Raj and I are having a fairly small wedding. We're mixing Hindu and Western traditions, and my sister will be my only bridesmaid. I also want you to be a part of my special day. Would you please be my personal attendant?"

"I'd love to. I am so honored." Ava placed her hand on her heart.

"I promise I won't be a bridezilla." Suni grinned. "I appreciate your calming nature and know you'll be prepared for any possibility or crisis that needs managing. Look at how poised you are today. I don't know how you do it. I'd also love your input on my gown, décor, flowers… all of it."

"You're so sweet, and I can't wait! Just call when you want to get together, and I'll meet you in the Cities."

"Me too. I'm getting married!"

"I'm thrilled for you," Ava said.

"Also, I've been meaning to ask, how are your headaches?"

"They've come back in the past week. The prescription is working when I take it at onset. I'm afraid with the recent crimes and my lack of a good night's sleep, I'm having one almost daily."

"We can try a preventative medication next. Schedule an appointment, okay? I hope you take some time off this week. You've been through some major trauma and need time to rest. I can't imagine a more stressful week for you."

"I'll work on both. Drive carefully and text me when you get home." Ava stood in her driveway and waved goodbye to Suni until she was heading down the road.

When Ava slipped back into her house, both Lauren and Shannon stood in the entryway laughing. "What's so funny?" asked Ava.

"You," replied Lauren. "We were just saying that you are the master of the classic, lengthy Minnesota goodbye."

❧

After the rest of her friends left, Ava told Lauren about her conversation with their cousin at Sweetwater farms. Mitch was their brother Reid's age, and they all had practically grown up together.

"He warned me that I'm a suspect, Lauren."

"Since when did Mitch become a total moron?" asked Lauren. "I can't believe this. We should have our mom call his mom."

"Ha, that would be funny!"

"You know he's only doing his job. There's no way he believes you are responsible for these horrible crimes."

"Unfortunately, I keep showing up at the wrong time." Ava felt a bit sick, recalling Pete's body and the bloody golf club. "I need to find my way out of this mess."

"You will, and I'll help you any way I can. I know how your mind works. You're going to put the puzzle pieces together."

"Thanks for staying late." Ava wiped down her countertop with a hand towel. "I could have cleaned up the dishes myself, but I appreciate your company."

"No problem. How many times have you helped me out at Woodcrest lately? You should be on the payroll, honestly."

The television was still on, and an advertisement startled Ava. A giant, polished-looking man with silver hair was announcing a huge sale on new cars at Montgomery Motors.

Ava pointed at him. "Hey, I recognize that guy in this auto commercial."

"Yeah. That's Mack Montgomery. He owns the biggest dealership in the tri-county area."

"I saw him at the pro shop this morning. I've heard the camera was supposed to add ten pounds, but he's actually larger in person. That man must work out daily. He was buying high-end golf clubs to surprise his wife for her birthday."

"He played professional football for like ten years before getting injured. You know he's Natalie Reinholtz's father, don't you?"

"I had no idea. I thought her dad's name was Malcom."

"It is. Mack's his nickname. Wait… don't you think it's a coincidence that he was buying golf clubs the morning after Pete was murdered? Perhaps Karen needed new clubs to cover up the murder weapon." Lauren's eyes widened. "Let's pay them a visit. We can snoop around and look for clues."

"You've been watching too many murder mysteries. How would we even manage to get into their home?"

"I'm serious. Natalie just lost her husband. I suggest we

offer to bring them dinner, my treat. I'm sure she'll invite us in. What do you say?"

Ava felt hopeful. "I think it's a great idea. How about tomorrow night? If we're lucky, the Montgomerys will be out of the house."

"Perfect!"

Chapter Nineteen

*A*VA WALKED DOWN *a dark hallway with the terrifying sensation that she was being followed. She turned to look over her shoulder and saw a large man several paces behind her. He was dressed all in black, and it was obvious he was pursuing her. Ava thought she was getting closer to her destination—to refuge—but the hallway before her continued to stretch out longer and longer. Additional doorways popped up out of nowhere, and the light at the end became dimmer. She began to jog to get farther away from him, but he also picked up his stride. Ava sensed the stranger was now on her heels. She felt a large hand grip her shoulder.*

"Ahh," Ava screeched, shaking off her nightmare. Sophie whined with concern. "Guess I'm not sleeping in this morning." She let Sophie outside, made herself a cup of cocoa, and plopped down in her breakfast nook, still in her pajamas. With her laptop in front of her, she intended to get some answers during her day off.

Her conversation with John Carlson kept replaying in her head because she felt like he was hiding something. A search of his name along with A to Z Medical Supplies led her to his profile on his employer's website.

Looking back at her in the photo was the same pale-faced man with thinning hair and black-rimmed eyeglasses she had seen at the country club. Ava dug further on the company's page but found only members of management listed.

She typed both John and Lindsey's names into the search engine. *Ta-da*! She found an engagement announcement with a photo printed in the *Duluth Tribune*. Ava read the article and discovered this was Lindsey's hometown and the location of their upcoming nuptial ceremony to be held in September. John had withheld this interesting piece of information. She wondered if John felt Ava wouldn't have taken his complaint last week as seriously if Ava had known about their relationship.

Now she was even more curious about John's claim that Lindsey was attending a supply chain conference in Brainerd over the weekend. Ava checked the websites for the two large conference centers in Brainerd: Madden's and Cragun's Resorts. Ava had attended regional human resources conferences at both. She quickly learned neither were hosting conferences that week or the week following.

After a few more searches, she discovered a large healthcare supply chain symposium was scheduled in Alexandria at the end of June. Was Lindsey planning to attend this event? She entered the code on her cellphone to disguise her caller ID, then dialed the resort. Ava stated her name was Lindsey Green and asked to verify her hotel reservation. After a brief pause, the friendly man confirmed her check-in and check-out dates and asked if she'd like to be transferred to the spa or restaurant to make reservations.

"No, thank you, but I really do appreciate your time. Have a great day," replied Ava.

She considered paying John a visit at his employer, but she had promised her mom that she'd take Grandpa to his haircut appointment that afternoon. And calling John would not likely yield what she was seeking, since she wouldn't be able to see his reaction. After all, ninety percent of communication was nonverbal.

Finally, she decided to share the information with Grant. He'd have a strong opinion on how to proceed. She left a message on his voice-mail, and a few minutes later, Grant's name appeared on her phone screen.

After listening to Ava's update and questions, Grant said, "This is interesting news but withholding their relationship doesn't mean he's a murderer."

"I know, but aren't you at all curious about why he would lie about this? I'm a suspect with less motive than these two have. Plus, I'd like to clear them if I can. Otherwise, I may need to share their names with Mitch, and I really don't want to do that."

"For all we know, he got the dates mixed up. But I hear what you're saying. Do you mind if I call him? When I tell John that I'm representing you and Ruby Park, he might confide in me."

"That's perfect. Thank you so much." Ava was relieved to have Grant's help.

⁕

When her boss heard from Ava that she was the one who found Pete, he insisted she take some time off. Intending to take full advantage of her day, Ava stopped at the Ruby Lake Community Center before visiting her grandfather. Although the building wouldn't officially reopen for another day, Heather had said she'd be on site. Ava wanted to access the scene of Brooke's shooting before dozens of citizens returned.

She entered the two-story brick building and stepped up to the registration counter. "Good morning, I accidently ran my ID card through the wash. Could I get a replacement?" Ava asked the teenager behind the desk.

"Of course. Your name please?"

"Ava Andrews."

"I thought I heard your voice." Heather approached the front desk. "Come back here and sit with me. Your card will take a few minutes to print. By the way, thanks again for hosting yesterday."

"Of course. I really enjoyed having you over. How does it feel to be back working in this building?"

"Strange, but somehow it feels like Brooke's attack happened much longer ago," responded Heather.

"Is everything all set to resume activities tomorrow?"

"Yeah. Do you want to take a look around?"

"You don't mind?"

"Go right ahead. I know you're investigating, and I want to help. First, I'll show you where we found Brooke."

They walked down the back corridor behind the office. At the end was a large storage closet for equipment on one side and the backdoor on the other.

Ava asked, "Do you think Brooke was trying to escape outside?"

"That's my guess. I must admit it makes my knees shake coming back here."

"I get that. Both of us found a crime victim this week—

talk about a nightmare." Ava pursed her lips, nearly frowning. They continued past the gymnasium, and Ava peered inside. "These floors look like they're new."

"The refinishing turned out great. Our temporary closing gave us time to polish and reseal the floors as well as deep clean the facility."

Back in the corridor, Ava spotted a Yeti rambler mug sitting on a ledge. It had the Montgomery Motors logo printed on it. Ava asked, "I wonder if this belongs to Natalie?"

"I don't think so. She always uses that pink and white Stanley quencher. I've never seen her without it."

"You're right. I haven't either, come to think of it."

"I'll take that mug back to the office for our Lost and Found bin." Heather said as she opened the office door for Ava.

Emma, the teenaged receptionist, looked up from her desk. "I have your new badge ready, Ava. Oh, you found Karen Montgomery's water mug. Do you want me to hold it here for her?"

Ava shot a glance at Heather at the mention of Natalie's mother, Karen.

Heather asked Emma, "Why do you think this is Karen's?"

"Because she's the only one I've seen carrying one with that auto dealership logo. Plus, it's neon green, so it's hard to miss."

"Thanks for offering, but I'll hold on to it for her."

Once Ava had returned with Heather to her cubicle, she asked, "Did you see Karen here the morning Brooke was shot?"

"No, it was just me and the custodian. After we found Brooke, I called 911. It was a blur of emergency vehicles after that. I don't recall seeing any visitors in the building. I'm surprised the deputies didn't see this during their search. It could've just been sitting there for a while though."

"Is your custodian here now?"

"He isn't on site today. We contract with a service, and they send someone each morning for an hour before we open."

"If Karen routinely attended classes, you'd think she would've missed her water jug? Do you mind looking up which date she last checked in?" asked Ava.

"No problem. I can look it up on my computer. Just give me a sec," Heather said as she clicked through a computer screen. "Here we go. Karen Montgomery checked in for Jazzercise last Tuesday. That was two days before I found Brooke. Since she normally attended the Tuesday and Thursday morning classes, then it's likely she planned to be there the same day Brooke was shot."

"What time does that class start?"

"Ten a.m. I'll let you know if she shows for class tomorrow."

"Super. I appreciate your help."

"Anything for you and Brooke."

May, who handled payroll and benefits, was limping toward the photocopier as Ava entered the Human Resources suite. Her shiny brownish-black hair was cut straight at her shoulders. Standing at all of five feet tall, May appeared overwhelmed by the box of print and copy paper she was holding.

"Here, let me help you with that," Ava offered.

May dropped the box with a loud thump on the workspace adjacent to the shared printer and copier. Ava watched her feed a ream of paper into the machine.

Previously, May had told her that she had started working at the Center about eight years earlier, right after she graduated from high school. She had tried out an accounting assistant role and then transferred to Human Resources a few years later. While May had an aptitude for numbers, Ava had observed her sheer enthusiasm for more creative tasks. She knew that May was currently taking a graphics design course though they hadn't talked about how this fit into her career goals.

"Hey, there. We weren't expecting you," May said. "Des told us you'd be taking the day off."

"That's true, but I'm visiting my grandfather. My mom had some work to finish up so I volunteered. Did I miss anything?"

"It's been fairly quiet so far. I got a call earlier asking if the security cameras are working. He said the guys were wondering if they are real or just there for show."

"Who was the caller?"

"He didn't say. The phone display showed the employee was in the Assisted Living dining room at the time."

"That's a strange question."

"Our employees have no boundaries. They ask whatever is on their minds. I got a call from one of the housekeep-ers recently asking if he could get reimbursed for his April health insurance premium because he didn't use it that month. I explained medical insurance works like auto insurance—it's there just in case. Can you imagine?"

Ava grinned. "No, but I want everyone to feel comfortable reaching out to us, and I believe in transparency. I'm just curi-ous about the fascination with the security system. By the way, I've been hearing great feedback about your T-shirt design. You're a talented artist. How long have you been doing graphic design?"

"I enjoyed drawing and drafting in high school, but I let that go. It wasn't in the cards for me to go to college. With four kids in my family, my parents didn't have the money to send us. Plus, my father said an art degree wasn't worth spending money on. They are very traditional that way," May said without making eye contact.

"So how did you learn to do all of this? The place cards and recipes for the dessert auction appeared to be printed by a professional."

"I'm glad you liked them." May stood up straight and turned away from the copier. "Initially, I took a graphics art class at the community center. One of the high school teachers held it in the evening last summer."

"Such a wonderful opportunity right in town."

"Yeah, they post a calendar of community education classes each quarter. I recently took an Excel course taught by Pete Reinholtz—I still can't believe he's dead. Finding him must have been such a shock for you. How are you holding up?"

"I was pretty shaken on Saturday, and now it feels surreal. You were saying that Pete taught classes at the community center. What other subjects did he teach?"

"I also went to his personal finance class last winter. The information was really good, though Pete wasn't a very engaging instructor. But I enjoyed graphics arts so much that I bought a software program for myself and started playing around with it. Now I'm taking classes at St. Cloud State. It's just that I can only afford to take one at a time."

"I'd love to see more of your work. Would you be interested in creating additional designs for our new employee swag?"

"Are you serious? I'd love to." May's face lit up with a smile.

"We'll do some brainstorming at our team meeting next week. Once we all come up with a theme, you can take it from there. I'd like to give each new employee a reusable lunch bag and water thermos to reduce waste. We can create a sense of community and encourage recycling at the same time. You can work on this project when you have spare time during the off-payroll weeks."

"I'll make the time. Thank you so much!"

May's desk phone began ringing. "I'll get that so you can finish copying," said Ava. "Human Resources, Ava speaking."

"I was trying to reach May," said the employee on the other end.

"She's currently busy. How can I help you?"

"This is Joe from the Laundry. I think I might be sick next month. Um, if I call in the day before the July 4th holiday, is it true that I won't receive holiday pay?"

"I'm sorry to hear that, Joe. Yes, that is the Center's policy. You won't be paid on the Fourth if you call in the work day before or after unless you already have approved paid time off. The policy was designed to encourage employees to request time off in advance rather than to call in on days when we have less staff coverage. If you anticipate needing a day off around the holiday weekend, I suggest you speak with your supervisor right away or find a coworker who is willing to trade days off with you."

"Okay, that's what I heard. Thanks."

"Bye, Joe. Stay healthy," said Ava.

May covered her mouth, trying to hold back her laughter. "See what I mean? They're quite bold. You wouldn't believe the calls I get from employees checking their paid time off balance to plan their next day off. The accumulated balance is listed on their check stubs, but they want an up-to-the-hour count."

"There's never a dull moment around here. I appreciate all you do for them." Ava glanced at her watch. It was time to take her grandpa for his haircut and beard trim. "I need to head over to Assisted Living. I'll see you tomorrow."

Ava strolled over to her grandfather's apartment. On her way, she received a text from Grant. *I spoke to John and his alibi checks out. I'll call you later.* Ava was glad she could check their names off her suspect list, but first she'd wait to hear what Grant had to share.

Ava stopped along her walk to read the activities calendar which hung on the wall. The board was full of crafts, clubs, movies, games, and entertainers. Her own social life was not nearly this busy or interesting. Retirement sounded pretty good, but naturally, she intended to remain healthy enough to live independently well into her old age.

She knocked on Charles' apartment door and was surprised to be greeted by Nellie.

"Hey there, good afternoon. I just finished cleaning Charles' room," Nellie said.

"Thank you very much."

"Don't mention it. I always enjoy our visits. See ya!" Nellie smiled brightly and proceeded to another apartment.

"Hi Grandpa, I heard you have an appointment at the beauty parlor today."

"Beauty parlor? Why do they have to be so fancy? We should have a good old-fashioned barbershop."

"You can certainly add that to the suggestion box. For today, let's go down and visit Doris," Ava suggested.

Charles turned in his chair. "Nellie was just telling me about her honeymoon plans. They're going to Paris and Rome for two weeks. Sounds like she found a really nice fellow."

"Good for her. Sounds like an amazing trip."

While Ava pushed him in his wheelchair along the route to the first floor, Charles introduced his granddaughter to several of his friends.

Several minutes later, they reached the entrance to the beauty shop. The door was open, and Ava greeted the friendly, middle-aged woman with short curly hair. "Good afternoon, Doris."

"It looks like this young man is ready for some pampering!" Doris flirted with Charles.

"Is that so?" Grandpa replied with a broad grin.

"Let me tie this apron around you. I'm gonna spin you around. Let's see what we've got here. Looks like your hair's getting a little long."

"That's true. I'd like you to bring my hairline up on the sides so it doesn't scratch the top of my ears." Grandpa placed his index finger above one ear. Charles had a beautiful head of white hair. That along with his overgrown beard gave him the appearance of a skinny Santa Claus.

"I can see why ya don't want that. How long would ya like to leave the length on top?"

Grandpa pointed at his head. "I think to about here will be fine.

Doris started trimming his white locks while they talked about the weather, lunch, and her grandchildren whose photos framed the large wall mirror. When she was finished, she turned him to look at his reflection. "Charles, what do ya think? Did I get it right?"

"I think so. Ava, does it look like the proper length?"

Ava bent down and smiled in the mirror next to her grandfather. "Yes, I think you look incredibly handsome."

"Oh gosh. You're a flatterer."

"Let's take a look at that beard now," Doris said.

"You can trim up the mustache too, please," Charles instructed Doris.

"You seem to be very busy today." Ava pointed to the hallway. "There are two customers waiting outside."

"My regulars get a little anxious. Often arrive a half hour early." Doris raised her voice so everyone in the hall could hear. "No need to worry. I won't go home until I take care of my favorite customers." She turned her attention back to Charles. "Now, how does that look?"

"Oh, I think I'd like the mustache trimmed a little bit shorter so you can see my upper lip. I don't want to get food stuck in it."

"You betcha. The customer is always right, I always say."

"I agree with that philosophy. Please add this to my tab," Charles said.

"You look pretty snazzy, Grandpa."

"You think so, do you?" His eyes widened.

"I'm sure of it. Thank you, Doris." As Charles began to roll himself to the doorway, Ava handed his stylist a cash tip.

Next, she accompanied her grandpa on a short walk through the gardens and then wheeled him to the activity center where he planned to enjoy bowling. A slide allowed wheelchair bound residents to push rubber bowling balls toward the pins set on the floor.

Ava heard her phone ding and saw a text from her sister. *Are you ready to go to visit Natalie? I've got their dinner ready.*

Ava sent a message back. *Pick me up in ten minutes.* She gave Charles a peck on the check and walked outdoors to the sidewalk in front of Ruby Park.

Once Lauren pulled up in her truck, Ava glanced at the back seat before climbing in. "Holy cow, you could feed an army. Don't you think this is a little much?"

"Well, I figured if we showed up with just a box, Natalie

might accept it at the door and not invite us in… but by bringing a few bags, she'll need help, right?"

"That's brilliant thinking."

"Well, you and Reid aren't the only Andrews kids with brains."

"That's for sure." Ava looked intently at her sister. "It must be hard being the youngest sibling sometimes, huh?"

"You've got that right. Try following a genius brother in school and a sister who does everything right—Miss Goodie Two Shoes."

"Really? I guess I tend to be a rule follower. You got to enjoy the perks of being the baby of the family. Grandma Andrews spoiled you rotten. It's not always fun being the middle child either. I was always running interference, and I didn't receive the same type of attention that the first born and the youngest seem to get."

Ava's cellphone began to ring. "I need to take this. It's Grant." Lauren shot Ava a curious glance while she answered her phone. "Hi, I got your text. What did you discover?"

Grant replied, "You were right. John was protecting Lindsey, but neither of them were involved in any crime. They attended a pre-marriage couple's retreat at a lodge in Duluth from Wednesday night to Saturday morning. John drove back early Saturday to attend his golf event, and Lindsey stayed in Duluth to make wedding plans with a friend."

"You were able to confirm this?" inquired Ava.

"John gave me the contact information for his pastor who led the program. It checks out. He was embarrassed about being dishonest, but he didn't want Lindsey involved in a murder investigation. Confidentially, she's been through a lot of trauma and counseling in her past. They're getting married in a few months, and he wants to focus on their future."

"I can appreciate that. Thank you so much for checking. I'm actually quite relieved for them."

"Me too. Where are you off to now? Sounds like you're driving."

"Lauren and I are on our way to visit Natalie Reinholtz at the Montgomery estate."

"Be careful," warned Grant.

"I won't be alone. Lauren will be with me the whole time." Ava looked at Lauren, who had a mischievous grin.

Grant said, "Also, I thought you'd want to know the blood on the club we found was consistent with Pete's blood type. No leads on its owner yet."

"Were there any distinguishing characteristics that can help narrow it down?"

"Only that it's a ladies' club. Otherwise, it's a popular brand."

"What's the size difference?" Ava asked.

Lauren's eyes widened as she registered this new information.

"They're about an inch shorter in length," Grant said.

"Got it. Thanks for sharing this update."

"Sure, I'll be in touch when I learn anything new. Call if you need me."

"I will. Have a good day." Ava placed her phone in her pocket.

Lauren turned the bend and spotted their destination. "Wow, this is the famous Mack Montgomery's residence?"

"It's the right address."

"I can see why Natalie doesn't want to return to her house.

It must be the largest property along the golf course. I'd never want to leave this place."

Ava responded, "I imagine she's going to want her privacy and live on her own with the kids again once things settle down. I hope it's just Natalie here, and her folks aren't home."

"Only one way to find out." Lauren opened her door and started grabbing bags out of the truck's back seat.

Ava pressed the doorbell and listened to beautiful chimes. They waited several moments, and Natalie opened the door. "Hi Natalie," Ava greeted her. "Meet my sister, Lauren."

"I've seen you at the Woodcrest Coffee Shop. Tess and I enjoy your weekly game nights."

"That's right," Lauren replied. "I hope you'll join us again soon. I'm very sorry for your loss. This is a difficult time, and we thought we could help out just a little by bringing you over a couple of meals for your family."

"That's incredibly thoughtful." Natalie smiled, looking genuinely surprised. "I feel so blessed to have your support. Please come in."

"Okay," Lauren gave a quick glance and smiled at Ava. "We'll help you carry these bags into the kitchen." Lauren followed Natalie and made herself at home in the sprawling cooking area. "I took the liberty of bringing Danishes, fruit, bagels, and cream cheese for breakfast as well. You may want to put them in the refrigerator."

"You're too much," Natalie choked up with emotion.

"We're happy to help." Lauren patted her arm. "By the way, this home is gorgeous."

"My folks have lived here for nearly ten years. The kids and I always enjoy coming over. Would you like a little tour?"

"Only if we're not interrupting," said Ava.

"I'd like that," Lauren announced over her sister's gentler voice.

"The main level has an owner's suite on the far end. The office is at the front, and you've already seen the kitchen. Here's the formal dining and living areas. And we have this four-season sun porch that overlooks the golf course."

"You have an incredible view from here," declared Ava.

"My kids are currently using the second level guest suites. The lower level is completely finished and walks out to the course. Would you like to take a look?"

"Absolutely," said Lauren, and they followed Natalie down the winding staircase that mimicked the one from the main floor to the upper level.

"As you can see, there's a family room and a second kitchen down here. Plus a full in-law suite just beyond." Natalie said. She led them inside a huge guest bedroom. "This is where I'm staying."

The vast space was larger than any owner's suite Ava had seen before. "It's almost like having a private apartment," Ava said.

Next, Natalie escorted them to the opposite side of the lower level. "Here's the media room where we watch movies and ball games on the big screen."

"It looks more like a movie theater to me," Lauren said.

Natalie smiled and pointed down the hallway. "Then, there's a home gym and a sauna to the back behind this room."

As they returned to the open family room, Lauren said, "You have party decorations up. Did one of the kids just celebrate a birthday?"

"Actually, it was my mother's yesterday. It was a downer of a day, but we made the best of it."

"Did you give her that golf bag?" Lauren pointed to the bag in the corner with a gift bow attached to it. "It's really nice."

"Yeah, that's from me and the kids. Honestly, my dad purchased it for her and said it was from us. He also bought her a new set of clubs. I've just had so much going on to even think about buying a gift, but I picked up the few decorations and a birthday card at the Short Stop convenience store. I'll take my mom out for a nice lunch once things smooth over."

"I imagine she completely understands," Ava said.

"It's kind of a bonus gift, because now I get to use her old set of golf clubs."

"Don't you already have a set?" Lauren asked.

"Nope, never had my own clubs. I rarely ever get a chance to play. When I have, I just rented them."

"That surprises me. I thought Pete was an avid golfer," said Ava.

"Well, he played a lot. I don't truly know how good he was. He's… or he was a bit of a bragger. Never wanted me to come along."

"That's too bad."

"He said we needed time apart. Which meant he could do whatever he wanted, and my place was in the home. Sometimes he wouldn't return until the sun came up. Being away so much was always a point of contention for me. I wanted the kids to experience normal family activities like having dinner together every night, you know?"

Lauren asked, "Where do you think he was going? It's not like we have a night life in Ruby Lake after the restaurants close. Except on the weekends."

"I'm not sure. Drinking at the bars, gambling, or possibly

having an affair. Honestly, I stopped caring about his whereabouts a long time ago."

Lauren gave her an apologetic look. "I'm so sorry. I didn't mean to pry."

"Don't be. I came to appreciate having more time away from him. We'd grown more distant in the past couple of years. He was becoming even more strict with the kids too. They could never live up to his perfect standards, especially Tyler. I've wondered if Pete was jealous of Tyler's athletic ability and popularity at school… Oh, don't listen to me. I'm probably rambling too much."

Ava leaned in. "Your feelings are quite understandable."

"Thank you. I'm grateful I've had the kids' activities and my work to keep me sane."

"I bet you're an incredible mother," Ava said.

"I've been thinking about buying a set of golf clubs and taking some lessons." Lauren said. "Do you think I could take a look at yours? I really don't know what type to buy. Matt thinks I might want to use a standard men's clubs rather than buying women's, but I'm not sure if it makes much of a difference."

"I'm happy to show you. Come this way. Dad has a weight room back here with a mini putting green." Natalie led the women down a hallway that led to an open space with another set of windows to the back of the house. The space resembled a high-end gym with a treadmill, a fancy universal weight machine, a Peloton bike, a stand of free-weights, and a bench.

Natalie handed a club to Lauren. "Try this putter. I've practiced with it a couple of times." While Lauren made a couple attempts at putting golf balls, Ava noticed that the three wood was in the golf bag.

"Ha, I obviously need some lessons," Lauren said with a laugh.

"Maybe we could take a class together?" Natalie asked hopefully.

"That would be fun. I'll let you know if I sign up," Lauren smiled and returned the putter. "Um, are you planning a funeral for Pete?"

"My mom has been in touch with his mother. She's planning a small celebration of life for his immediate family in Minneapolis. She divorced Pete's father years ago."

Ava said, "This must be so difficult for you and the kids. We're planning to attend the baseball game tonight. Will you be there? I completely understand if you're not."

"I'll be at the game. I told Tyler not to pressure himself too much, that the team can go on without him. But he wouldn't even hear of it. He insists on pitching tonight, and I guess that's not such a bad idea. He works hard and loves his team. Plus, it gives him something else to focus on. If they win their playoff game this evening, they'll advance to the first round of the state high school championships next week."

"The community is so excited. We'll be in the stands and hope to see you there. We'd better get going so you have time to feed your kids." Ava said. They headed up the stairs to the main floor. "Let us know if we can get you anything else."

"You both have been more then generous already. I really appreciate you more than I can express." Natalie escorted Lauren and Ava to the front door where they said their good-byes.

Ava climbed into Lauren's truck. "Our visit went better than I hoped. I'm really glad we stopped by and consoled

Natalie, even a little bit. I'm sure she really needs friendship right now."

Lauren turned her head. "It sounds like Pete was extremely controlling. I sure hope she takes time for herself to develop her own interests."

"I have to hand it to you, Lauren. You truly have a gift for being direct. I wouldn't have gained half the insight we learned without having you there."

"Because you're too polite and afraid of stepping on anyone's feelings."

"My jaw nearly dropped when you asked her if you could try out her clubs."

"It worked, didn't it? Plus, she's really nice, and I think she enjoyed our company too."

While Lauren backed her truck down the curved brick driveway, Ava noted the Montgomery estate included a four-car garage plus a golf cart garage. She also took in the new Mercedes sedan sitting in the driveway and assumed Natalie was now driving Pete's vehicle.

Chapter Twenty

AVA SAT ON the bleachers alongside her sister and Matt, enjoying the Ruby Lake Royals' playoff game. She was feeling toasty under the sun's heat despite wearing a baseball cap. "I'm going to get a bottle of water. Need anything?"

Lauren held up her nearly full water bottle. "I'm good."

Before visiting the concession stand, Ava took the quickest route toward the restroom, behind the bleachers toward the soccer field. She suddenly felt a quiver of dread and had the sense someone was behind her.

"Miss," a male voice called from behind her. She stopped her in her tracks. A hand tapped her shoulder, and she jumped.

"You dropped your sunglasses. I didn't mean to startle you."

Ava looked up at Mack Montgomery and scoffed. "Of all people, you should know better than to sneak up behind a woman."

"You're right. I do apologize." Mack handed over her sunglasses. "Are you Ava Andrews?"

Accepting them, she responded warily, "Yes."

"Thank you for what you've done for Natalie. Her mother

and I are just heartbroken over what she's been going through. Also, please extend my gratitude to your sister for generously providing dinner."

"We're happy to do what we can," Ava said, squinting against the bright sky. "Thanks for returning my sunglasses."

"Again, I'm very sorry I frightened you."

"I know you didn't mean to. I guess we're all a bit jumpy right now. Tyler's pitching extremely well. Have a good night."

Ava made her way to the restroom and then to the concessions stand before returning to her spot on the bleachers. Although she held an ice-cold bottle of water, her mood had soured.

"Are you okay?" asked Lauren. "Looks like you saw a ghost."

Ava nodded. "I ran into Mack Montgomery. He told me to thank you for dinner tonight." She returned her focus back on the field.

Soon afterward, Ava caught a glimpse of Jack Lindstrom sauntering to the bleachers, a bottle of diet cola in one hand and a regular in the other. She appreciated his athletic build. She raised her forearm above her eyes to block the sun's glare and caught Jack's gaze. He smiled back in recognition and easily strode up the stands, taking two at a time. Rather than asking if the space next to Ava was spoken for, he confidently claimed the seat.

"Would you like some pop?" he asked. "I didn't know your preference. I got both regular and sugar free. You're pick. Don't want you to get dehydrated sitting in the heat." She noticed the tiny wrinkles forming around his eyes as he squinted.

"That's so thoughtful. Actually, neither, I'm avoiding caffeine." She said, feeling sorry for his trouble.

"I'll make a note of that—likes beer, not cola," he responded in a light-hearted manner.

"Sorry, it's a long story, for another day maybe."

"How about dinner, tomorrow night?"

"I'd like that."

"Perfect. It's a date." Jack flashed a sexy grin, and a small dimple in his chin twitched.

Ava felt flushed. Jack was a smooth talker, and now she had a date. Ava hadn't gone on a first date in four years.

"Sorry I'm late," Jack said as he leaned forward to speak with Matt. "What have I missed? I see the score is three to nothing." He set the Coke bottle down by his feet and unscrewed the Diet Coke, which let out a hiss as carbonation escaped.

"It's the top of the fourth inning. Our team, the Ruby Lake Royals, is on the field. The team's pitcher, Tyler Reinholtz, is one heck of a talent. He just finished his sophomore year, and he's already our high school's starting pitcher. Wait till you see this kid's fastball."

Everyone in the stands focused on the sixteen-year-old commanding the pitcher's mound as Tyler struck out one and then two batters. The third batter approached home plate.

"I see what you mean. He looks so intent. Angry even, like he has something to prove."

"He probably thinks he does," said Ava. "Since his father recently died, I'm surprised he's playing tonight."

Matt turned his head toward Jack. "The authorities determined Pete was murdered. Everyone is talking about it."

"Yeah, I saw the news coverage. I'd say the pressure must be enormous for this kid."

They all focused on the field and watched Tyler's next pitch. "Strike," the referee called out.

Jack said, "Wow, look at that curveball. He has a future with a division one university if he can maintain his focus through high school."

"I agree, and a south paw is more likely to get a scholarship," replied Matt.

"Why is that?" Lauren asked.

"Because there are fewer of them, and lefties have an advantage over right-handed batters," explained Jack.

Ava smiled at Jack. "I learned something new today."

"Strike three—you're out," shouted the referee.

The two teams traded places, and the Royals were up to bat. Jack asked, "Did you discover any leads today?"

Ava filled him in on her activities while the game continued. The Royals scored another run, and Tyler was pitching again. In between the action on the field, Jack entertained Ava with tales about growing up on the farm.

Jack said, "I was goofing around in the barn with my cousins, and I fell out of the hay loft. Here's the scar to prove it." Jack pointed to a scar about two inches in length along his right wrist.

"You must have given your mom quite a scare. Did you have difficulty using your right hand for a while?"

"Not too long, but it was a good thing that I'm a lefty."

"Pay attention over there," said Matt. "We could be looking at a no-hitter."

Matt's prediction was correct. The Royals beat the Wolves by a score of five to zero. Family and friends began chanting Tyler's name. While Royals fans shouted and high-fived, Ava focused on the teenager. He looked up at his mom in the stands, gave her a salute, and walked off the field with his eyes directed at the ground.

"This is awesome. We're going to the State Championships," exclaimed Randy. To Jack, he said, "Our games will be played in St. Cloud. Do you want to go?"

"Possibly. Send me the schedule. I return on Saturday afternoon."

"Hey, I'll be back in a few minutes." Ava told Jack as she brushed his knee. "There's someone I'd like to say hello to."

"Take your time." Jack smiled back at her.

Ava found Natalie walking alone behind dozens of people heading toward the grounds surrounding the field. "I'm sure you're extremely proud of Tyler. He was sensational." She wondered where Mack had run off to. He was likely in a mob of fans congratulating him on his grandson's game.

"Yes, I am. They all played a great game... but Ava, he's barely spoken since Pete's death. I hope he snaps out of his trance soon and shares his feelings. I'm extremely worried about him."

"That's understandable. You're all dealing with so much right now, but we all process grief on our own timeline."

"I've heard you've been talking to people in the community and asking questions about Pete. Have you learned anything that will help? I mean, do you think you'll find the person who killed him?"

"No answers yet... but I'll keep trying."

"That gives me some comfort. Two deputies searched our home on Fern Street. They took Pete's laptop and his golf clubs. What does this mean? Do you think I'm a suspect?"

"I'm sure they're just searching for any information that may lead them to his assailant. It's normal for them to speak with you and all family members. Do you have an attorney?"

Natalie nodded. "My dad selected one for me. Thank you

so much for your help. Oh, look. I see Tess." Natalie touched Ava's forearm. "I'd better catch up with her. I'd prefer that we stay home for now, but I wanted to watch Tyler."

"Just one more thing. I don't think there's ever a good time to bring this up. When you're ready, please give me a call at the office to review Pete's death benefits. He had a 401k plan, plus his life insurance policy that remains in effect through the end of the month of his employment separation. You're listed as the beneficiary for both."

"I hadn't even thought about that. Thanks for letting me know. I'll be in touch soon."

"Of course. Congratulations on the team's victory."

Jack was chatting with Matt while waiting for Ava. The men were laughing as they said goodnight, and Jack turned his attention toward Ava.

"I can pick you up tomorrow evening at six-thirty," he said. "I'd like to try out The Orion Room. Have you been there?"

"Not yet, but I've been wanting to check it out. I read a great review about that place in the *Community Reporter*."

"I heard they have a new chef who created a farm-to-table menu," Jack said as they made their way to the parking lot.

"Sounds wonderful. I rarely get out to Wooddale except when I need to shop at the mall. As a matter of fact, I had to run out there for a chocolate emergency last week."

"A chocolate emergency, huh?" Jack grinned.

"We had a little snafu during our Employee Appreciation Week celebration. But I fixed it. Chocolate makes everything better."

"Good to know. You'll need to share your address with me so I can find you tomorrow. It might be easier if you enter your information into my contact screen."

"Makes sense," responded Ava. She and Jack quickly exchanged phones and entered their own contact information. "Would you like to join us at my parent's house for dinner? We're just grilling." She hoped that didn't seem like an afterthought, but it didn't feel right to exclude him since she, Lauren, and Matt were all headed there.

"I appreciate the invite, but Randy is expecting me at the auto shop. I need to make a few decisions before he can proceed. Let me walk you to your car."

They had strolled half-way through the paved lot when Ava stopped at her blue Ford Bronco Sport. "This is me."

"Awesome. I would've pegged you as a two-door coupe type."

"There's a type?" Her eyes widened. "To be honest, I did own a two-door in college. Then I discovered a crossover is the key to surviving winter driving. Plus, I have Sophie to cart around now."

"I like this for you. I'll see you tomorrow evening, Ava." Jack offered his full-wattage smile.

It worked. Ava was blushing again. "Good night." She found his raw sex appeal alarming in a good way.

Ava buckled herself in, turned the air conditioning on full blast, and then looked around. She needed to make a quick detour and pick up her faithful companion before heading to her folks' place. Lauren and Matt were staring at Ava from their truck. Not even the slightest bit embarrassed at being a voyeur, Lauren waggled her fingers at Ava before she and Matt drove out to the Andrews family home.

Walking through her parent's front door, Ava instantly felt as though she were wrapped in a warm hug. This had been her family home for most of her school years, and the furnishings had stood the test of time. Grace didn't fall for the latest trends. When she fell in love with a piece at a gallery or while traveling, she found it a dedicated space in her home.

"What was that in the parking lot?" demanded Ava while eyeing her sister and Matt in the kitchen.

"Oh relax. We thought you two looked so cute together," said Lauren.

"Hi kids! Come on in," called Doug. "We're in the sunroom."

"Guess who's got a hot date tomorrow night?" Lauren asked.

"You and Matt are going out on the town?" Doug guessed.

"No, not me, Dad—It's Ava."

"Ava's going out with Matt tomorrow?"

"Be serious."

Doug asked, "Really, who is the lucky guy? Or is he Grant?"

"What's wrong with Grant?" Ava asked in a huff.

Doug shook his head. "Just seeking clarification… I'm confused. I thought you two broke up."

"As a matter of fact, I'm going out with someone I met recently."

"Really? Tell us about him, sweetheart," Grace said.

Ava crossed the threshold of the cozy sunroom and sat on the sofa facing the view afforded by the room's wall of windows. "You already met him, Mom. His name is Jack Lindstrom. Matt introduced us at Woodcrest last week."

"That's wonderful," Grace said. "Doug, Jack is the young man I told you about who is restoring that 1973 Ford Mustang. I believe it's a Mach 1. You've really got to see this car. It looks brand new. I asked him to enter the Jubilee auto show on the Fourth of July."

"I really love those old muscle cars. Brings back a lot of memories. Remember when I owned that Chevy Camaro?" asked Doug.

"I do—that was our ride to the senior prom." Grace planted a kiss on her husband's cheek. "There was a mid-April blizzard the night before. One for the record books. Our prom pictures featured mounds of snow in the background. It was truly magical."

Ava envied her parents' relationship. Grace and Doug were a testament to opposites attracting, yet they complemented one other. Grace was flamboyant and adventurous while Doug was intellectual and reserved. They were true partners who supported one another's dreams, a foundation Ava wanted to emulate in her own marriage one day.

Sophie placed her head on Grace's lap in a pathetic bid for attention. Ava said, "I hope it's okay that I brought my dog to your house. I can move her to the backyard if you prefer. She likes being outside more than anything."

"Sophie is always welcome, honey, you know that. I still can't believe her original owner didn't come looking for this precious girl."

"An attendant at the shelter told me that some of their dogs run away from local farms where they roam free. They're considered farm animals rather than pets. Can you imagine?"

"Not everyone treats their dogs like members of the family. I miss our little Ginger so much. I loved having a dog around especially when your dad was out of town. It just doesn't make sense for us to get another pet now with the recent housing market boom and your dad's work schedule. I need to stay flexible for my clients."

"That makes perfect sense," Lauren agreed.

"Please let me puppy-sit whenever you need help," said Grace.

"I swear Sophie is more popular than I am. You're the third person who's offered to host her recently, and I'll definitely take you up on it. You've always been great with dogs. It's like you're the dog whisperer."

Lauren said, "Speaking of housing—Mom, is it true that you're going to be listing the Reinholtz place on Fern Street?"

"How did you hear about this so quickly?" Grace glanced at Ava who shook her head.

"I just met with Natalie's mother this afternoon to discuss it."

"Karen was at the coffee shop this morning, and we over-heard her talking to Rosie," replied Matt.

"Doesn't this seem rather soon? Pete's body isn't even cold yet."

"Lauren, you don't need to be crude. Yes, I will be listing it for sale before the weekend. I attached a lock box to the door, and I'll get an inspector and housekeeper out there before the first open house. I guess Natalie hasn't set foot in that house since she moved out last week. It's full of painful memories. What a sad story."

Ava was forming a plan. "Hey, Mom. Can you take me over to see their house tomorrow?"

"Whatever for? You just bought a new home."

"Not for me but to search for clues. I'm sure the sheriff's department has swept through their place, but it might give me some insight as to what happened last week and why."

"I don't know if that's such a good idea. I mean, Natalie might feel it's invasive."

"Natalie knows that I'm investigating these crimes, and

she's even encouraging me. It's not like I'd do anything illegal. I just want to look around. You said yourself that the house will be open to the public in a matter of days."

"I think she has a good point," Doug said. "Besides you told me you plan to go back to take marketing photos. I'd feel much better knowing that you had someone with you. That place has some bad history, and we don't know if Pete's murderer is hanging around."

"Okay, let's do it." Grace hit the palm of her hand on her knee like a judge lowering her gavel. "Can you meet me there at ten in the morning? I volunteered to be the bingo caller in the activities room tomorrow afternoon, and I want to have plenty of time to visit your grandfather beforehand."

"That's perfect. I don't have any other work commitments tomorrow, and my boss has been really accommodating. He's allowing me to flex my time this week." Ava touched Grace's shoulder before she led Sophie to the back door. Once outside, her dog took off like a race horse when the starting gates open.

Ava leaned over the deck railing and looked out over Ruby Lake. Smoke was rising from the neighbor's grill while its owners were sitting on their deck talking. A couple of teenagers sped by on jet skis, and Ava waved to a family cruising along on a pontoon. All seemed right with the world that night.

The double sliding patio door opened revealing Doug, carrying a Coors Light in one hand and a steel spatula in the other. "I hope I didn't startle you," he said. "I need to fire up the grill. Hey, I recognize that pensive expression of yours, Ava. What's on your mind?"

"Nothing. Everything. How did you know Mom was the one?" Ava turned to face her dad. He was tall and fit, his skin tanned from the yard work he enjoyed.

Doug stood over the gas grill. He started the flame using the electric start feature, and then he played with the temperature gauge.

"I'm sure I've told you the story of how we met. The first time I saw your mother was at a youth group function at our church. One of the gals brought your mom along as her guest. I noticed her smile first, and the way her hair moved really caught my attention. She was as pretty as an angel with her blond halo and big blue eyes. When she first looked at me, it was as if we were the only two people in the world."

"That's beautiful."

"After talking to her that night, I knew she was the one for me. I wanted to feel that way for the rest of my life, and I've spent every day since trying to make her feel as though I actually deserve her. What's this all about honey? Are you questioning dating someone new?"

Ava answered, "I guess so. Did I make a mistake breaking it off with Grant? I feel like I failed somehow."

"Grant is a good man, but I trust your judgement. Only you can make that decision. You'll find someone you can't imagine being without, and it appears you've been getting along just fine without Grant. There's no rushing love, honey. It'll happen when you least expect it, and you'll know because the right man will treat you like the queen you are."

"How did you get to be so smart, Dad?"

"Years of practice." Doug wrapped his arms around his eldest daughter.

⌘

Ava was sitting at the end of the dock swinging her feet, splashing cool lake water onto her legs when Lauren joined her.

"Dinner's almost ready. Say, now that we're alone, what are your intentions with Jack Lindstrom? He's really smitten with you."

"Smitten? Really Lauren." Ava swiveled around to dry off. "You sound like Dad."

"I hope you're not leading him on."

"Whose side are you on?"

"Yours… always. Jack's been hurt recently. If you still have feelings for Grant, you need to make that clear. It might be hard for Jack to trust again. Just think about it."

"I can honestly say that I'm completely over Grant. I felt nostalgic having dinner with him, but I didn't feel any chemistry. I have love for him, but I'm not in love with him. Haven't been for some time."

"That's a major revelation."

"He needs a partner to help him entertain clients, someone to take care of him and his home. He has a secretary and a housekeeper for that. And can you imagine me on a campaign trail? Please."

"No, I really can't." Lauren focused on a mallard and her ducklings while they paddled along the shoreline.

Ava picked up her shoes. "Remember my college boyfriend, Ben?"

"Yeah, the business major who was always pitching new product ideas. He was a bore. Whatever happened to him?"

"He's with a big marketing firm in Chicago. Anyway, I should have broken that off much sooner than I did too. I guess I want to fix things and see them work out. Likely part of my middle child syndrome. I'm always the mediator trying to negotiate a resolution. Looking back, I realize I've been too willing to change myself in relationships. I fell into the same trappings with Grant. Couples should cooperate but not give up their individual dreams."

"Absolutely. Matt is always encouraging me to pursue my hobbies and to go out with my friends. We're equal partners at work, too. You know, I can come up with some pretty wacky ideas, but he tells me to go for it."

"That's what I mean, and your business is super successful because of your creativity. And I realized something else. Grant is extremely persuasive. I'd been allowing some of his opinions to influence mine. I can make my own decisions, thank you very much. I think I surprised him the other day."

"I love this side of you," Lauren said.

"Tell me what you know about Jack's ex-girlfriend."

"Really? I thought you frowned on gossip."

"Out with it, Lauren. I can see you're dying to tell me."

Lauren tossed her hair. "Okay. Her name is Brittany. Apparently, she's pretty in a high maintenance way. Matt said she's the type who would wear high heels to the bowling alley. You know, she spends a lot of time at the salon, and she wears designer clothes."

"I get the picture."

"Well, apparently, she couldn't deal with him being out of town so much. She cheated on him, and Jack found out just before the holidays last winter," explained Lauren.

"Dang, that really sucks for him." Ava tilted her head. "Don't worry. I'd never mistreat anyone."

"Of course not. I'm sorry, Ava. I shouldn't have pressured you about Jack. You've got enough on your mind now."

Chapter Twenty-One

R AYS OF LIGHT appeared along the sides of the bedroom window shades. Ava glanced at the clock to find it was still quite early. Sophie heard Ava sigh, and she immediately whimpered to go out. The dog squeezed past Ava before she could even fully open the door to the hallway.

After feeding the eager puppy and letting her into the backyard, Ava changed her clothes. She was still unwilling to risk taking a nature hike on her own. Knowing she'd be more comfortable being in a public place with other summer joggers, Ava invited Sophie to jump into the Bronco with her. They would stroll around Ruby Lake's historic downtown.

Ava decided to follow Lake Boulevard past the site where she had found Pete, taking a healthy step toward overcoming her anxiety. As her car approached the first fairway, she glanced toward the now-infamous walking bridge and saw a young man sitting in the grass near the sight of the horrible murder.

She parked her car across the street and walked over with Sophie at her side. Ava intended to face her aversion to this section of the golf course and was curious about this boy who had placed fresh flowers on the freshly mowed grass in front of him. The floral stems were broken, as if he had pulled them from a garden nearby. As she reached the area where she had found Pete's body, a shiver ran down Ava's spine. She rubbed the back of her neck.

She now recognized the young man was Tyler Reinholtz, wearing black athletic shorts, a red T-shirt, and a baseball cap. The golden curls that escaped his hat fell against his slim neck.

"Hi." Ava said softly. "You're Tyler Reinholtz, right?"

"Yeah, who are you?" He looked up at Ava. The skin around his eyes was puffy.

"I'm Ava Andrews. I work with your mom at Ruby Park. I saw your game last night. You were awesome."

"I've heard of you from my mom. You've been helping her."

Ava sat on the manicured lawn next to him and pointed to the flowers.

Tyler shrugged. "I came by to pay my respects. I loved him, but I hated him so much, you know?"

Yellow and green marks covered Tyler's left knuckles. She asked, "What did you do to your hand?"

"I got hit by a ball during baseball practice."

"Ouch." Ava sat quietly for a moment. "How did you know exactly where your father died?"

Tyler's eyebrows raised into his forehead. He shifted his weight and pulled on strands of grass. He appeared anguished and panic stricken.

"Did you get in a fight with your dad the night he died?" Ava asked calmly.

"I didn't mean to do it," Tyler cried.

"Do what?" Ava waited patiently for a response.

"Kill him," Tyler sobbed. "I was so angry. I can't live with myself. I want to die." Sophie stood up and licked the boy's face and then sat down, brushing next to him. She was a good judge of character.

Ava didn't feel frightened listening to this poor weeping child, wrapped in a man's body. She only leaned in closer. "What happened that night?"

"I met a few friends at the clubhouse for pizza. It was the first day of summer break, and we were out celebrating. My grandpa said I could treat the guys on his tab. I left after the rest of them. I wanted to see the end of the Twins baseball game on TV and had to sign for the food. Dad was in his golf cart when I came out. It was like he was waiting for me."

"Did you talk to him?"

"He told me to get in the cart, but I said, 'go home'. I walked to the path to get my bike from the rack, and he came after me with his golf club. He was drunk and acting all crazy, saying he was going to go get my mom and sister to take us all back home. He took a swing at me, but he missed. That's when I hit him. He lost his balance and fell. Jesus, I should have come back for him. I let him die." Tyler glanced at Ava. "He was okay when I left."

"How do you know that?"

"Because he was swearing at me. He told me I was a worthless piece of shit. I could still hear him yelling as I rode off on my bike."

"Oh, I'm sorry. That must have been awful."

Tyler wiped his nose on the back of his arm. "I thought he'd get up and go back to our house in town."

"You punched him in the face, then?" inquired Ava. This would explain the bruises on Tyler's left hand as well as on the right side of Pete's face.

"Yeah, I got him in the cheek. Man, he deserved it so much. He punched me and my mom enough times."

"Was he looking up at you when he called you those names?"

"He was laying on his back. I heard he must have hit his head on something. Geez, it's so awful. They said he lost a lot of blood."

"Did you notice if he was bleeding when you left?" Ava asked.

"He wasn't bleeding," Tyler said. He cocked his head, looking puzzled. "He was just trying to get up."

"Tyler, did you also hit him with a bat, a rock, or something else?"

"God no, just with my fist, honest. I really didn't mean to kill him. You gotta believe me. I needed to stop him from going to my grandparents' house. Grandpa was furious at my dad for what he did to my mom."

"I believe you. You were just defending yourself, and I don't think you killed him either."

"You don't?" Tyler said. His eyes were empty and sad.

"You couldn't have punched him hard enough to cause the trauma that caused his death. What happened to the golf club he was swinging at you?"

"I took it with me and threw it in the garbage. It was trash as far as I am concerned."

"Where was this?"

"I biked back to my grandparent's house where we're staying. I wanted to warn my mom. My grandpa was up watching TV. Mom was already sleeping, I guess… Grandpa asked me to let her rest. I told him that I ran into Dad in the parking lot, but I didn't tell him about the fight. I don't want him to think I'm like my dad. I'm not!"

"Did you tell your mom the next morning?"

"I didn't get the chance. The cops came to the house early to talk to her. I was frozen when I heard he was dead. I didn't tell anybody… until now."

"Is your mom home?"

"I think so."

"How close are we to your grandparent's place?" Ava asked.

"It's that one across the fairway." Tyler pointed out the huge estate that backed to the course. Its rear elevation was equally impressive as its front facade had been. Majestic pine trees adorned the back gardens, and an oversized gazebo stood proudly to one side of the property. Ava noted the oversized picture windows, two stories in height, peered over the course. The club's path offered easy access to the clubhouse and driving range by foot, bike, or by golf cart.

"I'm going to call your mom, okay?"

Tyler nodded his response. Ava took her phone from the back pocket of her jeans. She snapped a quick photo of the home and then pressed the number for Natalie.

"Hello, Natalie. I'm with Tyler. We're on the golf course near the walking bridge. Can you drive over? Yeah, I'll wait here with him."

"I like your dog. What's her name?" Tyler ran his hands through the retriever's soft fur.

"Sophie," responded Ava. Her dog snapped to attention and wagged her tail.

"I hope we can get a dog. Our dad would never let us have one."

A few minutes later, Tyler relayed his story once again to his mother while Natalie embraced her son. Once they all got to their feet, Ava helped Natalie settle Tyler's mountain bike into the trunk of her new Mercedes. Tyler was already seated up front. He was bent forward, holding his head in his hands.

Ava spoke softly. "Natalie, you need to share this with the sheriff's office today. If you don't, I'll have to report it. Also, Tyler told me he threw Pete's golf club in the trash. You'll want to retrieve that for evidence, but be careful to avoid getting any further finger prints on it."

"I understand," replied Natalie. "I'll reach out to my lawyer for assistance once I get back to the house, and Tyler is settled in. His grief is much worse than I thought. I never expected he was feeling guilty. We have so much healing in front of us."

"You'll take it one day at a time," Ava said. "Now that he revealed the secret he's been bottling up, I hope he'll feel free to share even more."

"How did you know to find him here?" Natalie asked.

"Honestly, I didn't. I wasn't actually looking for anyone. I thought seeing the golf course again might give me some fresh ideas and perhaps, some closure. When I saw Tyler sitting on the lawn, I stopped and parked just across the street."

"I'm grateful you called me. I'll talk to you soon."

Chapter Twenty-two

REALIZING SHE NO longer had time to jog around downtown, Ava returned home with Sophie and prepared for the rest of her day. She had requested the favor of accompanying her mom to Natalie's house, so she knew she needed to be prompt. She arrived at the Reinholtz home on Fern Street several minutes before Grace, eager to look around in hopes of finding something—anything that could provide a clue to Pete's murder.

She walked around the perimeter of the home and peeked into the garage. On her tip toes, Ava was tall enough to look into its windows. The sight of a black Toyota Prius housed there sent a shiver down her spine. Had Pete been following her?

A lawn mower and snow blower were tucked into the side along with two bikes and garbage dumpsters. The large tool chest, wheelbarrow, and lawn tools took up the side wall. Everything appeared to be organized and tidy. However, she didn't see the golf clubs that she was hoping to find.

"Are you looking for something?" called a deep male voice. *Busted.* Ava's eyes widened, and she placed her hand on her heart. She turned to find Anthony Barone approaching the driveway. He continued, "Oh, it's you, Ava. I told Natalie I'd keep an eye on the house."

"That's very kind of you."

"Neighbors take care of each other in this town."

"Of course. I'm sorry for your loss."

"Yep." He shook his head. "They've been a second family to us."

"I'm meeting my mother here any moment. Here she comes." Ava could see Grace's car approaching. She pointed to the white SUV.

"Natalie is listing the house then." It was a statement more than a question.

"It appears that way," said Ava.

Anthony gazed at the ground. "Okay, see you later then." He began to walk back to his house next door but stopped to pull some dandelions growing at the edge of his lawn.

Grace stepped out of her Lexus and waved to Anthony. She nimbly opened the lock box attached to the door handle, grasped the enclosed key, and opened the front door to the home. The two women did a quick walk through of the main level. Ava was immediately drawn to the openness of the space at the back of the house where the bright kitchen, dining, and living areas were located.

"This is really pretty," said Ava. "Most of these old Victorians are boxy with small rooms. I like how they opened up the wall between the kitchen and living rooms."

"I agree. It was a wise investment. Young homeowners want to be able to keep an eye on their kids. I'm going to start taking photos back here. Go look around and tell me what you think."

Ava retraced her steps, heading back through the foyer. The room by the entryway had two wooden French doors. It likely served as the home's parlor originally but was now set up as a masculine-looking office. The staircase led up the opposite wall with a dark wooden railing in the same rich cherry wood.

Ava started her search in the office. She sat down in the leather desk chair and proceeded to open each of the desk drawers. She wasn't surprised to find them nearly empty. Only office supplies, an old calculator, and pads of notebook paper remained. The sheriff's department had taken all of their records. Ava admired the heavy wood paneling and the bookcase that lined the back wall.

She browsed the reference books, novels, and knickknacks on the shelves. One held college textbooks and a few three-ring binders. Ava pulled out the ring binders and flipped through their contents. Each contained a course syllabus and lecture notes for classes he taught at the community center. In the back of the third binder, Ava was surprised to discover legal documents regarding two lawsuits filed by Pete. One had a tab marked 'Sweetwater Farms' and the second was labeled 'Victoria, Minnesota.'

Rather than taking the time to read them, Ava searched for a photocopier and found one in the closet. She pulled the documents out of the binder, placed them in the copier's feeder, and pressed the start button. She put her copies in a folder which she stuffed in the large bag she carried with her.

While rummaging through the copier stand, Ava found a file labeled 'Cruises.' She thumbed through this and noticed that the Reinholtz's had taken a Caribbean cruise each year over Christmas or spring break, which made sense, because the kids would've been off school then. It was common for Minnesotans to plan week-long escapes during their brutally cold winters. Ava quickly copied the reservations for an upcoming trip in December.

"I'm going to take a look upstairs," Ava called out to her mother.

"Okay, I'll be outside taking pictures of the house and its landscaping."

Ava walked upstairs and peeked into bedrooms. The first was decorated in red, white, and blue and featured baseball memorabilia. Pennants for the Minnesota Twins and the Ruby Lake Royals hung proudly over Taylor's bed. The next room, decorated in lavender and silver, featured a white canopy bed. Large wooden letters spelled out "Tess" above the mirrored dresser.

Ava felt terrible for these two displaced children who recently lost their father. She forged ahead assuming the room on the end was the owner's bedroom. It was small but included a generously sized en-suite bath and closet. Ava guessed they had converted a smaller bedroom to make room for this modern space.

She quickly glanced in the drawers. Some of them were empty, and she assumed that Natalie had taken her belongings. Turning the light on in the walk-in closet, Ava was impressed with its storage system. It appeared that one side of this room was dedicated to Natalie and the other to Pete with open space on what was likely Natalie's side. A fancy watch display box rested on top of the built-in dresser. A glass lid allowed her to view ten very exclusive watches. She had heard of but never viewed the Patek Philippe, Rolex, Cartier, Breitling, Omega, and Tag Hauer brands up close and personal. A couple of them appeared to be gold.

The wooden display case also had a large drawer below the flip top display. When she opened it, she found a shallow space which held very nice yet less expensive models including Citizen, Fossil, and Seiko. There was a velvet bag which she opened to find a gorgeous woman's diamond Longines watch. She wondered if this was a gift for Natalie or another woman.

It didn't make sense to her that the tray was only an inch high when the drawer itself was several inches thick. Ava pulled the drawer entirely out of the display box and discovered two tiny metal levers at the back. As she pushed these down, the tray came loose revealing another compartment.

To Ava's surprise, she discovered a key, checkbook, bank deposit slips, and a small folder containing documents from a bank in Nassau, Bahamas. Ava opened a goldenrod envelope and withdrew a spreadsheet listing local businesses with names she recognized as their owners, their addresses, and phone numbers.

A creaking noise behind her made her jump. She spun around to see her mother.

"You scared the crap out of me, Mom."

"I'm sorry. Have you found something helpful?"

"I think so, but I'm trying to determine what to make of this. Pete has a very expensive watch collection. I know what his salary was at Ruby Park, and it wouldn't support purchasing these high-end pieces. I'm no watch expert, but there has to be well over $100,000 worth of new watches here assuming they're the real deal and not cheap imitations. I heard he had an appreciation for watches, but this is incredible."

"Perhaps he inherited these, honey."

"That's a plausible explanation," said Ava. "Or he had another source of income."

"I'm going to take photos of their serial numbers." Ava held up a small silver key with a round head. "What do you think this unlocks?"

"It looks like a key to a safe deposit box."

"I also found records for a bank in Nassau. I believe they travel to the Bahamas on an annual basis. He might have a bank account there."

"That's intriguing," Grace said. "Are you concerned that he could have stolen these watches?"

"I don't know. What if he was involved in some shady banking or business deals? I wonder if we should report this to Mitch or not."

"I think it would be best if I contact Natalie. I'll let her know that I'm concerned about her leaving valuable jewelry in her home while I'm showing it to potential buyers and that she should pick this up right away. Hopefully, she'll discover what you found, and she can decide what to do with it."

"You're right. That makes perfect sense. I'll go ahead and put all this back while you finish up."

Once Grace departed, Ava took out her cell phone and took photos of each watch making sure to capture both their faces and backs. Then she proceeded to photograph the checkbook and banking documents as well.

"I'm heading to the basement now," Ava called out to her mother before proceeding down the dark stairwell.

"There's not much down there. Be careful on those steps. They're very narrow."

Grace was right. This was a very old, musty basement that couldn't be used for living quarters. Ava found an old dehumidifier along with the furnace. She opened a closet door—

And a skeleton brushed against her as it fell to the floor.

Ava jumped back and tried to scream, but her voice was frozen. She managed to gasp and then yelled, "Holy crap!"

She caught her breath and realized she was looking down at a plastic decoration. The closet was stacked with labeled plastic bins clearly marked as Halloween, Christmas, and Easter holiday decor.

"Well, that's what I get for snooping," Ava mumbled as she stuffed the skeleton back in the closet. *Yikes.* Her mom might want to warn potential house buyers.

Her next stop was the garage. Ava didn't find anything of value inside that she couldn't see through the windows earlier. She took a couple photos making sure to include the Toyota's license plates.

When she returned to the kitchen, Grace was swiftly typing on her laptop. Ava could see that her mother was creating marketing materials. Grace had taken photography classes while in art school, and her advertising brochures were always top-notch.

Admiring her mother as she worked, Ava pretended to be occupied to avoid causing a distraction.

She wished she were more like her mother. Grace had an aura about her that naturally drew people in. She was not only kind but was also genuinely interested in the stories other people shared. Grace had many great tales herself, but it was the way she spoke to people with such enthusiasm that made her popular. Most folks were in too much of a hurry or were too stuck in their own worlds to take an interest in others. Mom took the time to make personal connections.

Ava asked, "Mom, have I told you how proud I am of you?"

Chapter Twenty-three

AVA WATCHED AS Grace assisted Latisha and her aide pass out cards for the afternoon bingo game. This activity always required a few volunteers to run smoothly. She approached the caller's table to offer Grace additional help.

"Uffda! I forgot my hearing aid," a resident said to his friend. "Can't hear any of you. Too much background noise. Don't know if I have time to wheel back to my room."

Ava knelt next the elderly, bald man. "I would be happy to give you a ride to your apartment."

"Aren't you an angel. I'm Ole, and my apartment is on the first floor down the left corridor. I'll show you."

"I'm pleased to meet you," Ava said. "I'll get you back here before you know it."

Ava easily navigated Ole and his wheelchair around the corner and down the hall. Once inside the efficiency apartment, Ole said, "Make yourself at home. I'll be with you in a minute." He wheeled himself to the night stand next to his bed.

Ava browsed the entertainment center under his television

where framed family photographs were displayed. Most were faded images from his past including a lovely wedding photo taken decades ago. One color photo stood out among the rest. Its shiny frame appeared to be new. Lindsay Green and John Carlson were holding hands under a giant oak tree.

Ava processed this information. She turned to Ole. "John's your grandson?"

"Yes siree."

"I'm so happy that he's engaged to be married."

"You know Johnny, then. His Lindsey is a fine gal," Ole said. "Isn't she lovely? She had such a tragic upbringing, though. Her mother died during childbirth, and her father was an abusive man. He served time in prison for selling illegal drugs."

"I wasn't aware of that."

"Poor girl transferred from one foster home to another. We're very happy to welcome her into our family."

"I don't know what to say. That's a sad but remarkable story."

"Heaven knows when you get to be my age, dear, you face many tragedies that you can't understand. Lindsey made it to the other side with therapy, and she has the love of the entire Carlson family. She's one of us now."

"I can see how lucky she is to have you as a grandfather." She appreciated his family values and pride in his new soon-to-be granddaughter. Ava wondered what extreme John would take to protect his fiancée.

"Here, let me give you a tip for transferring me." Ole held out a couple of dollar bills.

"No, thank you. It's been my sincere pleasure meeting you."

"Can I give you a hug instead?" Ole asked with a smile.

"Absolutely." Ava replied, and she happily leaned in and gave this gentleman a warm embrace. "Let's get you back to bingo before they start calling the first round."

Once she safety returned Ole back to the crowded community room, Ava caught a glimpse of Mitch walking out of the facility. She waved to Grace and then ducked outside to catch her cousin out front. It was mid-afternoon, and a band of clouds hung in the sky. The fresh breeze felt refreshing.

"What brings you by?" Ava asked.

"Official business. I understand you talked to Tyler and Natalie Reinholtz this morning. You provided her good advice. That kid is going through a rough time. Pete's golf club isn't the murder weapon, by the way, but it helped to piece together Tyler's story."

"I know. I heard the club Grant and I discovered was a possible match and that it's a ladies' club."

"Please keep that to yourself," Mitch said. "We'll keep an eye on Tyler, but his story checks out."

"Des Sparks told me that Randy has an alibi for his whereabouts the night Pete was killed. He was researching and ordering auto parts online for a couple of hours."

"That's correct. His computer records and order forms showed the timeframe he was working from his auto shop, and we followed up with the merchants to confirm his purchases."

"I'm happy for him. Do you have any updates on Brooke's condition?" Ava asked.

"Yeah, but this is off the record and must stay strictly between you and me. Her doctors brought Brooke out of her coma, and I spoke with her yesterday. She and Pete were arguing in the community center's office that morning. She threatened to turn him in for attempting to steal cash from the office safe, and he came after her. Not with a gun though. She was afraid he was going to harm her, so she ran trying to escape. A gunshot was fired, and that's the last thing she recalls. She claimed someone else shot the gun, and that it wasn't Pete."

"Does she have any theory about who would want to harm her or why?"

"No, but she said all the staff and instructors have contempt for Pete. Our leading theory is that Dave or another perpetrator was targeting Pete and accidentally shot Brooke," Mitch explained.

"Will Brooke be able to return home soon?"

"She was transferred from the ICU to the medical/surgical ward. She's facing a long road to full recovery and will require physical therapy."

"I'm glad she's improving. What a relief," replied Ava.

"You're certainly well connected in this community. Impressive since you've only been back in town a few months."

"It's all about building relationships, cuz."

"You'll let me know if you have other leads?"

Ava smiled sincerely. "As long as you return the favor."

Chapter Twenty-four

DRESSED IN A periwinkle wrap dress and sandals, Ava realized she was pacing her hallway. She stopped abruptly at the mirror to straighten the tie at her waist. When she saw Jack's car pull in, she said goodbye to Sophie and asked her to behave. She didn't want to be embarrassed by any doggie disasters should she decide to invite him indoors later. Naturally, that all would depend on how they got along during dinner tonight.

Jack was getting out of his vehicle as she engaged the deadbolt on her front door by pressing her security code. Just then, she noticed the sparkle of a metal object.

She reached down to pick up a lovely bracelet from behind her flower pot. It had the message 'Follow your Dreams' stamped on the front. While she didn't recognize this piece of jewelry, Ava figured it must belong to one of her girlfriends who visited over the weekend. She quickly wrapped the bracelet in a tissue and placed it into her purse for safe keeping until she found its owner.

"Wow, you look beautiful," Jack said as he opened the passenger side door of his Acura for her.

"You clean up nicely too."

The twenty-minute drive to their destination in the next town flew by as Jack entertained Ava with stories about transferring through various airports. He was kind-hearted, and she appreciated his sense of humor. Jack was finishing his latest story as they reached the restaurant.

"I guess it's the uniform. People see me and think I'm a 411 operator. I wanted to say to this guy, 'Let me introduce you to your gate agent. I need to get into the cockpit asap, or I can assure you no one is going to make their connection on time.'"

"I haven't laughed this much in a long time. Good grief, it would never occur to me to ask a pilot for gate information or directions to baggage claim," Ava said.

Jack escorted Ava into the restaurant and held the door open for her. Dozens of people were waiting out front, anxiously waiting to sample what this hotspot had to offer. She was pleased that he had made reservations.

They were soon directed by an efficient college-aged hostess to a table next to a window. She said, "Welcome to The Orion Room. Enjoy your dinner," and then set two menus and wine lists on the table while Jack pulled Ava's chair out for her.

"You're so gallant, Jack. I find that rare these days."

"I have older sisters, so that's what I know. Dad would have kicked my butt if I wasn't respectful. I figure he must know what he's doing. My folks have been married over forty-five years." The corners of Jack's mouth tipped up slightly.

A very serious-looking older gentleman appeared in a crisp waiter's uniform to collect their drink orders. "That's a glass of Pinot Grigio for the lady, and the Cabernet Sauvignon for you sir," he said. "Excellent choices. Our chef's special this evening is the smoked bison with sweet potato mash. Do you have any questions about the menu?"

"I've never tried bison before. Does it have a gamey flavor?" Jack inquired.

"Actually, our customers state that it's not a bitter taste, but rather, it's sweeter than beef. It's a lighter cut of meat."

Ava decided quickly and said, "I'd like to give that a try."

"Let's make that two. Thank you." Jack handed the menus to the waiter.

"Certainly, I'll be right back with your drinks."

Jack peered into Ava's eyes. "Now, it's your turn. Tell me a funny story about working in human resources."

"Let me see. I don't normally share specifics to protect the guilty, but this one is pretty innocuous. During my first job as a recruiter, I was interviewing candidates for an assistant administrator role. One of the male candidates was close to my age. When I asked him to describe his greatest attribute, he raised an eyebrow, and asked, 'You mean physically?'"

Jack chuckled. "Did he get the job?"

"No! I told him, 'I assure you, there are no physical require-ments for this position.'"

"That's hilarious."

"Some people really don't know how to make a good first impression. Once an external candidate brought her husband and three kids along to an interview. She was visibly upset when I asked them to wait for her in the lobby. I also had an applicant who answered her cell phone and proceeded to hold this whole side conversation while I waited."

"Wow, I'm speechless."

"Right? But, please keep these stories to yourself. I have my professional integrity to uphold."

"Your secrets are safe with me. Scout's honor." Jack's eyes sparkled, and she felt he was sincere.

"You'd think our high schools would do a better job of preparing the future workforce," Ava said.

"You're onto something there. You could look into volunteering and give those kids a great head-start on interviewing and workplace etiquette."

"That's a good suggestion. I'll give it some thought. I've always felt it would be fun to work in a career center. I'm curious whether people pick their careers or if their careers pick them. Did you always know you wanted to be a pilot?"

"Not exactly. I expected to become a professional football player for the Green Bay Packers, but I discovered by the sixth grade that wasn't in the cards. I fell in love with airplanes the first time I flew on a family vacation. There was no going back after that."

"Where did you go on that historic first flight of yours?" Ava asked. She was eager to learn about his adventures.

"Hawaii, now that I think of it." Jack smiled. "We visited Oahu, Maui, and the Big Island."

"The islands were beckoning for you to return."

"Maybe so. How did you get into Human Resources?"

"Well, I thought I would become a teacher when I was a kid. I loved elementary school, and I pretended to be a school teacher at home. Once I was in high school, I discovered my interest in human behavior. My college undergrad degree is in psychology. Back then, I thought I'd become a psychologist or get a Ph.D. and become a researcher."

"What stopped you?"

"I found my career path after accepting a student position at the University. There is so much more variety in HR than most people realize. We don't just hire and fire employees." She raised an eyebrow at Jack. "I really love helping people. Then, I went on to get my master's degree. I can't imagine doing anything else… Except when I'm really stressed out. During those moments, I wonder why I didn't become a florist."

Jack grinned. "A florist. Why is that?"

"Because flowers don't talk back."

"That's funny. How is firing people, by the way? Isn't that difficult?"

"Naturally, I don't like to see good people go, but in my experience, HR doesn't press to fire people unless they do something egregious. I'm usually coaching managers to set clearer expectations and to give people a second chance. I feel some people quit on the job by making poor decisions. What I mean is, people know the consequences of their actions, and sometimes we have to part ways. My job is to be fair and ensure everyone is treated with respect."

"I never thought about it that way," Jack said. "You seem to be very patient. What causes you to become stressed out?"

"Trying to help people that need more support than my company can provide weighs heavily on my mind. I hear some really sad stories. Fortunately, we can offer resources or make referrals in many cases. Sometimes, employees just want someone to listen, and I am definitely there for them."

"It sounds like you want to take care of everyone," Jack said.

Ava nodded. "My second stressor is very different. It's dealing with people who are intentionally difficult because they think it gives them power. I find it disrespectful, and it takes the energy right out of me. My time is better spent on other things, and reaching an agreement always takes longer with those people." Ava took a deep breath. "I apologize if I sound like I'm complaining. These are not the life and death decisions you are making at 35,000 feet."

"Actually, the flying is the easy part. Landing safely… now that can get a little tricky."

Ava laughed. "Thank you for being a great listener. I didn't mean to get so serious."

"I appreciate how genuine and empathetic you are. Dating can be so shallow with some people, but I'm really enjoying getting to know you."

"Truthfully, I haven't been on many first dates." Ava felt shy under Jack's continuous gaze. She noticed many of the other diners were spending more time looking at their cell phones than at each other.

"Interesting. Tell me more."

The waiter arrived with their dinner. Ava said, "Looks like I've been saved by this delicious-looking meal. What's your favorite type of cuisine? I'm sure you don't eat bison every day."

"Changing the subject now, I see. Does pizza count as cuisine?"

"Most definitely. Tell me about your family." Ava selected a dinner roll and passed the basket to Jack. "You said you have sisters."

"I have four older sisters. I'd like to think my folks kept trying for a boy, but I think I was an accident. The youngest of my sisters is six years ahead of me."

"You know what they say, if all children were planned, there would be no lines at amusement parks."

"Do they now?" Jack smirked. "I'll show you pictures of my nieces and nephews sometime. They're so cute."

"You seem to like kids."

"Love them." He spoke with genuine care in his voice.

"Yeah? How many do you see yourself having?" Ava was rather curious.

"About a dozen."

Ava almost choked on her wine. "You'd better get started then."

"I'm game if you are."

"That's not what I meant." Ava turned pink and reached for her water glass.

"You're cute when you're blushing. I think two or three would be great. And you?"

"I agree. That's a nice-sized family," Ava said with a smile.

"Okay, let's move on to the serious relationship stuff." Jack lowered his voice, "Dogs or cats?"

"Dogs, obviously."

"Pepperoni or sausage?"

"Pepperoni."

"Spring or fall?"

"Fall."

"Packers or Vikings?"

"Oh, is this our first argument?" Ava bit back a smile. She was enjoying their light-hearted banter.

"Skiing or skating?" Jack asked.

"Skating."

"The ocean or outer space?"

"Space... think of the infinite possibilities."

"Chocolate or peanut butter?"

"I can't live in a world without both."

"Touché!" Jack squeezed Ava's hand.

"Did I pass?" she asked.

"With flying colors."

❧

Ava couldn't believe how quickly the evening passed by or how naturally her conversation with Jack was flowing. When they reached her home, she asked, "Would you like to come in and see my new place?"

"Yes, I'd like that." He reached into the back seat of his car and retrieved a small gift bag filled with pink tissue paper. "I got you a little something."

Ava grinned as she lifted out the package. "Harry and David's dark chocolate truffles. These are incredible!"

"Hope you enjoy them."

"Truffles are the way to a woman's heart, but I'm sure you know that."

Ava showed Jack around her house, pointing out the highlights and her favorite architectural features. She still had items to purchase to make it complete, but that was half the fun.

"Your home is really nice, Ava. It's elegant but not pretentious, like you."

Ava laughed. "Are you saying that I am pretentious, but my house isn't?"

"Sorry, that definitely came out the wrong way. You are very real, and down to earth. I like that about you. This home seems perfect for you."

"I think I'm going to be very happy here. Can I get you a beer or a glass of wine?"

"Sure, I'll have a beer with you before I have to head out."

Ava withdrew two bottles from her refrigerator and set them on the counter top. Jack was standing so close to her that she could feel the warmth emanating from his body. She almost bumped into him while looking in the drawer for a bottle opener. Jack reached over, grabbed a bottle, twisted off the cap, and handed it to her. Then, he opened the second one for himself. Ava liked how he was taking care of her first.

"What's downstairs in your basement level?" Jack asked as he moved toward the staircase.

"Nothing really. There's a whole lot of storage space and the furnace room."

"Mind if I take a look?"

"Go ahead, be my guest."

As they stepped toward the staircase, Sophie raced down ahead of them. *I definitely have to take this dog to obedience school.*

Jack was mesmerized by the openness of the home's lower level. "This is awesome. You have a full walkout with an incredible patio door. You could do so much with this space. A wet bar could be installed against this wall, and you could hang a big screen TV over there. I bet you could fit a pool table on the far end. You already have plumbing roughed in, so it wouldn't be that difficult. This would be awesome for entertaining."

"I hadn't thought about all that. I have more than enough space for myself on the main floor. You sound like you know something about construction."

"I helped my dad complete renovations on the family farmhouse and again a couple of summers ago at their lake cabin in Wisconsin where they spend their summers."

"You are full of surprises. Are your parents snowbirds?"

"They are. Their main home is near Phoenix. I swear they are busier these days than before they retired. It's hard to catch up with them."

"Do you visit them often?"

"I try to. It's one of the perks of the job."

"Lucky you. I'd love to pick up and go whenever I liked."

"Yep, living the dream." Jack shot Ava a mischievous smile. "Is it too forward for me to ask if you're free tomorrow evening? I'm heading out of town again on Thursday."

"I'm free, and no, it's not too forward. I don't believe in those dating rules about waiting two or three days to call."

"Perfect. I need to get going, but I'll see you soon." Jack took Ava's hand into his own and raised it to his lips.

"Thanks for a wonderful evening, Jack."

Chapter Twenty-five

*A*VA WAS STANDING *in the hallway at the Ruby Lake High School in front of a bank of royal blue lockers. "34 right, 27 left, 18 right," Ava recited aloud. "Why isn't this combination working?"*

She felt panicked. Her fellow students had all vanished into their classrooms, and she was about to be late for Calculus. She yanked on the cold metal locker handle, but it wouldn't open. She tried again and again while a trickle of perspiration dripped down her back. But no luck, Ava was going to miss her final exam. She would fail this class. The bell rang overhead. This would not bode well on her college applications.

Ava jolted awake in her bed. *I'm missing something.* She peeled back her summer-weight down comforter. *I need to make a list of everything that happened last week starting on Monday.* Ava was eager to get into her office. She took a quick shower, grabbed a yogurt to go, and made it to Ruby Park in record time.

At her desk, Ava reached for her phone and dialed the internal number for Todd who worked in facilities management. He had reported to Pete Reinholtz.

"Good morning, Todd," she said. "I'm just following up on an inquiry. Can you tell me if the building's security cameras have been down recently?"

"Yeah. Last week Pete told me that he'd be calling the service provider to check on the security system. Apparently, he shut the system down because it kept erroring out, and the monitors went blank. I called the company first thing on Thursday to follow up, but the guy I talked to had no record of a call from Pete. I guess he never got around to calling before he was let go on Wednesday."

"It's been down this whole time?" Ava asked.

"No. After that call, I took a closer look. I tested the system a few times, and I didn't find any problems. I'm not sure what happened, but it's been back up and running since."

"Do you remember what day Pete told you this?"

"Let me think. It was at the end of the day on Monday. Probably about four forty-five. I remember because I had an errand to run, and he stopped me while I was leaving for the day. Is there anything you need?" Todd asked.

"Not right now. Glad it's working again. I'll call you back if I have further questions."

"Sounds good. Have a great day."

"You too."

Ava disconnected and called out, "Des, can you come here for a minute?" She hoped Des could hear her across the hall. It worked. Seconds later, Des poked her head in. "What do you make of this?" Ava relayed her last phone conversation to her confidante.

"You're thinking Pete disconnected the system. But why would he do that?" Des asked with an edge of concern.

"I'm not sure we'll ever know the truth." Ava leaned back and crossed her arms.

"Do you think he was planning to retaliate after receiving corrective action on Monday? That's a pretty scary thought."

"I don't know. He was pretty mad when I overheard him complaining about it."

"Pete was a hateful human being." Des dropped her gaze to consider the possibilities, then she raised her index finger with a new thought. "Perhaps it had to do with the financial audit. Cheryl said he's been acting stranger than usual, and I've heard him complaining about them being onsite. The audit team has been here longer than in previous years."

"That's certainly a possibility."

"What else do you think it could be?"

Ava leaned forward. "Maybe he planned to meet someone here after business hours. Let's assume he wasn't expecting a complaint from Lindsey Green and didn't anticipate being terminated."

"And he would've believed he had more time to carry out whatever he was planning."

"Exactly. If that's the case, he must not have completed his goal before he was fired. Otherwise, he would have turned the system back on. I wonder if he got into the building after his termination. If so, what was he doing?" Ava asked. "Maybe that's connected to his death."

"Well, you said Todd got the system back up and running the morning following Pete's employment separation. And Pete died roughly thirty-six hours later."

"It could be a long shot, but I think we have to take a thorough look at the security footage to see if he got into the building or met someone here."

"I agree with you. This is intense."

"We're going to need help," Ava said. "This could take many hours or even days. I'll contact Cheryl about assigning the security screening to Todd. In the meantime, I'm putting a timeline together to track the events of the past week."

"Let me know how I can help." Des started to leave.

"Thanks, Des." Ava smiled to show her appreciation. Then she reached for her medication to stave off an oncoming migraine. Her next destination was to visit Cheryl. Ava hoped she was available.

Ava knocked softly on Cheryl's slightly open door and stepped in. "Hi, I have a suspicion that Pete might have been planning to enter or harm the facility last week. I'd like to pull Todd from whatever he's working on today to conduct a thorough review of the security tapes… unless he's handling another urgent task. Can I let him know we spoke and that you support prioritizing this?"

"Go right ahead. I trust your instincts. While you're here, do you have a few minutes?"

Ava nodded. "Let me close your door." She returned to Cheryl's desk and sat down facing her.

"This is good timing. I wanted to fill you in on recent events. Jeff and I had a meeting with our auditors yesterday. They've identified inappropriate accounting practices and believe Pete was embezzling funds."

"Really?"

"I'm afraid so. They cited possible check tampering, false invoices, and loan fraud. We're bringing in a forensic accountant to track the activity and to estimate our losses. I reported this to the local authorities, and federal agencies may be brought in as well. I can't believe this. How did I not notice?" Cheryl's oval face was pale with a forlorn expression.

"Because it's natural to trust your accountant. Don't be hard on yourself. You'll get this straightened out." Ava suspected this was the reason for Mitch's visit the previous afternoon.

Cheryl said, "They found Center funds have been diverted to an offshore bank account in Nassau, Bahamas."

"Oh, dear Lord. I think I might have uncovered some information yesterday that could help. I need to run it by our attorney first to ensure the information remains privileged, and I'll get right back to you. Do you think any of his former staff are involved?"

"We don't know. I'll share updates as this evolves."

"Is the sheriff's department aware of this?" Ava asked. "Pete could have been dealing with some really shady people if there's any money laundering involved. That could lead them to find the motive for his murder."

"Yes, we've informed them. This is all really hard to believe, isn't it?"

"I've investigated some really shocking scandals, but I've never been involved in a murder investigation. This all doesn't even seem real. I can't wait to get this behind us."

"You and me both. Let me know if you discover anything else," Cheryl said.

"Absolutely."

Ava took the stairs back up to the second floor and entered her department. Grateful her team members were handling the day's business needs, Ava closed her office door again to use her phone.

"Good morning, Grant. Thanks for taking my call." Ava filled him in on her discoveries at Pete's home.

"You sure are full of intrigue. I'll reach out to the County Attorney's Office in case they want to request a search warrant.

Thanks for checking with me before turning over the copies you made. Even though Pete is deceased, we want to ensure all evidence is handled legally. We don't know that his wife isn't involved in this or how it will impact his estate."

"I can't imagine Natalie has a clue what he's been up to other than his obsession for purchasing high-end watches, but I'm not sure what to believe right now."

"Do you think the collection is still at the Reinholtz residence?"

"I doubt it. My mom said she'd ask Natalie to collect it. My best guess is that Natalie brought the watches to the Montgomery's house. She's staying in their guest suite. I'll text you their address in a minute. Before I forget, she's also driving Pete's new Mercedes. I saw it parked at their home when I visited on Monday. It still has the dealer's license plates on it."

"Got it. I'll talk to you soon."

Ava's next task was to speak with Todd. She headed to his office to follow up on their earlier conversation.

"Hi," Ava said to Todd. "I have an urgent project that I'd like you start working on immediately. It involves our business assets and physical security. I just spoke to Cheryl, and she supports you working on this. She said to let her know if we need to reassign any of your duties to your coworkers until this is accomplished."

"I'm glad to help. What do you need me to do?" Todd looked at her intently.

"I'd like you to screen all of Ruby Park's video feed beginning with the time you restarted the security cameras last Thursday. Watch it very carefully to see if Pete had been on the premises. Give the administration corridors and all the entrances your first priority. Also, note if there are any other unusual visitors or inappropriate employee behavior occurring. I know this could take a couple days, but it's important that you're extremely thorough. Do you have any questions?"

Todd seemed surprised. "How would you like me to document anything I find?" he asked.

"Can you make screen shots?"

"I can do that," Todd replied.

"Also, take written notes with the date, time, and location of any incident you find. Oh, and please make a backup copy of the video first before proceeding. I'd hate to see any computer glitches or power outages ruin these critical records."

"Good point. I'll do that right away!"

"Call me if you uncover anything that looks urgent. Here's my cell phone number." Ava quickly jotted down her number and passed him a sticky note. "I'll return your call or come over here as soon as I hear from you. If you don't contact me by the end of the workday, I'll check in before I leave. Please keep this confidential. Jeff, Cheryl, Des, and I are the only people who know about this assignment other than you."

"You've got it, Ava."

⌘

Ava's cell phone rang a couple of hours later, and Todd was on the other end of the call. "Hi Ava. I found something that you need to look at."

"Thanks, I'll be right there." She darted over to the facilities offices. "What did you find?"

"Take a look at this image here," Todd said. "This is last Friday morning. You can see Pete is wearing a jacket with his collar standing up and a baseball cap. He's walking to the rear entrance and appears to be carrying a building access card. He holds it up to the badge reader but can't get in."

"That's weird. I collected his ID and access cards on Wednesday before he left."

"He must have had an extra one, or he was using someone else's."

"Shoot, it didn't occur to me that he might take Natalie's."

"Apparently, he didn't, or he would've entered the building. Anyway, he turns around and heads back to the parking lot." Todd pointed at the screen.

"I wonder what he was attempting to do."

"Wait, that's not all. About fifteen minutes later, Renee from my department, is carrying two grocery bags out of the building. Pete gets out of his car, and she hands the bags over to him. He looks around, and then they are kissing. A minute later, Pete puts the bags in his car and starts driving out. Renee returns to the doorway and enters the facility."

"Nice job. This is exactly the type of information we're looking for. Let me copy down the times this occurred."

"That's not necessary. I've got it logged into a spreadsheet. I'll print this out, and you can take it with you."

"Thank you. I'm going to hold off on meeting with Renee until you view the rest of the video in case something else occurs. I want to make sure that I have all relevant information at once. As I mentioned before, this needs to remain confidential."

"You have my word," Todd said. "I have no idea what's going on, and I definitely don't want to be any part of it." He shook his head.

"Were you aware of a personal relationship between Renee and Pete?" Ava asked.

"Not at all. Though I had the feeling he liked her better than the rest of us in the office."

"This is great work. Would you like to take a lunch break?"

"No, I'd like to stay focused on this."

"How about I stop by the kitchen and order a burger for you? It's on me."

"Awesome. Guess I am getting hungry." Todd nodded.

"Do you want cheese on it and a side of fries too?"

"Yes, that'll be great. I really appreciate it."

"I appreciate you. Talk to you soon."

Ava completed her investigation timeline and then changed her focus to preparing her department's budget forecast. She checked her watch and realized she hadn't heard anything new from Todd. Needing to get up and move, she paid him another visit. She knocked at the entrance, and he waved her in.

"It's about time to call it a day. Have you come across anything else?" Ava asked.

"A couple of things, but I don't think it's what you're looking for."

"Oh?"

"I saw Nellie from Housekeeping taking a nap in the break room. It appeared to be a lot longer than the typical break time. A couple of nurses have been smoking on the non-smoking patio beside the north end of the building. Do you want me to print out that information?"

"No, thanks. I've drafted an employee handbook and will cover workplace expectations in an upcoming training. Please get ready to go home. How much of the video have you completed?"

"I just started on Sunday morning. There are a lot more people coming in and out of this facility than I was aware of."

"Hopefully, we won't find anything else that's alarming. I really do appreciate you focusing on this."

"I'm glad to help, and it's been kind of nice focusing on something different. Hope you have a great night. I'll see you tomorrow."

"You too."

Ava stopped at Cheryl's office. "Hey, I wanted to give you a quick update. The two of us need to meet with Renee tomorrow. Surveillance video shows her delivering a couple of bags to Pete in the parking lot last Friday after a failed attempt on his part to enter the building. Hopefully, she didn't give him anything more than some of his personal items."

"Dang it. That reminds me. Pete never called me to arrange a time to pick up his larger personal items. There are a few pictures, plants, and books in that office. What should we do about them now?"

"I'll ask Natalie if she wants any of it returned to her. I'm guessing not. If that's the case, we'll donate them," Ava said.

"I'm so disappointed with Renee. I gave the entire finance team explicit instructions to notify me if Pete reached out to anyone here."

"From what I observed on the video, they had a much closer personal relationship than anyone was aware of."

Cheryl sighed. "This really stinks. Dang it, anyway. Pete and Renee?"

Ava shook her head.

"I hope she has no involvement with the embezzlement… Her job as our contract coordinator shouldn't grant her access to any of that information, but it's possible he confided in her if they were really close."

"We'll ask her," Ava said. "If you have any concerns during

our conversation, I'd recommend that we suspend her until your financial investigation is complete. If anyone here is involved, they may tamper with evidence."

"I agree that's a major risk, but so far, we have nothing leading us in that direction."

Ava stood up. "I'm keeping my fingers crossed. Hang in there."

Chapter Twenty-six

A VA WAS FINISHING up at her desk for the day, when she received a call on her cell phone.

"Hi, I'm on my way," said Jack.

"Are you driving?" she asked. "I can barely hear you." The song he was playing, "Blinding Lights" by the Weeknd, overpowered his voice through the phone.

"One sec. Can you hear me now? I turned the stereo down."

"Much better. Great song choice, though."

"I'm on Highway 55, heading your direction. Nothing but farm fields and cows for miles. How's your day going?"

Ava grinned. "Busy. I'll fill you in tonight. What've you been up to?"

"I played tennis with Nash. He's my friend from high school. We stopped at Buffalo Wild Wings for lunch, and then I finished up some stuff around my place."

"Nash? He's the carpenter."

"That's right. Say, would you like pizza for dinner tonight?"

"Always," Ava replied.

"I can pick you up about six o'clock. Does that work?"

"Absolutely, I'll be at my place by then. See you soon."

Ava powered down her computer, dropped her phone in her bag, and padded out of her office wearing sneakers.

"I didn't realize anyone was still here," she said to Jenny who was reviewing background verifications for new hires. "Have a good night, and thanks for keeping things down to a dull roar this afternoon."

"I'm glad to help. Des said you're concentrating on the investigation, and we wanted to give you space. I'm about finished… Go enjoy this beautiful weather."

❧

The booming bass from Jack's car stereo announced his arrival. Standing on her front porch, Ava watched as he drove into her driveway, exited his car, and strolled up her sidewalk holding an armload of flowers.

"Wow! These are gorgeous, and roses are my favorite," Ava said. Sophie budged in between the two, and Jack reached down to scratch the dog's ears.

"The lady at the flower shop called them Summer Nights," Jack said with a smile. Ava recognized the hot pink wrapper from Rosie's shop.

"Let me put these in water." Ava inhaled the fresh scent of the yellow-to-deep pink variegated rosebuds. "I'm glad you're wearing shorts. I didn't want to be underdressed."

"Is there such a thing?" Jack winked. He closed the door and followed Ava from the entry way into her kitchen.

She caught him looking at her legs while she was grabbing a vase from a cabinet above her refrigerator.

Jack asked, "Are you getting hungry?"

"Honestly, I could wait a little bit. You know, I'd really love to see your Mustang. Can we do that first?"

"Really?" He raised his eyebrows in surprise.

"Absolutely. It's part of who you are and your family history."

"We can do that. I believe the shop is still open."

Ava filled the glass vase with water, added the packet of floral food, and carefully arranged the roses and greenery. The flowers were beautiful. She hadn't seen this new variety. Jack was smiling at her again, and she wondered if he was pleased that she liked his gift or because she was interested in his renovation project. Maybe it was both.

"I'm ready to go." Ava picked up her clutch and a jacket. The temperature would cool quickly after dusk.

Jack drove them into town and stopped his black Acura in front of a massive garage door that displayed the family logo: *Sparks Auto - Keeping your Motor Running Since 1965*. Randy came from a family line of auto mechanics. He was standing inside the garage and saw the couple approaching. Randy waved before he raised the large door.

"After you." Jack guided Ava into the enormous garage. His shining red muscle car was easy to spot.

"Oh, my goodness. It's gorgeous. Even prettier than I imagined. I looked it up online, so I had an idea of the body style."

"You did?" Jack asked.

"Yes, but I didn't expect this. It's so unique. This paint job is incredible. You obviously commissioned a custom painter."

"I fly with a guy who does paint detailing on the side. It was a hobby that turned into extra income for him. He actually hand painted this detail work and pinstriping himself. There's no pattern for this, and there's absolutely no tape on the body. It's truly one of a kind."

"Like you." Ava gazed into Jack's eyes and smiled. *Was he actually blushing?*

"See where 'Mach 1' is written on the back end?" He pointed at the feature. "This was done in gold leaf."

"I like the visual texture it provides." She stepped back to take it in. "This is the shiniest vehicle I've ever seen."

"Thanks to seven layers of clear coat."

"I think it's absolutely beautiful!"

"I'm glad you like it." Jack was holding her hand now and grazed his thumb over her fingers. She felt a jolt of electricity.

"You said this car used to belong to your dad?"

"Actually, my uncle Jim was the original owner. Unfortunately, he passed away years ago. He never married so my dad hung onto it to stay close to him. We kids kept Dad too busy to work on the car, and it was wasting away in storage. I offered to return it back to its glory days. You know, to keep the memories alive."

"Your connection to your family is awesome."

Jack took a moment before responding. He was clearly emotional. "I have pictures of my dad and Uncle Jim in the 1970's. I'm creating a photo album to show the original and restored versions at car shows." Jack opened the driver side door. "I'm not restoring this to its stock version. Actually, it's called a resto/mod because of the modifications. For instance, I've added air conditioning, Foose aluminum wheels, and an Alpine stereo system. Climb in. I had these custom leather seats designed too."

"It's absolutely amazing. I can't wait to see your photos. Do you have an update on when it will it be completed?"

"Randy said by the end of the month."

"Oh nice. That's great." Ava turned her eyes away.

"I thought you wanted me to enter it in the Jubilee show?"

"I do. It's just that once it's completed, you won't have a reason to come out here so much."

"Are you kidding, Ava?" Jack asked softly. He reached for her hand and helped her out of the driver's seat. "Do you think I've been spending each of my days off in Ruby Lake just for this car? I've been hanging around town because you're here. I hope that's okay."

Ava's face lit up. "It's more than okay. How long of a drive is this to your condo? It must be over an hour."

"Nah, I can make it in about fifty minutes."

She smirked. "Only if you break every speed limit along the way."

"I don't think of it as driving fast so much as flying low," he teased.

Ava wondered how Jack appeared out of the blue and into her life. Not only was he handsome, but he was sweet and funny too. She hadn't met a guy who shared his intentions so quickly, and he seemed very confident in his own skin.

Jack said, "I'd like your opinion on something. I have a choice of colors for the engine wiring harness. The engine is chrome so the wires will be highly visible when I leave the hood open at car shows. Wiring is available in standard black as well as red, yellow, white, or blue."

"Let me think." She closed her eyes briefly. "I'm sensing you are leaning toward red. That's a great option because it would match the body color. Personally, I would choose yellow. It's bold and would mimic the gold custom pinstriping."

"How did you do that? That's exactly what was going through my mind. I've been switching back and forth between red and yellow and was going to tell Randy to order the red.

I'm definitely choosing yellow now. I guess I needed the courage to pick the less obvious choice."

✧

Ava and Jack were seated at a dark booth on red vinyl-cushioned seats. Both were finishing their last slices of pepperoni pizza when Dawn Barone visited their table and greeted them.

"I hope you enjoyed your meal this evening?" Dawn was a full-figured woman with dark, shoulder-length hair and freckles, which were emphasized by her red, button-down dress shirt. *Anthony's* was embroidered in white stitching.

"Fantastic! This is one of the best pizza's I've tasted," Jack said.

"That's high praise from this guy." Ava smiled. "Jack is a pizza connoisseur."

"I appreciate the feedback and will share it with the chef."

Ava noticed Anthony was looking out the kitchen window at his daughter. He caught Ava's eye, turned his head, and retreated back into the kitchen.

"Jack, this is Dawn. Her family has been running this restaurant for generations."

"I hope you'll be visiting us again." Dawn turned to Ava. "Did you hear about Brooke? She's walking on her own."

"That's the best possible news," Ava said. "Have you heard anything else about who may have shot her?"

"No, but I know there was tension between her and Pete. Brooke and Dave ate lunch here a couple weeks ago, and Dave looked fit to be tied. I overheard him say that he was so angry he could kill Pete."

"Really? Any idea why?"

"That's all I picked up. I think Brooke was venting, but he

was getting riled up. I know she avoided Pete at the community center too," Dawn said. "Normally, I wouldn't share this with anyone, you know, but I heard you're investigating."

"I appreciate it. I have an unrelated question for you. Jack and I were admiring the portraits along the back wall. Are all of these family photos of the Barone family?"

"The display includes my mother's side too. That man in the center is Cecil Victoria, my grandmother's father. He established a supper club on this site in the early 1950s. He passed it down to my grandma who changed the menu to authentic Italian cuisine in 1980. When my grandparent's retired, my mother turned it into Anthony's Pizzeria as it is today. She and Dad managed it together until she passed."

"That's an impressive history. Will you take it over when your dad retires?"

"I'm thinking about it, but we'll have to see what the future brings." Dawn glanced back toward the kitchen as Anthony stepped into the dining room. "I should get back to work. See you soon."

"Can I get you kids anything else?" Anthony asked while passing his daughter.

Ava shot a glance at Jack. "Did you want to order dessert?"

"Not tonight, but thanks. The pizza was incredible, sir."

"Family recipe," Anthony said proudly, and he proceeded to greet patrons at a nearby table. He looked like a man who could have come from a long line of Italian chefs, just like his wife had.

Jack said, "I've got another surprise for you—if you're up for an adventure."

Ava grinned. She wiped her mouth with a napkin, folded it neatly, and set it on her dinner plate. "Ready."

Jack offered his hand and helped Ava to her feet. Fifteen minutes later, she found herself in a canoe on Ruby Lake. Jack rented the boat and started paddling them along the shoreline.

"I thought we could enjoy the sunset on the lake tonight," Jack said.

"I feel bad that you're doing all the rowing. We could have rented kayaks." Jack's T-shirt showed off his impressive biceps, and then she realized she wasn't feeling apologetic after all.

"This way I get to be closer to you," he replied.

"This is really nice. I want to share something with you. I was conducting some fact-finding discussions with Grant the other morning related to the murder investigation. I don't want to give you the wrong impression."

Jack arched an eyebrow in question, and Ava continued, "Honestly, it's really just business. We broke up several months ago, but I knew it was over long before that. We'd been stuck in the friend zone for ages. I think he wants someone devoted to his career goals, and I broke it off because I needed to follow my own dreams."

"I trust you, Ava. You don't owe me any explanations."

"There's a lot of gossip in this town. People say a lot of things, and I don't want it to be misconstrued. When I'm dating someone... well, I only date that one person. I'm not saying I expect that of you. We've only been on a couple of dates. Sorry, I'm not very good at this. I just want to be up front."

Jack smiled. "I think you're doing great. Loyalty means everything to me. I have a couple of close friends I know I can count on. I look for that in a partner too, but I haven't always picked the right women."

"Can you tell me about your last relationship?"

"I was seeing a woman named Brittany for nearly a year. She quickly grew tired of my schedule. She didn't care for the fact that I was out of town some weekends. She's very social and wanted me to attend every event with her. Anyway, I found out she was cheating on me."

"That's terrible. You must have been heartbroken."

Jack diverted his gaze and focused on rowing. "I was promoted to Captain about a year ago and didn't have the seniority to get time off for both Thanksgiving and Christmas, so I bid for Christmas week. I guess that was the last straw for her. She invited another guy to her family's Thanksgiving before even breaking it off with me."

Ava shook her head. "I don't understand why people don't communicate that to their significant other first. It's very disrespectful."

"I've talked to other pilots about this. The ones with successful relationships have partners who are independent, with careers or personal interests of their own. It just doesn't work if the other person needs your attention all of the time. I can't be in two places at once."

Ava attempted to lighten the mood. "I imagine you have no trouble getting dates. You must have women throwing themselves at you. You know, the uniform fetish, free travel, and all that." She gave him a mischievous smile.

Once again, Jack raised an eyebrow. Ava said, "Well, you're a good-looking guy. Are the rumors true that pilots and flight attendants hook up a lot?"

Jack shook his head. "Please don't believe everything you hear. I can't speak for others, but I've never dated a flight attendant or a pilot for that matter. I can't imagine flying with a woman I dated after a break up."

"That could be awkward."

"Some of the women I meet at bars or the gym are attracted to a perceived lifestyle. They think travel is all glamorous. Sure, I enjoy visiting new cities and meeting new people. But in the end, it's a job, not a vacation… Man, I can't believe I'm telling you all of this. You're really easy to talk to. I feel like I've known you a long time."

"I feel the same way. I'm not used to sharing information about myself quickly. I'm always honest… Perhaps even a bit too direct at times, but I usually reserve my opinions and personal experiences for my closest friends," Ava said.

"I'll take that as a compliment. Hey, look up at the sky. Doesn't that cloud look like a rhinoceros? See it's face and tusks?"

"I do. That's really cool." Ava pointed to the moving clouds. "I think that cluster looks like a cup and saucer. Oh, and I can make out a panda in that one right there."

Jack twisted his neck. "I can see that."

Once Jack paddled them back to shore, they stepped out of the canoe onto the sandy beach, and Jack returned their life jackets to the rental counter at the beach. They took turns using the spigot to rise the sand off their feet and then replaced their shoes. Jack wrapped his arm around Ava's shoulders as they made their way back to the parking lot.

"Is there anything else you'd like to do tonight?" Jack asked.

"I'm afraid I have to get back home. This has been a fun evening, and the sunset was amazing."

They listened to the stereo during the drive back to Ava's. When the car was parked, she turned to Jack. "I've really enjoyed our time tonight. I wish I didn't have to turn in, but I have a meeting with an employee first thing in the morning."

"Gotcha. Let me walk you up?"

"Hmm… very tempting, but I'm afraid I have to say good-night here."

Jack was holding Ava's hand. He reached closer to her and brushed a lock of hair from her face. "Oh, there are your gorgeous eyes," Jack said before leaning in and kissing her deeply.

"Good night, Jack," Ava managed to say after catching her breath.

"I'll wait here until you get inside. Remember to lock your doors after you take Sophie out."

Ava lingered a few seconds, collecting her purse and jacket from the backseat. She smiled then, "Okay, see you when you get back in town."

Ava stepped into her entryway and glanced out the side-light window until the tail lights of Jack's vehicle disappeared down the street. Sophie was bouncing around trying to capture her attention. After letting her buddy outside, she stopped in her kitchen to inhale the licorice scent of her roses. She smiled to herself, recalling that amazing kiss. She'd felt it down to her toes and found herself looking forward to seeing Jack again. This could be the start of something amazing, she thought. She hoped it wasn't only her imagination and that Jack felt a connection too.

Chapter Twenty-Seven

VA FLOATED DOWN a cool river on a black innertube enjoying the joyful sounds of children laughing and the waves hitting the river bank. The trees were showing off their various shades of green as she slowly drifted along. Groups of families and teenagers had tied their innertubes together at the beginning of their journey, essentially creating one large raft. In nearly each collection, one tube was dedicated to carrying a cooler full of beverages and snacks to enjoy during the two-hour trip, which would end at a beach. Ava relaxed with her eyes closed enjoying the summer sun.

Suddenly, she sensed darkness as clouds rolled in, and the wind picked up. Ava glanced around and wondered how she got separated from her friends who had made their way beyond the rapids. She could see Shannon in her bright pink suit at the sandy beach in the distance.

She held on tightly as she approached the small waterfall that led to the rocky rapids. "Bottoms up," a voice in her head reminded her. Ava complied to avoid hitting her bum on the wet stones. Her slim frame didn't carry enough weight to keep her tube afloat beneath her. Instead, it went flying up and over her head. The river's current pulled Ava under its dark water.

Ava was a strong swimmer. She had learned to swim by the time she was five years old. That was practically a birthright in the land of 10,000 lakes. She managed to get to the surface and take a deep breath before being pulled under again and again. A strong arm encircled her waist lifting her up and away. As he placed his other arm under her knees to carry Ava, her hero's husky masculine voice declared, "I've got you." He returned her safely to the river bank.

Ava's eyes flew open, and she stared up at the ceiling. Her heart was racing. She had experienced dreams involving bodies of water in the past and knew that it often represented emotion. In her subconscious mind, she was literally drowning in her own feelings.

❧

Ava went to Cheryl's office as soon as she arrived at Ruby Lake. "Are you free?" she asked.

"We have to stop meeting like this," Cheryl said lightly.

Ava took a seat across from the CFO. "I agree, but the sooner we get started, the sooner we can get to the bottom of this."

Thirty minutes after Renee joined Cheryl and Ava, their meeting was still in full swing. At first, Renee denied having any contact with Pete after his last day of work. She complied, however, when Ava presented her with photos of the security footage. One showed Renee handing bags to Pete, and the second was a picture of Pete and Renee kissing by the parking lot.

"I'm so embarrassed about this." Renee fiddled with her necklace. "I really loved that man. I can't believe he's gone… I know what people are saying about him, but he was kind and gentle to me."

"I'm deeply sorry for your loss, Renee," Ava said with a soothing voice. "I hope you're seeking support to help you through your grief."

"Does anyone else know about us?" asked Renee. Her face flushed, and she dabbed at her tears.

"We don't know who either of you shared your relationship with. Only a couple of us in administration are aware."

"He told me he was leaving Natalie, but that didn't happen before he was murdered. There's no reason to cause her more pain by telling her about our affair."

"I'll need to report your relationship to the sheriff's department," Ava said, "though I imagine they'll be discreet. Since Pete's murder is still under investigation, you should be prepared to be questioned. You may wish to consult with an attorney."

"Oh, my God. This is a nightmare."

Ava looked up to Cheryl for a sign, and Cheryl nodded.

Ava said, "Renee, we care about you, but we need to send you home while we complete our internal investigation. Your employment will be suspended pending the outcome. Your benefits will remain intact during this time, and you can call us with any questions. We'll be in touch in a few days."

Renee was inconsolable now, and Ava handed her a box of tissues to dry her tears. "Is there someone we can call to pick you up?" Ava asked.

"I'd like to contact my sister." Her voice was barely audible.

"Cheryl, can you stay with Renee until her sister arrives?" Ava asked.

"Of course." Cheryl looked at Renee. "You can stay here in my office if you'd like."

"Thank you both for your time this morning," Ava said as

she stood. "I know this is difficult. Please take care of yourself, Renee."

Ava left Cheryl's office and took the stairs up to the human resources suite. She called her cousin, Detective Sullivan, and informed him that both Renee and Natalie had a motive for Pete Reinholtz's murder. If Natalie was aware of Pete's intent to leave her, that could have started their violent episode last week. She also speculated that Renee might have learned Pete had decided to stay with his wife which caused Renee to take revenge.

Mitch listened and then responded, "A crime of passion is a solid motive. Your news about the affair isn't a shock, but it adds more to the puzzle. I'll look into it."

"Am I still a suspect?"

"Our primary focus is elsewhere."

Ava uttered a huge sigh. "What a relief—my anxiety has been doing a number on my head. Any news about Brooke's shooter?"

"We haven't found the gun, and Dave isn't a registered gun owner. We haven't determined the owner of the weapon used in Pete's murder for that matter. These cases can take weeks if not several months, but there's a lot of pressure on us right now at the department."

"I assume you discovered Pete's banking records and spending habits?"

"We did. Natalie turned over Pete's watch case thanks to you. Due to his financial entanglements, we're looking into another possible avenue. I don't want to go into that because I want to protect you. Please stay out of this investigation," Mitch warned. "We're talking about some very dangerous people. Avoid discussing the case in public. I don't want you to be targeted next."

"Are these suspects from out of town?"

Mitch switched to his bossy cop voice and commanded, "I said let it go, Ava. Geez, both of our moms will have my hide if something happens to you." He lowered his tone. "In addition to Pete's financial contacts, I'm keeping a close eye on Natalie and her father. Natalie was already a suspect due to the domestic violence, but off the record, we've identified a two-million-dollar life insurance policy that they purchased on Pete. She stands to gain the most with that man out of her life."

Ava felt a little lighter after disconnecting her call. She pulled up her investigation spreadsheet and highlighted Mack Montgomery on her suspect list. He knew his daughter had resources to fall back on. She rested her chin on her hand while staring at her computer screen. After responding to what felt like one hundred email messages, she stood up and gazed out her office window at the gray sky blending into the lake. Beads of rain formed on the glass, and their numbers rapidly increased. The weather forecaster on the morning news had predicted scattered rain showers.

Cloudy days always inspired Ava to get organized. First, she sorted her mail which consisted primarily of advertisements for benefits brokers, recruitment firms, and payroll software. Ava dropped all of the morning's junk mail in her recycle bin. Next, she tackled the paperwork on her desk, grouping documents by subject matter. She intended to scan and file the material for future reference. Ava signed the contract renewal for the employee photo ID printing system as well as a few invoices for office supplies. These went into an inter-office envelope for return to accounting.

Des had left a file containing a market analysis for Ava's review. Her report compared their competitor's pay rates for evening and weekend shift pay. Ava placed it in a red file folder and dropped it at the front of her file drawer to follow-up the next day.

After thoroughly cleaning off her desk, Ava grabbed her carryall bag and began to methodically determine what she needed and what she could toss. She removed the small clutch she carried on her first date with Jack. She peeked inside to grab her lip balm and saw the bracelet she had wrapped in tissue.

She had completely forgotten to text her friends to identify its owner. It was a lovely piece of jewelry, likely a gift, and she was surprised no one had called her to see if she had found it. Ava turned the custom piece over in her hands and discovered it was inscribed. Mystery solved. The name Dawn Victoria Barone was carved in tiny scrollwork. Ava decided she would deliver it to Dawn at Anthony's restaurant and placed it back in the small purse.

She tried to recall where she had seen the name Victoria recently. Ava pulled out the photocopies she had made at Pete and Natalie's home. Mitch had told her the originals were obtained by the sheriff's department as part of the investigation. She was familiar with the defamation lawsuit Pete filed against the Sweetwaters and set that file aside.

The other file was marked 'Victoria, Minnesota.' Ava assumed this was related to a business in a neighboring community with the same name. The contents included a loan document and a contract. She had only glimpsed at it then, but now she flipped through all of the pages and saw the loan document was signed by Maria Nicolette Victoria. The contract stated the building which housed Anthony's Pizzeria was collateral for the loan. In the event the loan payments fell behind by four months, the building reverted to Pete Reinholtz.

An image appeared in Ava's mind of a photo Dawn pointed

out to her and Jack the night before while they shared a pizza. The founder's last name was Victoria. *Maria is likely a descendant of Cecil.*

Ava quickly pushed back her desk chair and looked for Des in her office. Noelle caught her eye and said, "I think Des is with Todd in facilities management. Said he wanted to discuss a project he's working on."

"Great. I need to stretch my legs anyway… My foot is falling asleep. I'll drop by Todd's office."

A couple of minutes later, Ava knocked on Todd's door, and he waved her in. "Good morning, Ava," he said.

Cody from Nutrition Services arose from his seat. "I was just on my way out." He smiled as he walked past.

"Excuse me for interrupting," Ava said to Todd and Des.

"We were just finishing up." Des sat up straight, lacing her fingers together. "Cody reported that one of his cooks has been passing out business cards. He was wondering why our vendor printed them for him with the Ruby Park logo."

"I thought we only ordered cards for administration employees," said Ava.

"Exactly. When Cody asked Edward why he ordered business cards, he said, 'To impress chicks.'" Des grinned.

Todd rolled his chair backwards and wrote something brief on a notepad. "I'll call our vendor and make it clear they should only print our business cards when they receive a requisition from this office. Were you looking for me?"

"Actually, I wanted to speak with both of you. Do either of you know if we have a resident named Victoria?"

Des responded, "We probably have more than one. It was a popular name years ago."

"Sorry, I should have clarified. I mean with the last name

Victoria. Do you have a copy of the current resident census, Todd?"

"I don't, but I can call Stacey really quick."

Ava nodded. "Please do." Todd picked up his phone as Ava ambled toward the multiple computer screens that were displaying security camera footage from around the facilities. "Did you guys find anything today?" Ava inquired of Des.

"Todd discovered an older man walking into three different rooms in Memory Care. He collected three pairs of eyeglasses and what appeared to be a cookie canister. Todd thought it might be a visitor stealing items, but we confirmed that he was one of the residents in that unit. The nurse manager said some residents take things they believe belong to them, and she'll make sure the items have been returned."

Todd got off the phone. "Stacey said we have one resident with that last name. Her name is Maria Victoria, and her apartment number is 334 in Assisted Living."

"She's on my grandpa's floor. I've probably seen her." One of the security screens caught Ava's attention. "Hold on. What's going on here?"

Someone was carrying a very large blue bag into the side entrance of Assisted Living. He appeared to be intentionally turning his back to the camera. They all studied the image of a shorter, overweight man wearing a dark hooded jacket.

Todd moved closer. "Let me see. I'll rewind this and slow it down. Here, this guy is opening the exterior door on the south end. I'll enlarge the interior camera. Now, he's opening the door to access the interior stairwell, and that's all. We don't have cameras on the patient care corridors."

"What day is this video?" Ava asked.

"We're nearly caught up. This is for today. Hold on a sec…

we're looking at this morning between seven and seven-fifteen a.m.," reported Todd as he scratched his short beard. He froze an image on the screen. "This looks to me like an airline luggage bag. The kind you'd use to check golf equipment at the airport when you take it on vacation. My dad has one similar for golfing in Florida and Arizona."

"Dang, I have a really bad hunch." Ava placed her left hand on her temple. "Des, please print a photo of this guy, make color copies, and distribute them to the front desk greeters. They need to ask anyone who resembles this man to have a seat in the waiting area, and press the security button at the desk to silently alert Facilities."

Ava continued to give instructions. "Todd, I need you to issue a Code Gray to alert all staff to be on the lookout for suspicious activity. We also need to organize a search for this bag."

A loud siren cut into their conversation. "It's not Wednesday… it's Thursday," declared Ava attempting to process this diversion. "Oh geez, that's a real tornado siren. Todd, hold off on the Code Gray and announce a Code Twist over the intercom immediately. Everyone needs to prepare for a possible tornado. Please monitor the emergency radio."

"Got it. Will do."

"Des, we need to get to our designated stations immediately. Let's all meet here once the 'all clear' is given." Ava looked at Des and gave her a look of concern. "Grandpa can't get downstairs with the elevators locked during the storm. I'll be on the third floor of Assisted Living." Ava dashed across the facility and sprinted up the central staircase to the third floor. She was proud to see other employees rushing toward the nursing care units.

Ava stopped at the nursing station to collect the emergency

door tags used to indicate that a room had been checked. All of the Ruby Park employees practiced emergency response during routine drills. The support team made sure all windows and blinds were closed and assisted residents to a safe, central area. Mobile residents were escorted down to the first floor, and those in wheelchairs gathered on their respective floors.

Ava was relieved to see a nurse guiding her grandpa, along with a few other residents with wheelchairs and walkers, to their community room. She started down her designated hallway with the resident apartment closest to the nursing station and began knocking on doors.

She spoke loudly and knocked before entering each room. "Hello, this is Ava. I'm here to help." Once the room was checked, she placed a door hanger to show other staff that the room had already been inspected. She quickly worked her way back to the far end of the hallway.

The tornado siren stopped blaring after a few minutes, having served its purpose of alerting county residents to take cover and tune it to emergency announcements. Ava knew they were not out of harm's way, but at least she could think more clearly without the loud noise reverberating in her head. The wind was howling outside, and thunder shook the facility.

Once she finished one side of the corridor, Ava stepped across the hall to work her way back to the central nursing station. She knocked, received no answer, and entered the room.

Ava approached the south-facing window that revealed an ominous, greenish-gray sky. She quickly closed the window shade and turned toward an open closet.

There sat a tall blue luggage bag. An assisted living resident didn't have much need for a bag of golf clubs. She quickly unzipped it—the same bag she had seen on the video earlier.

Ava discovered a partial set of clubs, and the three wood was missing.

She took the phone out of her sweater pocket to take a photo. Her back was to the door, and she heard a female voice ask, "What are you doing in here?"

Ava turned her head and found Dawn Barone in the doorway. She was wearing a charcoal-gray hooded rain jacket. As she looked back toward the closet, Ava noticed a phone number appear on her cellphone. It was an incoming call. *Thank goodness I silenced my phone.* She clicked the green button with her thumb to engage the call and immediately dropped it back into her left pocket.

She raised her voice. "Hi, Dawn. I'm helping the nursing staff check the residents' rooms to ensure everyone is out. It's a safety protocol, but you know that. HR is assigned to Assisted Living. I assume you're looking for your grandma?"

"This is her apartment. She wasn't in the community room so I came to check on her," replied Dawn. Her voice was strained, and she was shaking.

"I bet the nurses took her down to the first floor already." Ava was eager to get out of the apartment fast, but Dawn was blocking her exit. "By the way, I found a bracelet that I believe is yours. It must have fallen when you delivered pizza to my place over the weekend. Your name is engraved on the back. It's in my office. I'll go get it for you."

"Thank goodness. I've been searching all over. My mom gave it to me after she was diagnosed with pancreatic cancer," said Dawn, who didn't budge an inch from her stance in front of the closed door. "She died a year later."

"That must have been terrible for you and your dad."

"She passed a couple of years ago, and I still miss her every day. She was mentoring me to take over the restaurant one day. Her chemotherapy and medical care were really expensive, so she and Grandma were forced to mortgage the property. I wish they had asked for my help sooner. Dad might lose the pizzeria now."

"There must be other options. I'm sure the bank would be open to renegotiating the loan."

"I would've done that. But because of some outstanding debt, my family took out a high interest loan from Pete Reinholtz. I don't know what they were thinking. Dad was so depressed, and I guess they were desperate. Now the restaurant is going into default. I don't know how we'll take care of Grandma now. We can no longer afford this place."

"Have you spoken with a social worker here to explore your care options?"

Dawn shook her head. "You must think I'm the biggest jerk because of my discrimination complaint."

"I don't think that at all. You have the right to present your side. Besides, I wasn't working here when you left, and I don't know the circumstances of your departure."

"It really hurt. I thought I was doing a good job. And my dad was furious. He said I needed to stand up for my rights."

"I understand. He's looking out for you. That's what father's do."

"He hasn't been the same person since my mom died, and he's become more bitter in recent months." Dawn moved into the kitchenette.

"I should make sure someone has checked on the rest of the residents," Ava said. She started for the doorway. "After the storm passes, I'll go get your bracelet. It's a beautiful gift."

The apartment door swung open. Anthony Barone stomped in, looking furious, and he flung the door closed behind him.

Ava attempted to squeeze past the heavy man. "I was just leaving," she said.

"Not so fast." Anthony pushed Ava into the apartment. "I see you figured it out."

Dawn gasped. "Dad, what are you doing?"

Ava's skin began to crawl.

"Don't trust this woman. She's not your friend." Anthony lunged toward the closet door and placed his hand on the unzipped luggage bag. "I'm not stupid," he said as he pulled out a gun from his jacket pocket. "I know what you're doing here."

"Please put the gun down," implored Ava. "I don't know what you're talking about. I was making sure the apartment was vacant. It's part of our safety protocol."

"You know exactly what I'm saying. You've been poking your nose into everyone's business, asking too many questions. You were spying on me and Dawn last night."

Ava gasped. "Honestly, I wasn't… Listen, Jack is new to town, and we were just having dinner."

"Dad!" Dawn yelled. "That's enough. Let's get you home. You're acting crazy."

"It's not bad enough that creep Pete destroyed your future, but now this woman intends to turn me in. Over my dead body. Or should I say yours, Ava. Back up against the wall," Anthony demanded. He gestured toward the living room wall with his gun in hand. Then he said, "Dawn, get out of here, now."

"Dad—stop this!"

He pointed the gun to his head. "I said now!" Anthony shouted. "Get out. Go as far away from here as you can, or I'll shoot myself, too."

Tears streamed down Dawn's face as she opened the door and exited the apartment. Anthony redirected his gun toward Ava.

Ava tried to wrap her head around what she was witnessing. Anthony had to be out of his mind. No rational person would believe they could murder someone in this crowded facility and get away with it. She hoped Todd was still listening to this conversation through her phone. She prayed help was on the way. Surely, Dawn would say something, right?

I need more time. Keep Anthony talking.

"You called from the dining room the other day to ask about the security cameras because you were planning to hide these golf clubs in Maria's room," Ava stated, her heart stammering in her chest.

"What if I did? It was a damn good hiding space until this stupid storm brought you in here."

"And, you drove Dawn's car to the golf course that night to murder Pete Reinholtz. That's why you had her golf bag."

"You did your homework. I guess you think you're pretty smart. Yeah, I saw him at the golf course. His foursome was golfing one hole behind mine. That idiot was drinking all day, bragging and spouting disgusting insults. He was so drunk he took off with a golf cart. Parked it by Lady Luck and continued his binge drinking."

"You spoke to him again at the bar that night. What happened?"

"He wouldn't negotiate. Said he was going to buy a fancy house on the golf course once he sold Maria's restaurant. I told him the pizzeria was my wife's legacy for Dawn, and then he had the nerve to call my girl a worthless whore. He treated his wife and my daughter like garbage since high school. Always been a bully. So, I followed him back to the golf course that night and gave him what he deserved."

Ava inclined her head. "You murdered Pete because he was abusive?"

"Pay attention. That man has ruined lives."

"Including yours?"

"He was my family's CPA for years," Anthony stammered. I didn't realize he was stealing from us until I started doing the bookwork on my own. That was Nicole's job… my wife who passed. The restaurant belonged to Nicole and her mother. They took out a high interest mortgage from that lowlife scum when she learned she had cancer. Pete took advantage of my family when my wife was dying. He was evil."

"You confronted him near the country club that night?"

"I watched him from the car at first. He was fighting with his kid. When his son took off on a bike, I grabbed a club and confronted Pete. It was for my own protection."

"Did you shoot Brooke Sweetwater?" Ava took in a sharp breath.

"That was an accident. I knew Pete worked out at the community center early most mornings, so I went there to reason with him about paying back the loan. Instead, I heard him yelling at Brooke. She caught him opening the safe, and he chased her out of the office. She jumped when I pulled the trigger. Rather unfortunate that Brooke was shot, and Pete escaped."

Anthony pulled back the window blinds and quickly peeked outside. At that same time, Ava reached a few inches with the hand behind her back and pulled on the emergency cord that was attached to the wall. Each apartment was equipped with one in every room.

He stepped away from the window, frowned, and jerked his head to the door. "Looks like you're coming with me. Don't make a sound. I saw Charles down the hallway, and I swear I'll kill your grandfather if you say a word."

Holding the gun at her back, Anthony opened the door and shoved Ava out ahead of him. Grandpa Charles shuffled his feet as he pulled his wheelchair along the passageway. The door to the stairwell nearest to her opened, and Ava caught sight of her cousin, Mitch. "Put the gun down," he ordered.

Anthony slammed Ava against the wall and ran down the wide corridor toward the opposite stairwell. Charles lifted his walking cane and tripped Anthony who fell to the ground. Anthony scrambled on the vinyl floor to retrieve his pistol.

"Grandpa, no," Ava cried out. Another uniformed deputy stepped out from behind the nursing station, threw himself down on Anthony, and wrestled him for the gun. A shot fired. Ava's vision went black, and she felt herself falling.

A muscular arm encircled Ava's waist and lifted her. "I've got you," declared his deep, husky voice.

Am I dreaming? Ava felt like she was floating, and then she opened her eyes. "You're wearing your captain's uniform. Damn—you look hot."

"You're not so bad yourself, darlin'," replied Jack. "Hey everyone. She's coming back around."

"Ava, you fainted when the gun went off," said Stacey, the Director of Nursing. "No one was injured. Everyone is safe now thanks to you."

"Where's Grandpa?" Ava asked with deep concern in her voice.

"Right here, honey," responded Charles.

Ava sat up straight and surveyed the small group sitting in the common area on the third floor. "What are you doing here, Jack? I don't understand."

"Mitch was visiting me and Randy at Sparks Auto. I drove into town this morning to drop off a couple of custom chrome valve covers. I was about to leave for the airport when Des called him to report your discovery. Mitch was also alerted that 911 calls came in from Ruby Park at about the same time. I was worried you were in danger, so I followed him here. I had to know you were safe."

"What about the storm?"

"The tornado threat is gone. It's just a thunderstorm now."

Mitch and Todd were holding a conversation at the nursing station. Todd gave a slight wave of his wrist, and both men approached. Mitch focused on Ava. "That was smart thinking leaving your phone line open. Todd heard Anthony's full confession. I'd like to get your statement while this is still fresh in your mind."

"Of course." Ava looked up at Jack. "I guess you have to leave for the airport now."

"Not a chance. I'll call scheduling and let them know I have a family emergency. One of the reserve pilots will cover."

The elevator opened revealing the Center's CEO who joined the small group. You displayed remarkable leadership, Ava," said Jeff. "Deputy Hildebrand is taking Mr. Barone off to the county jail. I understand you and Charles saved the day."

"That was incredibly brave, Grandpa. But why do you have a walking cane?"

"Well, I'll show you." Charles reached down to lock the brakes on his wheelchair and held his cane perpendicular to the floor. Ava watched in amazement as he slowly pulled himself to a standing position and took a few steps toward her. "What more do I have to do for a hug?"

Chapter Twenty-eight

As Ava and Jack entered the large dining room at the North Star Inn on Ruby Lake, staff and seated guests applauded, congratulating Ava for her part in solving the recent crimes. Ava waved shyly. As she passed by, she personally greeted several people that she recognized.

"Here's our guest of honor!" Grace said. She greeted Ava and Jack with hugs.

Ava turned to her mother. "I wasn't expecting this kind of attention."

"Better get used to it—you're a local celebrity now," Grace said proudly. "Relax, honey. I reserved a private room for our dinner celebration."

They entered a modest-sized room decorated with roses, and one large round table was set for Ava's extended family. The North Star was the oldest, yet most elegant resort on the lake. Doug joined them and gave Ava a kiss.

"I really appreciate you and mom for throwing this party. I love having the whole family together," she said.

"You're our superhero, honey."

"Here's the real hero." Ava bent down and kissed her

grandpa Charles on the cheek. "Hi, Grandpa. I'm surprised your friends at Ruby Park let you go out tonight. I hear you're even more popular now that you're a crime fighter."

"You cracked the case, my dear. I was just in the right place at the right time, or the wrong place at the right time. The important thing is we're all safe, and we're together."

"Aunt Helen, I'm so glad to see you. You look amazing!" Ava said to her mother's sister, Mitch's mom. "This is Jack Lindstrom."

"Thank you, sweetheart," Helen said. "It's a pleasure to meet you, Jack. Grace has told me quite a bit about you. Have a seat next to me during dinner, so I can get to know you."

"Don't mind if I do. I understand your Mitch's mother." Jack took her hand in his own.

"That's right," said Mitch. "Sounds like you're moving in on my girl."

"Don't worry, detective." Jack held his hands up slightly. "I've already set my eyes on this one." Jack placed his arm protectively around Ava's waist.

"Hey, everyone!" The group turned to see a young man who was the spitting image of his father. Ava's brother, Reid, had driven straight from the airport—his first time back home in three months. It was a true celebration.

"Reid. You made it, son." Doug placed his hand on Reid's back. "You got here just in time to enjoy dinner."

"I'm glad you remembered how to find us," Lauren teased her big brother.

"I just followed my nose. The North Star is my favorite food joint in Ruby Lake—next to Mom and Dad's, that is."

"How are you coming along with testing the new software?" Doug asked his son.

"I think I resolved that snafu we talked about earlier in the week."

"Fantastic! Are we on track for release this fall?"

"Yeah, I think we'll be within two weeks of the projected go-live date."

Matt leaned in toward Jack and Mitch. "These two guys have been speaking in a conspiratory geek-mode for the past year. I just smile and nod."

Jack laughed. "What is it that you're working on?"

Reid explained, "We've identified a new code that will eliminate foreign cyber-attacks. Our mission is to offer a secure environment for banking systems that make transactions with each other worldwide."

Jack nodded with interest. "When Ava first told me you were in the IT security field, I didn't understand the extent of it. I understand you founded your company, Andrews Intelligence."

"That's the one," Doug said proudly.

"I've read about your company in the *Minnesota Business Review*. It was a very impressive article, sir."

"Please call me Doug. Reid here is the true genius behind the next generation of online banking."

"I have no doubt about it after meeting the rest of your family," replied Jack.

"I heard you're a pilot," said Reid. "That's got to be exciting."

"When my flying becomes exciting, it probably means I'm doing something wrong."

"He's a wiseass too," Reid said to Ava. "He'll fit right in."

Seated on a dining room chair for the first time in months, Charles enjoyed having his family gathered around him. His wheelchair was tucked away against the back wall. Matt said, "I didn't realize you were still in physical therapy. Glad to see you're making great progress."

"It's all due to my therapist," said Charles. "Yvonne is amazing and so strong. Oh, she's a big girl. A big, big girl. About your size, Lauren."

"Hey, I heard that," exclaimed Lauren. Reid, Ava, Mitch, and Matt all burst into laughter. Grandpa had a gift of exaggeration that sometimes caught them by surprise.

Doug raised his glass. "I'd like to propose a toast to Ava, Mitch, and Charles. Ruby Lake owes you a debt of gratitude for solving this case so quickly. Thanks to you, everyone can take a deep breath and enjoy the summer."

Everyone raised their glasses and said, "Cheers!"

Mitch followed Doug. "Allow me to toast Ava. Thank you for making my job a little easier. If you're ever interested in changing careers, you have a future in detective work."

"Cheers!" The group said in unison.

"Thanks, but I think I'll retire from crime fighting and leave it to all you," Ava said, her eyes wide.

Mitch announced, "Anthony Barone will be in prison for the rest of his life. He's facing charges of attempted murder for shooting Brooke Sweetwater and second-degree murder for killing Pete Reinholtz. I also want you all to be the first to know that I accepted a permanent transfer to Ruby Lake. We'll be neighbors again soon."

"That's wonderful news!" said Helen. The whole family applauded.

Grace spoke next. "Ava's suggestion to have the Chamber's Fourth of July Jubilee sponsor the family emergency shelter has really taken off. Media attention regarding Brooke's shooting and Natalie's story of domestic abuse has rallied folks in the Twin Cities area as well. The Garrett County Family Safe Home has received tens of thousands of dollars in donations. They'll have a dedicated tent at the Jubilee with counselors on sight all day."

Ava set down her champagne flute. "That's incredible. Save me a shift to work at their booth. Speaking of the shelter, their website lists items their patrons need most. I was thinking about creating several types of care packages for distribution."

"What do you have in mind?" asked Lauren.

"A backpack designated for kids or women with toiletry and clothing basics plus a special item like a teddy bear, game, or book. They can be displayed at the booth for folks to sponsor—people can see where their donations are going, and it could build an emotional connection."

"That's very generous, honey," said Grace. "I know many of the women and children enter these safe homes with only the clothes on their backs."

"Sign me up," Lauren said with a warm smile. "I'll help with those sample packs. Plus, Matt and I will be handing out free lunches to all the kids who stop by."

Reid looked around the table. "Impressive. Let me know how I can pitch in."

After the family completed their surf and turf dinners, Lauren shared, "There's live music in the Wilderness Tavern tonight. I thought we could enjoy the band before heading back to Mom and Dad's place for a campfire."

"You kids go on ahead." Grace pulled back her chair. "We'll take Grandpa to his apartment and meet you at the lake house after sunset."

Once everyone hugged Charles goodbye, the younger generation searched for outdoor seating at the tavern adjacent to the restaurant. Mitch and Reid bought a round of beer at the bar and set the mugs on the wooden picnic table they were sharing with the family.

Ava approached Mitch and whispered, "Do you think Ruby Park will recover any of the embezzled funds?"

"Highly unlikely. Pete was using a foreign bank. His account balances were low anyway because he was a big spender. I hope the facility is insured."

Ava nodded. "Cheryl said she filed a claim on the business crime insurance policy."

"Glad to hear that. Employee theft is a lot more common than people realize," Mitch said as he and Ava rejoined their group at the table.

Jack was saying, "Spending time in Ruby Lake reminds me of growing up in Wisconsin. We can actually see the constellations here."

"I know what you mean," Reid said. "Don't get me wrong—working in Austin offers a great nightlife. But there's nothing like being home, especially this time of year."

The sun had gone down, and the temperature was becoming noticeably cooler. Jack ran his hands up and down Ava's arms, sending electrical currents throughout her body. "Hmm, I hope you don't mind hanging out with my family for a while longer," responded Ava. "Dad and Reid are really proud of their s'mores."

"I'll follow you anywhere... Besides, your family is awesome."

Ava tilted her head. "Do you think your folks and sisters will like me?"

"Are you kidding? You'll blend in better than I do," replied

Jack with a smile. "I can't wait to introduce you to them over the Fourth of July weekend, after the Jubilee, that is."

"It's a date." Ava smiled. Jack was tapping the rhythm of the band's music onto the tabletop. "Would you care to dance?"

Jack took her by the hand. "I'll give you fair warning that I'm not much of a dancer, but I'll definitely take any excuse to hold you close."

Ava and Jack moved onto the dance floor where they attempted a few different dance moves. Ava did her best to avoid his toes, though Jack didn't seem to mind when she bumped into him.

The band's female vocalist announced, "We're going to slow this down. I dedicate this next song to the lovers out there."

Guests crossed paths as several returned to their seats and others joined the dance floor. Jack pulled Ava closer. She brushed her hands up against his muscular chest and wound them around his neck. Jack was a few inches taller than Ava, and she found it comforting that she could rest her head on his shoulder. The lead vocalist sang "How Long Will I love You" by Ellie Goulding. Ava took in a deep breath of the fresh outdoor air. *Embracing this man, on this perfect evening, under the starry sky, feels exactly right.*

Epilogue

July 4th

AVA AND GRACE Andrews stood on the steps of Ruby Lake's original town hall and surveyed the bustling crowds on the square. This Fourth of July Jubilee drew in more vendors than the Chamber of Commerce had recruited during any year prior. Crowds of locals and visitors had flocked into their quaint downtown for their first official summer festival which promised great food, an art fair, a grand parade, the auto show, and ultimately, a fireworks display after dark.

Grace said, "The kiddie parade was a huge success. It doesn't seem that long ago that you, Reid, and Lauren were riding bikes around this square."

"I remember wearing a princess costume one year. I didn't want to take it off." Ava laughed.

"That reminds me, I saw Brooke and Dave Sweetwater with their daughter Zoe. Brooke told me she's doing well in physical therapy."

"That's wonderful!" Ava said.

White tents lined both sides of the three streets surrounding them. Arts and craft vendors, a farmer's market, local politicians, and various service providers were busy greeting people while showing off their goods and services.

They strolled over to Rosie and Shannon's booth. "Take a look at Shannon's new jewelry line," said Ava.

Grace browsed the selections and said, "These are remarkable, Shannon. I think you'll be sold out before long." Grace held up a pair of earrings next to her face while looking in a small mirror. "I'll take these!"

"You bet. I didn't have time to make as many pieces as I would've liked." Shannon said, looking up at Grace from her folding chair. She placed the earrings in a small gift bag and passed it back to her along with her change. "This show gives me the opportunity to gage customer tastes. Then I'll decide what to sell in my shop."

Rosie said to Grace, "You and the other chamber members must be so pleased with the turnout."

"We are, and the weather cooperated just perfectly. Didn't it?"

"I'll say."

"Ava, I thought you'd still be at the auto show," Shannon said.

"I hung around for over an hour before noon. Jack brought his friend, Nash, and they've moved on to the Sparks Auto booth. Randy received a lot of compliments on the engine work he did for Jack."

"That's great for business. Did you see Natalie and her daughter? They were here earlier and bought a couple pieces."

"Lauren and I spoke to them at the emergency shelter tent. Natalie told me she dropped Pete's lawsuit against Sweetwater Farms," Ava said, and Shannon nodded in return.

Ava pulled Grace aside to make room for shoppers to view the jewelry display. She spoke quietly, "Natalie also said that she intends to make a large donation to the county safe home when she receives Pete's life insurance funds. She wants other women to benefit from her experience. Isn't that amazing?"

"That's powerful. It sounds like she's healing," Grace said. "I need to run. Make sure Jack gets to the north stage by two o'clock sharp where the judges will announce the auto show winners. I have my fingers crossed."

"We'll both be there." Ava smiled.

Grace turned to leave and said, "I'm going to check in with your dad. He volunteered to line up the vehicles and participants for the parade route."

Ava started back to Shannon's booth and overheard her say, "You'll have to ask Ava. Here she is now. Ava, meet Elyse and Katelyn. They're both teachers at Ruby Lake High."

Katelyn said, "We hear you're responsible for importing new men to the Jubilee. You should receive a reward for beautifying this old town."

Ava laughed. "What do you mean?"

Elyse pointed to the Sparks Auto booth which was now surrounded by several men.

"Now, I get it. Okay, the first guy in sunglasses and cargo shorts is my brother, Reid. Next, to him is my cousin, Mitch Sullivan. They're both single, and Mitch just moved into town. You probably know Randy from Sparks Auto, and Matt is my brother-in-law. He owns Woodcrest with my sister."

"And the remaining two gorgeous men on the end?" asked Katelyn.

"The one wearing the black polo with the Mustang logo and jeans is my boyfriend, Jack." Ava smiled proudly, trying not to blush. "Nash is the taller guy with the ball cap. I'm heading over there in a second. I'd be happy to make introductions."

"Would you? That's so nice!"

Ava leaned over to Shannon and spoke softly, "Why don't

you join us? Nash is a contractor. Maybe you can find some quiet time to discuss your renovation project."

Shannon tried to hold back a grin. "I'm sure I can get away for a few minutes." She said to Rosie, "Mom, I'll be back to help you close up our stand before the parade begins."

"Don't worry about me. You girls go have fun."

The four women walked over to the Sparks booth, and Ava made introductions. While everyone was getting acquainted, Jack rested his palm at the small of Ava's back. He was holding two blue ribbons in the other hand and held them up for Ava to see.

"What are the ribbons for?" she asked.

"The judges handed out several quality awards early. They were working up the crowd for the awards ceremony. I received one for outstanding custom paint and the other for outstanding custom engine. I'm really happy for Randy. He built the engine and deserves all the credit."

Ava couldn't stop smiling. She was so happy for Jack and their friends.

Des approached with her two sons. "I hope we got here in time to join you for the awards ceremony."

"You did, but we should head over early if we all want to sit together," suggested Randy.

"Good plan," Des said. "Why don't you guys go now and save our seats. I need to talk to Ava for a minute."

Jack, Randy, and the two boys left the group while Des and Ava stepped aside. "What's up Des? You look so serious."

"I just took the kids to the pizzeria. Dawn closed the dining room and has high school kids serving pizza by the slice from the front counter. She told me that Natalie Reinholtz is not going to take ownership of her mother's property.

They've agreed to create a new payment plan. But business remains slow… probably due to Anthony's arrest. She's planning to re-open the dining room in August as Victoria's Italian Kitchen."

"That's a nice way to recognize her family history. Let's hope the community embraces her through this crisis, and the new restaurant does well," replied Ava. "By the way, I heard Renee just started working for the hospital."

"I guess it was too uncomfortable for her to return to Ruby Park, even though she was cleared of any wrongdoing in Pete's embezzlement."

"A fresh start can do wonders. That reminds me, I saw both Brooke and Natalie this morning at different times. They also appear to be moving on with their lives."

Des said, "That's partly due to you, my friend."

"Well, I think you and I make a great team," Ava replied. "Let's go catch up with the guys—I've never been this excited about a car show."

Des and Ava reached Randy and Jack just as three judges approached the podium.

The eldest man addressed the crowd, "I'd like to thank everyone who participated in this year's Jubilee Auto Show to share the history and art of automaking. We'll announce the awards for the best in each category followed by best in show. These winners will receive a trophy and the honor of leading the grand parade. Let's begin. If your name is called, please come to the front to accept your award."

"First, is the award for the Best Classic Vehicle pre-1945. The winner is the 1925 Ford Model T owned by Gary and Phyllis Johnson from Wooddale."

Everyone clapped for the retired couple as they proudly accepted their trophy and shook hands with the judges.

"Next, is the award for Best Hot Rod. The winner is the 1957 Chevrolet Bel Air. Come on up, Boyd Zimmerman."

The crowd applauded as Boyd walked to the front wearing his farm overalls. Everyone in town new Boyd. He and his family regularly sold fresh produce in the Ruby Lake farmers' market.

"The third category, is the award for the Best Muscle Car. The winner is the 1973 Mustang Mach 1 owned by Jack Lindstrom of Eden Prairie. We learned this is the first car show in which this vehicle has been entered. Come on up Jack, and welcome to the Jubilee."

Everyone clapped their hands together while Ava, Des, and the boys screamed in excitement.

"The best performance vehicle is the 2002 Ferrari Enzo owned by Don and Stephanie McKnight," declared the head judge. A very tan Don McKnight accepted his award during the applause. Ava guessed he didn't live in town year-round.

The announcer continued, "The Best Truck is the 2018 Toyota Tacoma owned by Phil Ferguson." Phil had a large following of fans that hooted and hollered for him while he accepted his trophy.

"Now, one of these vehicles will be named best in show," continued the emcee. "By a unanimous vote, this year's best in show is the 1973 Mustang Mach 1 owned by Jack Lindstrom. Let's all give Jack a big hand."

Ava couldn't hold back her tears. She was overwhelmingly thrilled for Jack. He put so some much love and effort into restoring it for his family. She could only imagine how proud his dad was going to be when they drove the beauty to Wisconsin the following day.

Jack received shouts of congratulations and shook many hands. "I couldn't have done this without you, Randy," Jack called out. Now everyone was on their feet applauding.

As Jack and Ava broke away from the crowd, Ava found Shannon standing next to Nash. Her green eyes were glowing.

Ava gave her friend a wink. "Catch up with you later? After the parade, Jack and I will drop off his car at my place, and we'll bring Sophie back with us. Join us for a picnic dinner by the bandshell."

"Sounds great. I'll wave to you on the parade route!"

While walking hand in hand with Jack, Ava became lost in thought. A month ago, she'd been so wrapped up in her work that she felt she'd heard it all, but she wasn't even close. That had been foolish thinking on her part. Her life was only just beginning, and there was so much more to experience. She knew life was filled with unexpected challenges along with the joy, but Ava now dreamed she could be spending a million more moments like this on her journey with Jack.

"What are you thinking?" Jack asked.

"Just that I can't remember being happier."

Doug was in complete control lining up the parade participants according to the sequence on his clipboard. He directed a rowdy team of teenage boys wearing Royals jerseys to gather behind the high school marching band. The entire town was proud of their baseball team's second place finish in the state tournament.

"Congratulations, Jack!" Doug spotted his daughter alongside Jack who was placing his trophies in the prize-winning vehicle. He handed each of them a flag to wave along the parade route. As Jack ushered Ava into the passenger side of his Mustang, Doug smiled and nodded his approval.

Jack started the ignition, and the powerful engine roared. He took his place as second in line behind the mayor's limousine. Ava recognized many faces as she waved at her community full of old friends and new ones. *I'll never forget this moment—I feel like a queen.*

Acknowledgements

My darling husband, John, I deeply appreciate your unwavering encouragement, your eternal optimism, and your honest feedback. Thank you for suggesting the book title now featured on the cover. Also, many thanks for your willingness to turn down the stereo and for cooking countless meals, allowing me to focus. You're the best!

I am immensely grateful for my beta readers: Judy D., Bradley S., Debra F., and Patti R. Your thoughtful feedback and brilliant questions kept me on my toes, and the smiley faces you left in the margins brightened my days more than you can imagine.

My heartfelt appreciation goes to my proofreader, Robyn Ender, for your razor-sharp attention to detail and for your valuable insight. I also owe a big thank you to my copy editor, Bryn Donovan, for sharing your knowledge of style.

Many thanks to the talented art and design team at Damonza for creating the beautiful cover design and for rendering the layout of the interior pages.

Tremendous love to my parents for their unconditional support and for giving me the courage to reach for the stars. I am forever grateful to my exceptional extended family and to my dear friends. Thanks to each and every one of you for inspiring me along this incredible journey.

And finally, a huge shout out to Team HR. You're the most amazing professionals that I've had the privilege to work with. Your dedication to helping others and your tireless work ethic have greatly enhanced the lives of your colleagues.

About the Author

Born and raised in Minnesota, Kirstin Dianne has a deep affection for small-town living and all four seasons. After enjoying a human resources career that spanned three decades, she retired from corporate life to follow her passion for writing. She holds a Master of Education degree from the University of Minnesota.

When not plotting her next mystery, she can often be found curled up reading a book, practicing her drawing skills, or planning an upcoming travel adventure. She shares a home with her high school sweetheart and their quirky labrador retriever.

You can follow her at: kirstindianne.com